Dying to Dance

(A Maddie Fitzpatrick Dance Mystery)

by

Kate O'Connell

Copyright © 2014 by Kate O'Connell

For information, email **Cozy Cat Press**, cozycatpress@aol.com or visit our website at: www.cozycatpress.com

COZY CAT
P R E S S

ISBN: 978-1-939816-40-5
Printed in the United States of America

Cover design by Nicole Spence
http:/covershotcreations.com

1 2 3 4 5 6 7 8 9 10

Special Thanks

I would like to thank several extraordinary women in my life for their effortless support.

Martha Kepner for being with me when I first uttered those words, 'I think I'd rather write a novel' and never once believing in the statistics. Jane Notten for reading that first draft and taking it, and me, seriously. Sue Conradie for being with me during so many of my surreal and mundane moments and showing me what it means to be an artist. Shire Kerrod for being there week-in, week-out (with coffee) and never bugging me because I didn't let you read the drafts. You are all my inspirations.

I also want to thank my husband, Paul, for never, not even once, mentioning that the pile in the sink was getting dangerously high. (Though you did get snarky about the laundry on occasion. I forgive you.)

And I want to thank my daughter, Eden, because she made it incredibly easy to write a book and because I love watching her dance.

I will never underestimate the power of you believing in me.

Dedication

This book is dedicated to my dance partner, Paul.

Prologue

The gloved hands tremble, the binoculars in their grasp, momentarily losing sight of the picnickers and resting on the scattering of clouds. Several shallow breaths later, the binoculars find the couple and focus again. They sit on a blanket; the remains of lunch pushed negligently aside. Her arms are now wrapped around his upper body while he holds one arm at his side as the other lifts a cigarette to his mouth. Had the couple been closer to the one who was watching them, they would hear the intake of breath and the growl that came after it. The man was inconsequential, but the woman had to be stopped.

The binoculars slip past the prey again as the woman on the picnic blanket screams, one hand flapping against her neck, the other one pointing at something on the ground. She staggers on heels inappropriate for the uneven ground and immediately the man is at her side. With a practiced movement, he rifles through the woman's handbag and withdraws something. A syringe. The binoculars are forgotten for a moment, then raised again to narrowing eyes as they watch the man effectively administer the medication, then fuss over the woman as he guides her back to a seated position.

The one who is watching, backs through the undergrowth, breathing unsteadily; punching a number into a cell phone as a plan began to take shape.

Chapter One

It was her heels. The three spiked inches of pure Italian leather designed by Inez Ponderosa in an alluring shade of blood red represented both the surest way to fail in your first Argentine Tango class and an irresistible temptation for many women.

Maddie Fitzpatrick watched with a growing sense of alarm as the woman in front of her, Alice Walters, a thirty-something, doe-like creature with a pointed face and vein-lined limbs, teetered precariously on her heels again. The teacher in Maddie deliberated the benefits of intervention. On the one hand, changing shoes could destroy forty-five minutes of hard work; on the other, ignoring the increasingly spastic wobbles could leave her first student in Pembroke with a bruised ego at best and at worst, a broken ankle.

Unable to convince Alice to wear the more sensible two-inch heels she had on when she arrived at the lesson, Maddie had spent the better part of an hour easing Alice's weight and balance into the position she would need to walk the Argentine Tango. It had been an arduous task, but she saw Alice was making progress.

"When am I going to be able to do those leg things?" Alice asked, muttering Maddie's instructions under her breath while performing her version of passing her weight through her center.

Maddie sucked air through the small gap between her two front teeth, an imperfection she had resolutely refused to fix, though choreographers and partners alike had begged her to.

"What leg things do you mean, Alice?"

Maddie released the tension in her neck by dropping her chin to her chest, savoring the dissipating pain as she took several deep breaths. She knew exactly which leg things Alice was asking about. Steps like the *boleo* or the *gancho* required the dancer to lift one foot off the ground in a sharp movement reminiscent of a knife blade slashing through the air. They were the traditional steps that attracted dancers and non-dancers to Argentine Tango.

She wondered if she was ever going to get a new student who understood that learning to dance was a skill that took years to master, not days. This was particularly true of the Argentine Tango, because the initial classes focused on a connection between two people and the music, not the steps. She lifted her chin, pushing several golden-brown curls that had escaped her ponytail back behind her ear, and sighed. She knew she would never say anything to discourage Alice or any other student.

Alice's expression took on that of a hopeful spaniel. "You know, the ones where I get to lift my leg and do this."

Anticipating the upcoming show of enthusiasm, Maddie slid away from her student, neatly avoiding the leg Alice had lifted and then waved about her, as if trying to fend off a ferocious dog.

"Those bits come later, Alice. Good job today. Let's stop and recap what we've done and make sure you know what to practice before our next class."

Alice let her leg drop to the ground uncertainly. Maddie had to motion for her student to sit, before she reluctantly did so.

The two women sat side by side and changed into street shoes. Maddie's movements were languid as she performed the ritual of removing dust from the bottoms of her shoes with a wire brush before placing them in a protective bag, and were a foil to Alice's uncoordinated attempts to unbuckle her own shoes. Maddie dropped her gaze to her water bottle, reassuring herself that Alice was an enthusiastic student and this was enough for her.

"Oh, I love it. I love all of it. I've done swing and two-stepping and salsa. That's where I met Henri. It's all just so great." Maddie watched as Alice turned pink saying the name 'Henri,' omitting the 'h', as the French would.

"Is Henri your boyfriend?" Alice nodded vigorously. "Does he dance too?"

"Oh, does he dance! He's excellent. I met him at a salsa night but he said right then and there that salsa wasn't his dance. It's Argentine Tango that he loves. So that's why I'm here. He wants me to learn so that we can go to Buenos Aires together."

"Did he learn to tango here in Pembroke?" Maddie was certain the answer would be a negative before she asked it. She'd done her research before relocating back to her hometown and knew that the nearest Argentine Tango teacher was in New Brunswick, half an hour down Route 287.

"Oh, my goodness, no. I don't think he would have thought that was good enough." Alice must have realized how that sounded, because she turned a brighter shade of pink before she continued.

"I mean, he's a world traveler, so he's danced just about everywhere—New York, London, Paris and Argentina, of course. He said I had to learn so that when we go to Buenos Aires we can go straight to the *salons*."

Again, Alice colored slightly at the word *salons*. Maddie wondered whether she was embarrassed because she knew her boyfriend sounded like a tango snob. Maddie picked at a pile of brochures and the day's newspaper and rearranged them before looking up. She didn't want to watch the competing emotions wash over Alice because she wasn't sure she would be able to keep what she thought of the boyfriend off her own face. He sounded like a jerk, but what bothered her more, was that Alice had the word 'victim' all but inked on her face. It looked like Alice had been hurt in her life, and history was due to repeat itself.

Maddie continued, "Let Henri know that I'm going to begin *practicas.*"

Alice looked puzzled, so Maddie added: "it's a place to practice what you've learned in class. It starts this Tuesday night and it would be nice for both of you to come."

"Oh, well, gosh, I'll tell him but he's really busy until late most nights. I usually only get to see him at nine o'clock or so."

"Okay. I'll be here from seven, so you're welcome."

Maddie left Alice at the front door of the St. Claire Dance Studio and made her way down the hallway to the office where she hoped to find Peter St. Claire, her new boss. Maddie had joined the staff of the dance studio as the resident Argentine Tango teacher two weeks earlier. Peter taught International Standard and America Smooth and Maddie immediately liked his combination of dry humor and fatherly concern, particularly because at thirty-three, they were the same age. She poked her head into the office, but turned to leave when she saw that it was empty. A frustrated grunt stopped Maddie in her tracks and when she turned back to face several exasperated expletives, she saw Peter pop up from under the computer console.

"I am, at this moment, not happy," Peter raised his hand and revealed a dead mouse.

"Ahhh … Peter, what are doing?"

"Dear child, exactly what it says on the box…collecting the body and disposing of it."

"I hope you're going to wash your hands before your Viennese Waltz class."

"Yes, well, remind me to fire Frank when he finally makes it in. I have asked him time and again to catch them, not kill them." Peter squinted at the dead animal as if ascertaining that it really was dead and sighed. "If only it were still alive, I could take it home for Ernie or Bert to eat."

Maddie had heard about the various animals that Peter and his wife Kristy, collected. They habitually housed numerous stray dogs, cats, rabbits and their most recent additions, Ernie and Bert, two supposedly gorgeous ball pythons. With his wife now pregnant, Peter decided that it would be a health hazard to have any more animals in the house and so, as soon as Kristy brought a new one home, he looked to re-house it.

"You're not interested in a snake are you?" Maddie shook her head and stepped away from Peter's outstretched arm.

He averted his eyes from the mouse as he moved to the wastebasket and unceremoniously plopped it in. "Imagine all the money I could save if I could get Frank to box them up for me," Peter began rummaging in a drawer. "Otherwise I'm going to tell him that I can find an animal-friendly custodian."

"You can't really fire someone who's not on the payroll, can you, Peter?"

Frank was really more like one of Peter and Kristy's animals, a stray human in need of a place to feel welcome, rather than someone who needed a paycheck. He had ostensibly come to the dance studio to take dance classes after he retired. However, Peter couldn't remember him taking a class. As he remembered it, Frank showed up and started to fix things. Two years later, he was still there, fixing things.

"May I inquire, please, how it is you know so much in such a short time working here? In fact, have you even been paid yet? I don't think you're considered an employee with full employee benefits, and that includes gossip and impudence, until you've actually received money from me."

Maddie laughed. "Hey, watch it, Peter, or I won't take Ricky's samba class tonight."

Peter's facial expression changed from mock gravity to mock fear. "Ye gods, woman. You absolutely cannot go thinking down that line. You committed to it. You're there and good luck to you."

"Peter, I'm tired of asking this question and not getting an answer. What is it about this class that sends everyone into a tizzy?"

"What do you mean by that? I'm not in a tizzy. Trust me, you'll know when I'm in a tizzy. This is simply a bit of a titter and I certainly don't know what you're talking about."

"Yes, you do. When I told Philip that I was taking the class for Ricky, he actually made the sign of the cross in front of me." Philip was twenty-three-years-old, *a very young twenty-three,* Maddie thought. He taught the hugely popular Lindy Hop classes at the studio, with his equally young girlfriend Claire. Lindy Hop instructors were barely containable balls of energy.

Peter reached for the pair of glasses in his shirt pocket and positioned them delicately on his nose, a habitual attitude that lent him a look reminiscent of John Lennon. "Maddie, there's nothing sinister going on. Ricky has his favorites, the same way Philip does. And the same way you will too. Remember, I have never had an Argentine Tango specialist of your caliber at the studio."

Maddie coughed self-consciously into her hand and reached for the tissue box next to the computer screen. She didn't consider the fact that she was known as the choreographer of the final Argentine Tango performance on *Dance for Your Life* as a valid reason to praise her abilities, but everyone else seemed to.

Peter and Maddie had spoken about the infamous performance when she first arrived at the studio and, by tacit agreement, had never brought the subject up again.

"That Abigail was, let's just say, developed."

Maddie snorted before she could stop herself. The girl who had deliberately sabotaged her career was, to say the least, developed. She was also vindictive and patient, two qualities that together spelled disaster for Maddie. When Abigail took her clothes off on national television and then swore to the producers that she'd been instructed to do so by her choreographer, the fact that it was a ridiculous fabrication meant nothing when the network censors were on the phone seconds after the episode aired. A flash of nipples in a wardrobe malfunction during the national anthem had nothing on Morgan LeRoux's fully exposed genitals while she executed several elaborate *piernazos* and *boleos*.

Maddie was, of course, fired, but what she didn't expect was that she would be fined. She went from the prospect of making more money for the three-month stint as a reality television choreographer than she had in five years of teaching, to having a bank balance of exactly $345 when she left California. After she'd had to watch Abigail sign a lucrative deal with *People Magazine*, she wasn't sorry to leave.

Maddie bunched the unused tissue into her palm and tossed it into the wastebasket, careful to avoid looking at the dead mouse.

Peter continued as if placating a toddler. "You know I appreciate your effort. But it's only for tonight, then I promise I will never ask you again."

"Why aren't *you* doing it?"

"Samba! Are you mad, girl?" Peter asked as he stomped away, playing the wounded artist. "I didn't spend ten years of my life sneaking down to Mrs. Primrose Devine's basement to learn the intricacies of the fox-trot to sully my reputation with a Latin dance. And by the way, another student asked to have a private with you. His details are on Laura's desk."

Peter tossed this last piece of information over his shoulder *like a treat*, Maddie thought, hoping she'd forgive him for suckering her into teaching the Thursday night samba class. Again, she wondered what she'd gotten herself into.

While keenly interested in a new student, Maddie needed a break and a cup of coffee first. She didn't even spare a glance at the ancient percolator, which sat unplugged atop the filing cabinet, as she picked up her handbag and left the building.

The dance studio was built on the edge of the business section of Pembroke, New Jersey, a revolutionary-era town consisting of mostly 18th century clapboard and 19th century red brick buildings. Maddie smiled as she passed buildings she had grown up with, although most of the buildings' original purposes had been lost to modernization. She was happy to arrive in the fall, her favorite season, but more importantly, it coincided with her parent's departure for a two-month tour of South Africa. Perfect for Maddie, because she needed time to save money before moving out on her own, and the two-bedroom home her parents had scaled down to was the ideal place to do that. The fact was, she was grateful her parents were away. She would never have been able to afford to rent in the area, but she would have gone crazy if she'd to live with them. The three days they spent together before she drove them to the airport were already filled with her mother's on-going perplexed inquisition and her father's precise action plans. She didn't want to have to produce explanations that she didn't have, even though it had been six months since her split from Craig and three since *Dance for your Life* had aired.

Luckily, she didn't have to provide answers. Not for another month, anyway. What she needed to do was make some money and the only thing she was trained to do was teach dance. It felt remarkably unsuccessful to be living at home at the age of thirty-three and she wanted to make sure that the current situation did not become permanent. For that to happen, she'd have to attract students and quickly.

Following three other pedestrians across Main Street, who were all headed in the same direction, she arrived at Vito's, a deli owned by Vito and Rose Bonelli, the parents of her old high school friend, Linda, now a lobbyist in DC. The deli was situated off Main Street, on Elm, leading south to the river. Most of the buildings south of Elm were more industrial in flavor than the ones on Main Street, but again, their personas had changed in fifteen years. There was the old mill that now shipped in wood from a 'good wood' rehabilitation program. Next to that was the carpet factory, now selling rugs for a fair trade exchange program in Guatemala.

The building closest to the river, and by far the largest, was currently a matter of dispute. Maddie had read in the local paper that there were three factions, all vying for ownership of the property. The Pembroke Historical Society had been kicking up a fuss for more than a year and had garnered the support of the majority of the town. As Maddie entered Vito's, she could see official-looking people milling about and cars pulling up to the building.

"Madeleine!" Vito's voice boomed out as soon as she stepped through the door and caused Maddie to jump. She hadn't readjusted yet to the levels of affection the Italian family threw at each other. Vito came out from behind the deli counter and gave Maddie a hug that lifted her off the ground. He then placed her squarely in front of him and took her by the shoulders.

"You are, of course, too skinny." Then, nodding as if making up his mind. "You will have the lasagna." Maddie lifted her hand in supplication.

"Vito, thank you, but I can't. I have to go back to teach."

"What would your mother say if we let you starve? What would your father say?"

Maddie laughed. She knew she wasn't going to leave without the lasagna but she really couldn't stay to eat. A meal with the Bonnelli family was a long and loud affair, and though she was reveling in the warmth of their welcome, she wasn't ready to divulge all the ins and outs of what had happened in California.

Vito pursed his lips, shaking his head slightly.

"What you need is some family and some food, but, aghh … you young ones always know best, hey? Come, I'll wrap the lasagna up and you take it for your dinner. And you want a cappuccino, yes?" Maddie nodded and handed over her travel mug. Vito took it, while raising his eyes to the heavens.

"And while you wait, you give this a read and if you agree, add your signature." Maddie took the clipboard Vito held out to her and read.

"KEEP MULTI-NATIONALS OUT OF PEMBROKE" The three paragraphs under the heading detailed the possible acquisition of the riverfront complex by U.S. Mall Corporation and catalogued the injustices that Pembroke would suffer if this were to happen. Signatures followed and took up three additional pages. Maddie added her name to the end of the list, at number 342.

Leaving the deli, with her mug of coffee in one hand and the foil-wrapped lasagna in the other, Maddie noted that the street had grown more crowded. Now, television crews had joined the small crowd and several dark, glossy sedans pulled up. However interesting the events turned out to be at the riverfront, Maddie had to get back to teach her lesson. After another sip of coffee, she headed back to the studio.

Detective Joe Clancy crouched in his unmarked Chevrolet Impala, on the corner of Main and Elm. Hunched over the bag in his lap, he breathed deeply, pleased that the meditation techniques his sister had shown him were actually working, and that he'd been able to keep the BLT he'd eaten in his stomach. Using a paper napkin, he absorbed the beads of perspiration that had accumulated on his forehead and considered the fruit salad resting next to him warily. Better not.

Instead, he slouched further and glanced out the window to his left. She was still there. Her presence caused his stomach to somersault again. Wishing he were anywhere but where he was, he inhaled through his nose several times before choking on her name. Maddie Fitzpatrick.

Joe had been rhythmically chomping the last bite of sandwich when a flash of golden-brown hair and a tall, lean body caught his eye. What he first suspected was an apparition was wearing something purple that hung from her shoulders and swung in time to her graceful steps, as she cautiously drank from an insulated mug. He knew who it was; in the same way you would know the person you've slept beside every night for thirty years, even if all you glimpsed was the back of her head as she turned a corner. Even so, Joe couldn't immediately trust his instincts. He prayed for the first time in years, begging God that he wasn't just seeing what he wanted to see. Maddie Fitzpatrick had come home. For what reason, or for how long, he didn't know.

Joe had also moved from Pembroke when he was eighteen to go to college, but had returned ten years ago as a junior detective in the police department. In that time, he had risen in the department, gaining respect across the community, and keeping his relationship with Mr. and Mrs. Fitzpatrick cordial, yet distant. He scowled at the memory of his last interaction with the couple and their daughter, the anger and embarrassment still ridiculously alive. He knew that, even after fifteen years, he would not be welcomed back into their home.

Chapter Two

Maddie crossed Main Street and walked north on Pine to return to the studio. She had a private lesson before she had to teach the samba class. The regular samba teacher, Ricky Russo, had been on holiday for the past two weeks, so Maddie hadn't met him, but word had spread and his words were infamous. It was said that Ricky required students to sign confidentiality agreements before they could enter his class. He also demanded the utmost loyalty from his students. If you were taking a class with him, he didn't want to hear about you taking classes with anyone else. Furthermore, it was said that men, while not exactly banned from his classes, were not welcome and were certainly not allowed entry without a woman on their arms. Ricky was supposed to return from his holiday to teach his intermediate class that evening but had called Peter to say he couldn't make it, irritating Peter because it was the third class that Ricky had cancelled, with little consideration for the effect it could have on the dance studio's reputation.

Maddie learned all of this, not from Peter but from the studio's secretary Laura. She'd been with Peter since day one and she knew the studio, with its stories and secrets, better than anyone, including Peter, if you took her word for it. Maddie walked up the front steps to the studio and found Laura watering the plants lining the entrance.

"Your private is here and he's already knocked over the table with all the brochures on it." Laura emptied the last of the water into an overflowing pot of Impatiens.

"That boy needs help, and I'm sure it's not the dance variety that I'm talking about." Laura's natural speech included several huffs per sentence and this last comment was made with her regular sound effects and then a couple of extra ones for good measure. Maddie raised her eyebrows as she eyed the pack of cigarettes bulging from Laura's shirt pocket. Though she'd never seen Laura smoke, she never seen her without an unopened pack somewhere on her body.

The studio secretary stood four feet, nine inches tall and unlike other smaller-statured people, didn't augment her lack of height in any way. She owned several pairs of Keds in bright colors and wore them with jeans most days. From behind, she looked twenty years old; the only clue giving away her sixty-odd years was her head of white hair which refused to be tamed regardless of the gusto with which new styling products were applied daily. With Maddie's height a full foot taller than Laura, she felt like an Amazon next to the petite woman, and this, coupled with the intense huffing, always ensured that Maddie kept a couple of feet between them when they met.

Maddie had also heard the stories about Toby, her next student. He had tried just about every dance style offered at the studio and was found to be rhythmically challenged in each one of them. It didn't bode well for Toby and the Argentine Tango.

After collecting her shoes and taking a mint from a glass pig on Laura's desk, Maddie entered the studio and saw a man she presumed to be Toby, sitting ramrod straight in a chair against the mirror. His eyes were closed, allowing Maddie the opportunity to stare at the most remarkably chiseled jaw line she'd ever seen, and while living in L.A., she'd seen many. He seemed to be humming just under his breath but his only movement was made by his left hand that held a peach, as it rose to his mouth, then relaxed into its original position in his lap after he had taken a bite.

Maddie drew closer and saw that he wore earphones and was listening to something from an iPod gripped in his right hand. He must have sensed her, because his eyes flew open, giving Maddie view to a pair of astonishingly turquoise eyes, as he simultaneously jumped out of the seat, knocked the chair against the mirror, dropped both his iPod and the peach and somehow managed to send his glasses across the room.

"Oh...Ah....Sorry. I just didn't see you." Toby had turned a bright red as he bent to rescue the iPod left dangling from his ear. He then scuttled across the floor to retrieve his glasses that had slid almost out of the door. Maddie stifled a laugh and told him that it was no problem.

She continued to smile to herself as she put her shoes on. Toby looked exactly like the stories she'd heard. He was tall, not impossibly, but tall, probably 6'3, and all gangly, in the manner of teenage boys when they've just hit that growth spurt. But he wasn't a teenager. He already had some attractive silver coming out at his temples, though the hair-style was a decade out of date. Maybe a bit on the nerdy side but altogether a very good-looking nerd, and Maddie had always liked nerds.

"Sorry...I know....I just don't seem to have any coordination. I mean, I've tried all the dances and I just don't get them. This is it. If this doesn't work, I'm just going to go back to my books." Toby looked spent after that revelation. He took a deep breath and remained quiet, but Maddie sensed that it was taking all of his concentration to remain still.

"It's no problem, Toby. I'm Maddie. The fact is, today we're going to work part of the time without music and without really moving much at all." She smiled at his inquisitive expression. "I know, it sounds a bit ridiculous coming to a dance class and not moving, but actually, Argentine Tango is an intellectual dance as well." At this piece of information, Toby brightened. Maddie gestured to the center of the room. Her words had struck a chord.

She began the class by asking him to stand still, then she had him move his weight forward to the tips of his toes, then shift it back onto his heels, realigning his posture as he swayed between the two extremes. She eventually got him to keep his weight on the arches of his feet in a way that was comfortable for him, then, led him through exercises that helped him to release his hips and stretch his torso. Half an hour later, while not an entirely new man, Toby looked like he was ready to start walking.

Toby's problems arose when he had to take Maddie in his arms. In the embrace, Toby lost everything he had achieved when standing on his own. While Maddie had expected it, Toby was caught off guard. After being in the embrace only a half a minute, he ripped his arms away from Maddie.

"I knew it was too good to be true. This isn't going to work." Toby looked as if he was about to storm out the door and Maddie had to think fast to keep him there.

"At the beginning of the process, it's easy to be frustrated. Argentine Tango is primarily about three things. The first aspect is walking. Then you find the connection to your partner and then you connect to the music." Toby's mouth had formed the shape of an *O* and Maddie wasn't convinced that he wouldn't hyperventilate. She sped on.

"During the first couple of months we'll spend our time working with these components, layering them slowly, over and over, so that it becomes instinctive."

Finally, Toby relaxed his facial muscles and released his breath but he continued to shift awkwardly from side to side as he moaned.

"It was all going so well and now it's going wrong again. Why?"

"It's normal." Toby didn't look like he was going to be placated so Maddie continued. "Your muscles haven't learned these movements yet. You've got to give it time. "

"But you put the music on and everything fell apart. It's always the music."

"Remember I said that Argentine Tango is an intellectual dance? That's part of it. It's a head game. You learn the movement first, then you learn to do it with another person. And to do that, sometimes you have to stop thinking about it so hard. For some dancers, that's the most difficult lessons to learn."

"Great, so there's more than one hard part?" Toby had become rigid again, his hands clenching in a way that reminded Maddie of someone holding stress balls.

The remainder of the hour passed with less enthusiasm from Toby, although by the end of class, he told Maddie that he'd learned more from her than any other teacher at the studio and he would be back the following week.

"I'm also running a *practica* on Tuesday nights. It would be a good time to come and practice with other new students."

Toby gulped. "Other students?"

Maddie swallowed another chuckle. "Yes, other students. You'll be dancing with other people before long, believe it or not."

Maddie watched as Toby transferred his weight from left to right, resembling an enthusiastic robot, rather than a dancer.

"Don't worry, Toby. We'll take it slow and I'll see you next week. Tuesday if you can, 7 pm."

Toby gathered his iPod and the peach pit that had rolled under the chair. He had his head turned away from Maddie when he spoke.

"I can't do Tuesday nights. I take a chemistry class at Pembroke College." He went on in a self-deprecating manner, still unable to look Maddie in the eye. "I'm not a full-time student or anything. I just never got a chance to do it when I was younger and thought, what the hell? I've always liked chemistry."

"That's great. The last time I saw a chemistry lab was in high school." Toby simply nodded his head towards Maddie in a gesture she read as a farewell and left the room.

Maddie collapsed in a chair near the window after Toby left. He had taken more energy than she'd anticipated. *What was it that made him try all these different dance styles?* Maddie wondered. The most common reason for a single man to take a dance class was because he was trying to impress a girl, followed by a man whose mother had intervened and insisted that he take up dancing to meet a nice young woman. There was always the guy who hoped that women who danced were also women who would have sex with him and she wouldn't rule that one out completely in the case of Toby Downs. She noticed he wasn't wearing a wedding ring, but that didn't mean anything these days. She figured she could ask Laura for the scoop tomorrow.

Maddie turned the sound system and lights off and closed the studio door behind her, only to find her way blocked by three women in flowing robes reminiscent of Arthurian legend. The shortest of the three turned to face Maddie and smiled. It was all Maddie could do not to reach out and touch the elfin creature who hovered before her with hair falling to her waist. Maddie marveled at its color, as she forcibly held her hand down at her side. It looked like strawberries picked on a hot summer day. The creature spoke with a wispy, ephemeral voice that said she was only on this planet for a short time.

"Oh, Madeleine. It is Madeleine, isn't it?" Maddie nodded.

"I've left the large classroom open for you. I heard that you will be in there tonight." She tilted her head and looked at Maddie through half-closed eyes. "Such a light spirit. You will work so much more smoothly in this space. Richard is, well, let's just say his presence is heavy."

Maddie snapped her mouth shut when she realized that she'd been staring at this woman with it hanging open.

"And rest assured, I've already cleansed the room. My class called many daring entities and I wouldn't want any of them staying behind to cause mischief unintentionally." With that, she turned on her toes and floated away as dandelion fluff does in the wind, her two companions wafting behind her.

As the three women moved to the front entrance, Laura came out of the office and looked as if she was ready to propel the three forms out the door with her broom.

Maddie gasped. "What was that?"

Laura's huff was accompanied by several vehement head shakes this time. "That was Cathwrynn, spelled with a *W*, a *Y* and two *N*s. She rents the space from Peter for her WiccaJoyDance, an amalgamation of joyful, soulful, spirit-filled dance involving mind, body and soul." Laura stopped sweeping and peered over her glasses at Maddie. "I'm quoting directly from her blurb in the brochure, just in case you're getting any funny ideas about me." Maddie laughed as she promised Laura that she was definitely not getting any funny ideas about her.

"Peter certainly has a motley crew surrounding him, doesn't he?

Laura nodded. "That's exactly right. He likes broken or strange things." She seemed to give up the pretense of sweeping and leaned against the broom. Maddie felt a shiver run up her spine, empathizing with the words strange and broken.

"Not me, you understand, and I'm sure, not you." Maddie felt Laura's breath on her face and took a furtive step away from the woman and her broom.

Laura shook her head as she continued. "It's all I can do to keep things running around here, what with all that goes on. Peter letting all these crazy teachers use the building. Next thing you know, there'll be a bad element here and then what will we do?"

Maddie wasn't sure if she was supposed to answer, but the issue resolved itself when the phone rang and Laura gave a final huff, then a tap to her cigarettes, and departed.

Maddie followed Laura into the office and collected her dinner. She left the lasagna from Vito in the refrigerator and took her rice bowl leftovers, nodding to Laura who was on the phone explaining to someone that, no, the studio did not have a pole dancing class. Maddie glanced back at Laura to see the secretary holding the receiver a foot away from her ear with an exaggerated look of disgust on her face.

Leaving the office, she found Cathwrynn floating back down the hallway, her eyes wide. She wafted within three inches of Maddie's face and whispered moodily.

"There's an evil presence waiting for you." Maddie couldn't help but giggle at the theatrics when Cathwrynn lifted both hands in the air and let them flutter down to her sides. "I mean really. It's that Nina LePore and she says she wants to converse with you."

Maddie turned to Laura, who'd finished her conversation and was standing at the door of the office again. "Do you think this Nina LePore actually said that she wants to converse with me?" Laura didn't answer but inhaled, then rose on her toes to lift herself over her 4'9 figure. "Should I know who Nina LePore is?" This time, Laura raised her eyebrows and jiggled her head about before disappearing into the bathroom as she spoke over her shoulder.

"Let's put it this way. You're about to and I don't envy you."

Maddie cautiously looked into the classroom she'd be using for the samba class. Standing up against the full-length mirror, staring at her image as she opened and closed her mouth in alternating wide and small circles, a woman with deep auburn hair straight out of a bottle ignored Maddie's entrance. She was about 5'5, but with her three-inch heels, she almost reached Maddie's height. She had a toned body, but the sleeveless shirt she was wearing revealed bruises on her inner arms, faint and somewhat obscured by make-up, but bruises nonetheless. She also had a bandage on the right side of her neck, lending her the appearance of a recent vampire victim.

Maddie tore her gaze away from the woman's arms and found herself looking directly into her eyes. Maybe evil was a strong a word for Cathwrynn to use, but there was definitely something not altogether nice about this woman's eyes. She had the telling signs of plastic surgery that Maddie had seen exhaustively in Southern

California, but she estimated that Nina LePore was in her late 40s.

The woman turned slowly. "You're Madeleine and you're teaching Ricky's class tonight." The strained and overly distinct voice could have been issuing an accusation or asking a question. Maddie couldn't tell.

"I just want you to know I'm Nina LePore. I'm Ricky's girlfriend and dance partner and I assist his class. I will assist you tonight."

Maddie waited a couple of Buddhist seconds before she responded, but found she'd lost her opportunity. Nina had turned on her heels, picked up her handbag sitting on a chair and walked towards the door. When she was halfway out she stopped and turned to Maddie again.

"You look familiar. You didn't have anything to do with that show, did you?" Nina looked appraisingly at Maddie, her lips pursed and nose twitching as if she were sniffing Maddie out. Maddie knew she was going to have to come up with something to say once people made the inevitable connection with *Dance for Your Life,* but she hadn't yet, so she remained silent. Seeming to have come to a negative conclusion, Nina pivoted and was gone.

Wow, Maddie thought. If Nina LePore was a portent of things to come, Peter really was going to owe her one.

She sighed. She had just enough time before the samba class to eat. On her way out she ran into Peter piling bags into his Mazda MX.

"Want a lift anywhere, sweetheart?"

"Nope. I'm going to eat in the gardens and prepare myself for the dreaded samba class."

"Hey Maddie, don't hate me for it. Have a good night. Frank will lock up."

Maddie waved good-bye as Peter sped off a little too quickly to be legal.

The dance studio parking lot backed onto the gardens of the Museum of Colonial Life, and a hole in the fence meant that Maddie didn't have to walk around the building to get to them. As she stepped through the opening, a hand reached out and grabbed her shoulder. Maddie screamed and her assailant let out a yelp of his own as he dropped his arm.

"Oh, sorry, I ..." The boy, still a teenager, staggered away from Maddie, clearly surprised to find her there.

"I... Sorry, I was just..." The boy hadn't yet finished a sentence and the way he was swaying in front of Maddie made her think he was drunk.

"Um, are you looking for someone?" Maddie looked back towards the studio to see if there was anyone around in case she needed help. His clothes were soiled and she realized the moldy smell in the air was coming from him.

"Sure, sure. I need some. He's here isn't he?"

Maddie could barely make out the words the boy mumbled, but as she watched his eyes roll back in his head, she understood that he was on drugs. She was going to head back to the studio to avoid having to deal with him, but before she could, he darted through the hole in the fence and weaved his way across the parking lot and out of sight.

She breathed deeply, hoping he didn't return and went to what she now considered her spot, a bench in the eastern corner of the garden that held onto the last rays of the autumn sun. Each day she sat and noticed how much more quickly the sun disappeared and missed sunny California. She was a creature of habit, so the book she held, *The Blind Assassin*, was one she was reading for the fourth time and the rice bowl was one she'd eaten hundreds of times in various combinations with her ex-boyfriend.

Nostalgia almost overwhelmed her, but she shook it off when she realized that at least she had called Craig her ex-boyfriend. For two months after he broke up with her, she continued to think of him as her partner. They'd been broken up for six months now. While she did sink periodically into self-pity, those moments were growing increasingly infrequent and she accorded that accomplishment to the fact that she was no longer in proximity to the intense, beautiful and self-absorbed Craig.

She finished her meal, marked her place in the book and told herself that this was where she wanted to be right now. She had a job, which in this economy was fortunate. She had the space to think her next steps through because her parents were conveniently away. They were loving and supportive, but had she and her parents been living in the same house during this time of transition, Maddie would have gone crazy.

Packing up her dinner, she climbed back through the fence and had to thank her lucky stars that she had quick reflexes, because they saved her as she sprang back to avoid being run over by a red Toyota Prius with realtor advertising on the doors. She stopped dead in her tracks, not because of the near collision, but because of the name on the car. The decal read, *Clemments Realty—Let Me Make a House Your Home.* Maddie pulled her eyes from the writing on the door to the person behind the wheel. Katy Clemments, in the flesh. Katy gaped at Maddie in equal bemusement and Maddie had the distinct impression that Katy was thinking about driving off, but reconsidered and lowered the window with the push of a button.

"Maddie Fitzpatrick. What a surprise." Katy shook herself, as if trying to wake from a dream, then lowered her oversized sunglasses, revealing piercing green eyes. "Wow! What are you doing here?"

Maddie swallowed and wondered why Katy's question irked her. She'd returned to town and should expect to run into people from her past. Katy, on the other hand, couldn't have expected to bump into someone she hadn't seen in fifteen years.

"I'm back in town, actually. I moved back last month and I'm teaching at the dance studio." She pointed to the back door. Katy followed Maddie's finger and appeared to be digesting this information. "How are you?" Maddie tried to maintain a cool façade she didn't possess. She felt her words tripping over themselves and she was already conjuring up the thoughts in Katy's head. Had she seen *Dance for Your Life*? Did she know that Maddie coming back to Pembroke was admitting failure? But Katy hardly paused to consider the reasons for Maddie's return as she pushed her sunglass back up her nose.

"Great. In fact, I'm better than great. I've got my own business. See?" Katy tapped the words that sat just under her fingers resting on her door. Her nails were long and painted, Maddie noticed with a groan, and the exact color of her car.

"I'm mostly into residential sales so if you're looking for a place, you know who to call." At this, Maddie was horrified to anticipate, Katy reached to the space above her steering wheel where Maddie could see an envelope of business cards attached to the dashboard. Katy handed her one clasped between two fingers. Maddie looked at it and saw once again, Katy's name and her position and printed underneath: *Pembroke. I'd never live anywhere else.* Katy had already released the brake and the car was inching away.

"But Katy, what are you doing here? Are you taking a class?"

"Oh, good grief, no, not me. My mother wanted me to pick up a brochure for her. She wants to take waltzing classes or some such thing. Is that something you teach?" The question was asked with such disdain that Maddie thought she must have been imagining it. She and Katy hadn't been close friends, but they'd known each other for twelve years of elementary, junior and high school and Maddie was annoyed that Katy didn't appear interested in why she'd moved back.

"I can get you a brochure if you'd like. Peter St. Claire teaches the International Standard dances and he's a fantastic teacher." Maddie thought back to Katy's family and remembered that her father had died during their freshman year. It was devastating for Katy's mother to find out that her father had had a girlfriend and that they had had a child together.

"How is your mother?"

"Oh, she's great. Listen, I have to go. I'll come back and stop in for a chat tomorrow." Her car was already three feet away when she shouted out that it was really weird, them running into each other after all these years.

Maddie realized, with unexpected clarity, that she had thought that her return would elicit more excitement from some of her old classmates. As she crossed the parking lot, the reality of the situation exploded in her head. She was here and ready to start all over again, but all the people she'd known in her teens, people she'd systematically cut from her life when she moved to California, had gone on with theirs and were, at most, only peripherally interested in getting to know her again. She took a deep breath and went back into the studio to teach the samba class.

"Did you know?" Joe's voice came through the phone in a rush of emotion that told Maureen she'd have to answer carefully. Joe Clancy was one of the best police officers she'd ever known and she wasn't saying that because she was his secretary, or because she was his sister. Joe had been honored by the town, county and state during his career and was recognized as a leading contender for the next Assistant Chief of Police. Yet Maureen heard his voice and knew immediately that he'd either heard or seen that Maddie Fitzpatrick was back in town.

"Well?"

"Well, what, Joe? People usually say hello when they call someone. Or did you forget that social grace?"

"Did you or did you not know that Maddie was here? And don't even answer that. I know you did. How long is she here for?"

Maureen exhaled. She was at home, stirring a pot of white sauce for a potato bake, and hadn't seen Joe after he left the office at 3 pm in search of a late lunch. She'd wondered why and now knew. He was thirty-three, five years older than Maureen, but at times like these, Maureen felt like the elder of the siblings.

"Yes, Joe, and calm down. I haven't seen her and I only heard about it over the weekend." She thought about ending it there, as she tasted the sauce and added more garlic, but knew that full disclosure would be necessary to get her out of this conversation. "Tracy told me."

"Tracy?" Maureen expected sputtering and rage, but what she got was a more threatening and worrisome whisper.

"Yes, Joe, Tracy. Now, you listen here. Tracy said she saw Maddie on Friday and wondered whether she should say something to you. She asked me what I thought she should do, and do you know what I told her?"

Joe cleared his throat and when he spoke he'd lost some of the edge in his voice.

"Yes, Maureen. I think I can imagine what you said." Joe wanted to hang up, but Maureen wasn't done with him.

"I said, Joe Clancy, that you and Tracy weren't dating anymore and she doesn't owe you anything. And," Maureen hit the wooden spoon she'd been waving in the air hard against the pot of sauce in front of her, "that you and Maddie are adults and whatever it is you have to say or do with one another, you're old enough to do it. Do you hear me? And make sure you eat something. I'm making a potato bake; come over if you want."

Maureen hung up, leaving Joe lying on his kitchen floor with the dial tone echoing in his ear. He thought about what his sister had said. She was right, of course. Then he thought about the potato bake and his stomach turned again. He slowly got to his feet, grabbed a six-pack from the refrigerator and collapsed on the sofa.

Chapter Three

Maddie had a couple of minutes to freshen up and get a bottle of water before her class. In the office she found the janitor, Frank Monroe, on a ladder navigating a box onto a shelf above Laura's desk. Frank was the happiest person she'd ever met, hands down. Always smiling, always ready to say something to make you laugh, Frank oozed cheeriness. Maddie loved it, but she hadn't been working there long enough to have had a bad day; one of those ones when you see a person like Frank and just want to throttle him.

"Hey, sunshine, how're you doing?"

Maddie grinned. "I'm great, Frank. Just ran into someone I haven't seen in fifteen years. How are you?"

"Super. Super." He said it like he meant it and added a rub to his abundant stomach as if somehow his good cheer was related to what he'd just eaten.

"Guess you're going to have to get used to that. Running into all sorts of ghosts." He said this with a laugh and another rub, this time to his head. Then he touched his nose and winked at her.

Maddie reached over to stabilize the ladder as Frank climbed down. "You're right. I haven't put much thought into some of the people I could end up running into." Maddie looked up at the ceiling, sure that Frank could see through her lie. She'd put quite a bit of time into thinking about seeing Joe Clancy again. There was hardly anyone from her graduating class still living in Pembroke and it was her bad luck that one of them was

Joe Clancy and not just living there but a prominent member of the town.

While her parents hadn't bothered to provide any information about Joe over the years, they had, of course, discussed the situation in detail with Maddie's sister, Sylvie, who'd dutifully passed news on to Maddie. She knew that Joe had gone to college in Maryland and she knew that he'd returned and joined the police force, a fact that surely bemused her parents.

"Oh, it sounds like there's a story. Too bad you can't sit down now but I know you have some teaching to do. I'm just going to putter round here until you're done." Frank looked at his feet, as if hearing something from them. "Seems like I was just doing something…"

Frank trailed off, then lifted his head, smiled and waved at Maddie before leaving the room. Brushing a slight concern for Frank aside, Maddie picked up her dance bag. She had five minutes before she expected the students to arrive and she wanted to warm up so that she'd have a chance to chat before class began. She hadn't been given instructions, only told that it was an intermediate level class and that she should teach them a stand-alone step, as Ricky Russo would have his own syllabus to follow when he returned.

Maddie wore her Cuban heels again and entered the room to find an astonishing sight standing in the centre of the room. A woman had her hands on ridiculously curvy hips and was pouting at herself in the mirror. Maddie was so taken by the sheer image of this woman—hips and breasts clad in a lilac cat-suit, platinum blond hair, heels that raised her at least four inches off the ground—that she only noticed as an afterthought that the woman was rolling her ankles in the semblance of a warm-up. Maddie stopped at the threshold of the door and prepared to say hello, when the woman lifted her hand in what looked to Maddie like a sign that said 'don't talk to me, I'm busy.'

Ignoring the signal, if that was indeed what it was, Maddie walked into the room, determined not to have a Nina LePore repeat performance. "Hi, I'm Maddie. I'm teaching the samba class tonight. Are you in it?" Maddie walked by the woman as she spoke and put her dance bag and water bottle on the table next to the sound system. The woman surprised Maddie and did an about face, then walked toward Maddie with an off-centre smile.

"I'm so sorry." The woman drew out every letter in those three words, as if she could make them true. "I get so involved in my dancing, sometimes I don't even notice other people in the room. Ricky says it's a sign of true talent. My name is Andrea." She didn't offer her last name, but she held out her hand for Maddie to shake. Maddie took it as gracefully as she could but before she could close her fingers around Andrea's hand, the shake was over. Andrea stepped back and began rotating her ankles again.

"I'm always very careful to warm up before all classes, though I think you'll find that not everyone is so diligent." She enunciated the word *diligent* as if she thought Maddie had never heard it before.

"Yes, well, showing care for your body, and the work it can do, is admirable." Maddie turned away quickly and took a sip of water. She noticed Andrea turning back to the mirror looking like she'd just won a contest.

"You're older than I thought you'd be. What are you? About forty?"

Maddie, not sure she'd be able to control what came out of her mouth next, was actually grateful that Nina LePore came through the door.

Maddie watched with interest as the two women made elaborate eye contact in the mirror and then promptly ignored one another. Nina didn't even glance at Maddie but stalked to the far side of the room and rooted around in her shoe bag, producing from it a pair of shoes to rival Andrea's. Maddie wondered if she should go back to finish her PhD in dance studies. She could title her thesis *Do Shoes Make the Dance?* It would be a study on whether adding height to shoes increased dancing ability or just made the dancer look desperate?' Maddie winced at her own thoughts with an unexpected pang of sympathy for these two clearly sad women.

Finally, more students arrived to dissipate the tension. The couple who came through the door next walked hand in hand and appeared to be the complete opposite of the two women already in the room; naturally blond, fresh-faced and clearly in love with one another. They were giggling between themselves and when they saw Maddie, their faces sparkled like Christmas tree lights. With none of the affectations Andrea and Nina exhibited, these two came directly to Maddie.

"Hi. We're Robyn and Jesse Booth. Are you teaching class today?" The woman spoke with a Southern accent that reminded Maddie of her dance history professor from Louisiana. Maddie was so taken aback to have enthusiastic words spoken to her, she couldn't help but grin back at them. Then he spoke with a similar accent.

"We're sure glad to see a new face around here." His voice was clearly audible and at his words, Andrea and Nina, who'd been occupied with their own reflections, simultaneously glared at him. Judging from his reaction, he didn't care a bit that they'd heard him and he grabbed Robyn's hand again and started swinging it between them. They may have been from the South, but *they looked like they were from Utah*, Maddie thought, all clean wholesomeness and white teeth.

"I'm Madeleine Fitzpatrick—call me Maddie. It's a bit of a surprise for me, teaching today. I think Peter had expected your teacher to be back."

Robyn laughed again. "Well, we're certainly glad to have some different input. We love dancing, but this class has been challenging." Robyn said all that with a smile, but there was an undercurrent of anger in her words. She let her eyes slide over to Andrea and then Nina, before jabbing Jesse playfully in the ribs. "He's really good. You'll see tonight." Jesse looked sheepishly at Maddie and coughed unnecessarily into his hand.

"How did the two of you hear about the class?"

Again, the gleeful exuberance of youth flew out of their mouths as they finished each other's sentences.

"Oh, we won it…"

"…at the College…

"…Jesse is a lecturer…"

"…We were the best in the limbo-duo."

Jesse grinned. "We're very limber." Robyn then grabbed Jesse saying she wanted to practice a bit to warm up.

While she'd been talking with Jesse and Robyn, three other people had arrived at the class. One woman came directly into the room without making eye contact with anyone. She was as hard as Andrea and Nina but in her own way. She was clad entirely in black and her hair was tied back in an impossibly tight bun midway up her head. Maddie had been a dancer for twenty-eight of her thirty-three years and she knew just how tight a bun could be. She looked like the ideal dancer, with a tall, graceful body, and unlike the two divas, her body looked natural.

Maddie was so engrossed in contemplation over this woman's perfectly proportioned body that she was startled by the woman's face when Bun-Head finally looked up. It was a hard face to look at and Maddie instinctively turned away. It was flat, her eyes were too far apart and her nose too small. In fact, all of her features looked as if they hadn't had time to grow before they decided they were done. Bun-Head registered Maddie and read her reaction before turning her attention back to her shoes.

Focusing on the other people who'd entered the room, she was unsure whether the man and woman were a couple. The man stood several feet away from the woman and then began to circle the perimeter of the room. The woman stood at the door, her nose inches away from the inside of her bag so that Maddie couldn't see her face. When the man had circled the room once and had come to a stop next to the windows, he whipped his head towards the door and snapped his fingers. Maddie watched as the woman jumped and stumbled her way to his side. It was then that Maddie recognized the woman as Alice Walters, her earlier private Argentine Tango lesson and he, Maddie presumed, was her boyfriend—the infamous Henri.

Maddie took an instant dislike to him. He looked slimy, no better way to put it. His hair had receded and was brushed over the top to try to disguise the fact, and his sideburns were an inch too long. He was chewing gum with his mouth open, his hands stuck into the tops of his jeans, as if he was about to rip them off and expose himself to his adoring female fans. However, no other woman in the room paid any attention to him, save for Alice, and she looked at him with a mixture of what Maddie read as adulation and fear. She looked like a puppy that desperately wanted to lick her master, but knew that if she did she would be kicked.

Henri surveyed the room, looked directly at Maddie with a leer, then passed over her, dismissed Jesse and Robyn, lingered over Nina and finally let his eyes collide into Andrea and actually grunted. Andrea, to give her credit, ignored him.

Maddie didn't think it could get worse and she contemplated actually hating Peter for this. She glanced at the clock and knew she had to start class when the door opened again. Toby lingered at the threshold and Maddie didn't hide her surprise.

"Toby, what are you doing here? Are you in this class?"

"Oh...no, absolutely not." He entered the room and stopped short of Maddie as if he'd tripped, although she could see nothing he could have stumbled on.

"It's just, I was talking to Peter before he left and he said you were taking this class and he said if I wanted to watch it might be okay." His words came out of his mouth like an avalanche, as if he needed to get the words out as quickly as possible lest he choke on them. He continued:

"He said that I wouldn't be able to watch when the regular teacher came back and that maybe you wouldn't mind." He then gulped loudly and rubbed his eyes behind his glasses.

"That's great; you're welcome to stay, Toby. I'm just starting class now." Toby looked relieved and went quickly towards a seat by the mirror. He walked by Bun-Head, who resolutely turned her face away with a look of disgust making her face even uglier. It looked as if her reaction got to him and he was about to bolt but instead he took a deep breath and continued to move further into the class. When he saw Andrea, Maddie noticed him stumble. An alluring smile practically jumped off her face and landed at Toby's feet. He blushed all the way to his hairline and seeing that, Andrea pushed out her enormous décolletage.

"Right; let's get class going. As you can see, your regular teacher was unable to come tonight and I've been asked to take this class. My name is Maddie Fitzpatrick and I'm primarily an Argentine Tango teacher." As Maddie spoke, she took in the myriad of responses from the people around the room. At the mention of Argentine Tango, Alice perked up a bit and, for the first time, let her eyes fall away from Henri. Henri, on the other hand, rolled his eyes and continued watching Andrea. Andrea looked coolly at Maddie, as did Nina. Bun-Head's face was blank but she nodded at every other sentence. Jesse and Robyn were still holding hands and still smiling broadly and Toby remained seated, but looked as if he would gladly fade into the mirror if he could.

"Okay, I don't know exactly what Ricky has been doing with you…"

Nina interrupted. "Obviously, I can tell you that."

At this outburst, Andrea snorted and Henri rolled his eyes again and everyone else seemed to be suffering various degrees of embarrassment.

"It's true," Nina continued and then made up her mind with a shrug of her shoulders as she walked to stand next to Maddie. She smiled broadly and stood so close to Maddie, she almost knocked her over with the scent of her perfume.

"I'm sorry; I didn't explain the way that Ricky teaches and offer you some suggestions for instruction."

Unable to contain herself, Andrea stamped her foot. "Oh, please, can we just get on with it? Obviously, you didn't practice with Ricky before this class because he's not here."

Nina spun her head to face Andrea. "Actually, I did. And, just so you know, we're back together so you can just take your slutty eyes off him." She punctuated her sentence with a smack of her lips as she turned back to face Maddie, clearly planning to further instruct Maddie on how she should teach the class. However, Henri took the opportunity to add his own thoughts to the spectacle.

"Now, now, ladies, there's plenty of men to go around, if any of you should need a little attention." Maddie watched, relieved as every woman in the room made faces ranging from disappointment (Alice), to outrage (Robyn), to contempt (Andrea) and disgust (Bun-Head). Maddie felt as if she was in kindergarten.

"Yes, Andrea is right. Let's get started. I'd like it if everyone would come out to the dance floor and tell me your name." Surprisingly, all the students did as Maddie had asked. Andrea stated her name loudly and with flair. Next, Henri introduced himself first, omitting the 'h' in his name and adding Alice as an afterthought. Alice said nothing. Bun-Head introduced herself as Renée Lambert. Then Robyn introduced herself and Jesse himself. Nina looked disdainfully towards the windows and Maddie didn't push it.

"And what about him?" Andrea pouted and motioned over to Toby.

"Oh...I mean, I'm not in the class. I'm just going to watch." Toby looked as if he'd have willingly jumped into a hole in the studio floor if one had opened up.

"Don't be silly," Andrea sashayed closer to him. "You can see that we need an extra man, can't you?"

Toby appealed for support from Maddie while Henri's expression said that he'd be all the man any of these women would ever need.

Nina's voice broke the silence. "Oh, for heaven's sake, just join us. We're working on *solo spot voltas*. You can just be a support while the woman turns around you." With that, she gave Andrea another dirty look and then turned toward the mirror to practice her *voltas*.

Maddie thought she was going to scream. She knew she had to take control of the class or she might as well just apologize and tell them all to go home. "Toby, please join in." Then turning to the rest of the class, she continued. "I start my class differently from Ricky and I think you will all benefit from the change."

Jesse and Robyn looked clearly relieved and signaled Maddie with thumbs up. Whether the relief came from Maddie taking control or the different class structure, Maddie appreciated their enthusiastic response.

"Okay, everyone out on the dance floor. Please bring your feet together, release your pelvis into the floor, bend your knees and I'd like you to sink your tail bone into the floor and bend into a *plié* in parallel."

She'd gotten everyone's attention and the class followed her instructions without grumbling—Andrea and Nina doing so in what looked like an effort to outshine one another, but doing it, nonetheless. Even Henri stopped his constant roving eyes but he couldn't seem to stop himself correcting Alice. As Alice had performed the very same exercises that afternoon, she was doing just fine and Maddie let her know. That elicited a glare from Henri but when he saw Maddie looking at him in the mirror, he gave her an ingenuous smile and shut up.

"Now keep your arms weighted and bring them up over your head, reaching for the ceiling, stretching tall until your heels are off the floor and your weight is in your toes. Hold this position and breathe. Let your stomach relax and move in and out with each breath." Maddie couldn't suppress a giggle because the moment she said the word *stomach*, all the women and Henri, had sucked theirs in.

"Now let your heels come back to the floor and...."
Before Maddie could continue, the door flung open and
both Andrea and Nina threw their arms in the air and
screamed.

Chapter Four

Nina and Andrea simultaneously flew into action, each using the other to propel herself towards the man in the doorway.

"Ricky, Ricky, you're here!"

"Oh, Ricky, you've come back!"

The man held his hands up as if protecting himself, as both women tumbled toward him. However, within an instant, he'd stopped the nonsense with another flutter of his hands, as if shooing annoying flies.

"Girls, girls." In a flash, he grabbed the hand of each woman and pulled one to either side of his body. "Class, I do apologize for the inconvenience of my late arrival. It couldn't be helped, but I'm here now, thank goodness." Ricky paused to survey the room and gave Maddie an inquisitive look, followed by a weak smile.

Maddie hadn't met Ricky Russo, although she'd seen several photos of him, but he didn't look like the images she'd seen. In those, he had a superficial look achieved by slicked hair, perfectly manicured eyebrows and a knowing smile aimed directly at the viewer. The photos were choreographed. The man standing in front of Maddie was, first off, older than the photos, more like fifty than the projected image of an eternal thirty five year old. And he had a rumpled look, as if he hadn't slept or changed his clothes in several days, leading Maddie to wonder what kind of vacation Ricky had been on.

As if reading Maddie's thought, Ricky appeared to awaken out of a reverie. He pushed the two women towards the rest of the class, who were still gaping at the spectacle of the three of them, and spoke to the whole group.

"Again, I apologize for my abrupt arrival and my appearance. I hadn't thought I'd be able to make the class; however, at the last minute, an alternative arrangement presented itself and I made haste to take advantage of it." Then, presenting his disheveled look with a flourish of his hands, he continued, "Thus, the state of my appearance. Nevertheless, it's time we move on with class."

With that, he took Maddie by the hand. Nina and Andrea both glared at Maddie, then Andrea flipped her head as she walked to the far end of the room, as far as she could be from the rest of the class while still remaining a part of it. Nina, however, did not take Russo's not-so-subtle hint and slid in between Ricky and Maddie and, much to Maddie's discomfort, began stroking Ricky's neck. It looked as if she was readying to kiss him, when he swung his arm up to block her face. She continued, apparently unfazed.

"And thank you so much for taking care of me. The swelling's gone down now," she said.

As one hand continued to grip Maddie's unwilling one, Ricky's other hand reached up to the bandage on Nina's neck. He lowered his voice so that only Nina and Maddie could hear him.

"Good, I'm glad to hear that. Now get back with the rest of the class and behave."

If Nina had been hoping for a touching reunion she was disappointed, and judging from the way she paled at Ricky's words, she was not prepared for the brush-off. Maddie was sure there were tears forming in the corners of her eyes but she turned away and was three feet from the two dance teachers before she spat.

"I told her what we were doing, darling, but we hadn't even started anything."

Ricky's arms flapped about again, before he regained control with a melodramatic sigh. He surveyed the room with what looked like disappointment, In the same instant that Ricky noticed him, Maddie remembered that Toby was there uninvited. Toby had been slinking away from the group, but stopped when he felt Ricky's eyes on him, an expression of absolute rage spreading over the teacher's face. Maddie stepped in before he had time to say anything to Toby.

"Hi, I'm Madeleine Fitzpatrick. I'm glad to see that you've returned from your vacation, as I see your class is too."

Maddie tried to pry her hand away from Russo's, but he held on tighter. The anger that had seemed about to boil over five seconds earlier was replaced by a charm-filled smile, as he brought Maddie's hand to his lips.

"My dear girl, I'm so pleased to finally meet you. And to have you here to demonstrate to the class today, is an honor."

He kissed Maddie's hand again and then turned to the class, still clutching her hand in his. His gaze hovered over the heads of all the students and Toby took that as his command to leave. Maddie tried to catch his eye to give him some encouragement as he slunk out the door, but he appeared not to be looking beyond the lenses of his glasses.

"And so, we're working on *spot voltas* today. Everyone take a partner." Russo immediately took Maddie in his arms and danced three *voltas*, added a couple of *whisks* and ended with an inappropriate dip.

"Ah, perfection," he murmured close to her ear. "I will have to bring you over to samba, Madeleine. Over to the dark side, as they say."

Maddie was so flummoxed she said nothing, but gave a bemused smile as Russo finally broke away from her to talk to the class. Part of the problem, Maddie admitted, was that he was a good dancer. Better than that, he was excellent. Maddie could tell in those thirty seconds of dancing that he had complete control of both himself and his partner, moving as if in liquid. It was just the kind of expertise that women fell for and she understood now why the women in this class idolized him. *Too bad he's so creepy*, she thought as she wiped her hands on her skirt.

While Maddie moved toward her bags, determined to leave before the night became any more carnivalesque, Ricky moved around the room, giving cursory attention to Robyn and Jesse, completely ignored Henri and offered more detailed ministrations to the women. He glided over to Nina, who lapped up his words as if they were thick cream. She couldn't seem to help herself from looking over at Andrea and gloating. Andrea just tossed her head, however, and went on with her practice. Then Maddie saw Nina's demeanor change, deflating from the inside. When Ricky moved on to dance with Renée, Nina looked around herself in an apparent panic and, for a moment, Maddie thought she was going to run after Ricky and make a fool of herself again. However, in an abrupt change in behavior, Nina made a spastic motion, as if she'd received a message from aliens, grabbed her handbag and ran out the door, slamming it behind her.

Maddie collected her water bottle and dance bag, but her plans to leave were thwarted as she passed Jesse and Robyn.

"Please, Maddie, can you show us how the end of the step goes?" Robyn implored Maddie, with her eyes as round as saucers and speaking volumes. Maddie instantly felt sorry for them, such a wholesome couple stuck in the middle of this soap opera.

"Sure, the trick is making sure your weight doesn't move into your chest but stays in your hips." Jesse and Robyn were actually pretty adept, proving to Maddie that she wasn't wanted so much for dance instruction as for her ability to add some normality to the class. As Ricky was deeply engrossed in dancing with Renée, and she saw Jesse and Robyn were ready for a *whisk*, she added it onto the step they were working on. Ricky had, by this time, partnered with Andrea and had pulled her into an embrace so close, her already straining bust looked as if it was going to escape and run from the room.

Edging toward the door, Maddie glanced around the room and caught sight of Alice's expression as Henri hauled her across the dance floor. Maddie deliberated. She had no interest in talking to Henri, but she thought she owed Alice some support against the brute.

As she walked up to them, she caught the last words Henri was snarling in Alice's ear. "You don't know anything about it so why don't you just shut up and dance."

Alice blanched at Henri's words and then blushed when she saw Maddie approach.

"Oh, hi, Maddie. We were just trying this move out. I'm not so good at it, as you can see." Maddie felt such a loathing for Henri she wasn't sure she could stand there and not spit at him. Impulsively, she took Alice by the hand and led her into three *voltas*. When they stopped dancing and Maddie released her, Alice looked at Maddie in awe.

"No Alice, actually you can dance those *voltas* perfectly." Turning to Henri, she thought she might regret what she was about to say. "Henri, why don't you try them with me and let's see where you're going wrong."

Maddie watched as the color in Henri's face turned from pink to scarlet to purple. If it had been different circumstances, she would have marveled at the fact that the human body could change colors in such rapid succession. As it was, she took a step back from Henri, unsure whether he would spring at her. However, Henri surprised her by opening his arms and lifting them in the air.

"Ah, you 'ave got me, *mademoiselle*. The samba is not yet a dance under my profession, is that what you call it? The Argentine Tango, you see, is my specialty." Henri then bowed his head briefly before looking down onto the top of Alice's head, taking her by the hand and pulling her close to his body.

"This *trés belle* woman is learning so that we can dance the *salons* of the world together." Alice, for her part, grew rosy pink and looked adoringly up into Henri's face, a difficult task, as he was holding her head in a vice grip against his chest.

As Maddie regretted offering Alice support, Nina came back into the room and walked past them, carrying a small box held proudly in front of her like a prized possession. Maddie noted, in exasperation, that Nina had dumped her bag directly on top of Maddie's. As Nina passed Andrea and Ricky, she thrust the box toward them and cooed, "Thank you, darling, so thoughtful." With a dumbstruck class for an audience, Nina elaborately opened the box, lifted out a chocolate and proceeded to make pseudo-erotic sounds as she placed the piece in her wide-open mouth and swallowed.

This woman can't possibly be for real, Maddie thought as she watched Nina swallow the chocolate. She turned her attention back to Henri as he led Alice again, then stopped to chastise her for an incorrect weight exchange.

As Maddie considered telling Henri to shove his 'dance expertise' up his rear, Nina giggled from the other side of the room. She had walked up to the mirror and was now standing just inches away from her reflection, her laugh growing increasingly loud as she stuck her tongue out and wiggled it, so that the tip touched the mirror. Maddie frowned as she made a mental note to tell Frank that the mirrors would need extra cleaning.

Most of the class had tried to get back to dancing and were only looking at Nina obliquely. Maddie however looked back and forth between Nina and Ricky and wondered if he was going to be man enough, or teacher enough, to do something about Nina's behavior. Nina left the mirror and danced a pseudo waltz around the classroom on the tips of her toes, swaying from side to side so that Jesse had to pull Robyn out of her path to avoid a collision. Nina gave a hoot and popped several more chocolates in her mouth, exclaiming as she did that they were the most fantastic things she'd ever put in her mouth.

At that comment, Andrea snorted, crossed the room and took her shoes off. *Leaving was a very sensible decision,* Maddie thought and also made her way to the door.

With no warning, Nina wobbled on her heels and flailed her arms to the sides in an apparent effort to steady herself. She'd dropped the box she'd been so elaborately holding and then stumbled into the mirror. Renée, in what looked like an uncharacteristic instinct, reached out to Nina to try to steady her inevitable fall. However, Nina seemed to have lost all ability to stand and fell to her knees too quickly for Renée to be of any help. Nina's hands had flown up to her throat, where she scratched as if wearing a too-tight scarf.

Ricky had stopped, seemingly paralyzed for a moment, before he rushed to the bench and brought Nina a bottle of water. Upon reaching her, he seemed unsure of what to do and unconvincingly slapped her on the back. Everyone else in the room had stopped moving and watched in awe as Nina tried to stand up, only to fall to the ground, emitting a desperate, high-pitched noise.

Andrea, as silent as the rest of the group, went from shock to distress in a matter of seconds. "Oh, my God, do you need your epi-pen?" she screeched as she ran to Nina. "Somebody get it, it's in her handbag." Andrea immediately grabbed Nina and turned her over as best she could.

Both Maddie and Ricky ran to Nina's belongings but Maddie reached the handbag first and dumped the whole thing out. She instantly found what looked like a pen with a needle on the end of it and ran to Andrea. Andrea took the contraption and moved to use it, then froze. Maddie looked at her and wondered why she'd stopped, then realized what she should have seen when she pulled it from the bag—it had been used.

Andrea lifted it closer to her eyes and looked at it incredulously. She turned to Nina and she screamed. "Nina, do you have another one?"

Maddie went back to the handbag where Ricky knelt, staring at the items strewn across the floor and shaking his head. Maddie didn't see another needle either. She opened the door to the studio and screamed down the hall, "Frank, call an ambulance! We need an ambulance."

There was a sound at the end of the hall but Maddie had turned back into the room and watched as Nina's hand dropped away from her throat. She looked directly at Ricky and seemed to be saying something, but only a strangled noise came out. A final cackle erupted form her mouth and she was dead.

Chapter Five

There was utter silence for three seconds, a silence so complete that Maddie felt she would suffocate. Then screams came from three different areas of the room. Renée had drawn back towards the windows in horror and screamed as if she couldn't believe her bad luck at being present. Robyn grabbed Jesse around the waist and screamed as if she had lost her best friend. Alice clutched herself and did a little dance as if she had stepped on something unknown and screamed in a high-pitch meow.

Maddie heard herself and realized she couldn't stop whimpering. The only woman who hadn't made a sound was Andrea, unable, it appeared, to loosen her grip on Nina. Maddie watched as Andrea started mouthing the words *Oh, my God* but no sound came out of her mouth.

Standing above Andrea, Ricky started shaking. He edged away toward the wall, his hands tightly clasped in front of his chest. When he reached the hard surface, he plummeted to the ground as if someone had kicked him in the knees and once firmly on the floor, placed his face into his hands and started silently sobbing.

Henri paced back and forth, saying, "What the hell? What the hell just happened? What are we going to do about this?"

Jesse had Robyn securely in his arms, her face buried in his chest, and was leading her out of the classroom. At the door, he turned, found Maddie's gaze and shook his head with a frantic look before he disappeared with his wife. Frank and Toby appeared at the door as Jesse and Robyn left the room, Frank holding a green first aid box with a bright white cross on it and Toby gripping Frank's elbow in what looked like an attempt to restrain him. Frank looked as if he was going to take charge, but upon seeing Nina lying on the floor, stopped short while his hand came to rest on his heart.

"Holy Mary, Mother of..." His voice trailed off after that and he stood in the doorway seemingly unable to move closer. Only Toby came all the way into the room and knelt down beside Nina to feel for a pulse in her neck. Before he could say anything, Andrea seemed to wake after a bad dream with a start and yelled out.

"She's dead, you moron. Dead. Can't you see that? She's freaking dead." Her voice continued to rise as tears poured down her cheeks.

Maddie watched all this as she heard the sound of sirens coming down Main Street. The municipal building was only minutes away, and while it had seemed like hours since Nina had fallen to the floor, it had been only four minutes. The sirens reached the dance studio and the noise of doors slamming shut and people talking over radios filled the air. Everyone in the room avoided eye contact, as if each had been caught in the act of something illicit until Jesse appeared from the hallway and pointed two paramedics through the door before disappearing back outside.

The paramedics entered and moved swiftly to Nina. Both were men, although Maddie could hear a woman's voice in the hallway. Everyone else from the class wordlessly moved to the perimeters of the room as they waited for the silent paramedics to rise from their crouched positions and say something. One of the men, younger than the other by at least two decades, announced that she was dead, as if he couldn't believe it. His face had whitened to such a ridiculous extent that the freckles covering him seemed as if they were going to jump off his body and hide in the closet. His red hair glowed like a flame against his yellow paramedic shirt, giving him a clown-like appearance. He stood up as the older man lifted his hand to the younger man's shoulder and squeezed it. The older man spoke to the class for the first time.

"I'm really sorry about this, folks. For all of you." He looked at everyone in turn.

"I'm going to call this in to the police. Could everyone get comfortable? They're probably going to need to talk to each one of you."

At this remark, Henri and Ricky both looked at the paramedic in alarm. Ricky just let his head sink back into his hands, but Henri began pacing the room in agitation. The older paramedic took his walkie-talkie out and turned to the window as he spoke into it.

In those seconds, Henri stormed over to the younger man. "What the hell's all this about? I want to get the hell out of here," he said, jabbing his finger at the young man. To his credit, the paramedic didn't back down and Henri immediately changed tactics.

"Look, can't you see my girlfriend's in a terrible state. I'm going to take her home." Everyone in the room turned to look at Alice. She didn't look to be in too terrible a state, but she shrank under the universal gaze and obligingly made an effort to look more visibly upset.

More sirens converged on the studio and the female voice Maddie had heard earlier entered the room. She was somewhere in age between the two men, probably about thirty-five. "Brian, Officer Henry is here and the detective's on his way. I'm outside with the other woman." At that, she turned abruptly and left the room. Maddie looked at paramedic Brian and wondered what she'd meant, 'the other woman'. Toby met her eyes and nodded toward the door. Maddie looked at him quizzically until he whispered.

"That other couple. She fainted in the parking lot. She may have hit her head." *Oh, great,* Maddie thought, *just what Peter needs, a lawsuit from someone with a concussion.* That's when she remembered that she should call Peter.

Before Maddie spoke to the paramedics, she glanced at Ricky to see if he was going to step up and act like a teacher at the studio. She relinquished any idea that she would be able to sink into the woodwork herself when she saw him on the ground in a fetal position.

"Um...I'm sorry, I'm Madeleine. I'm a teacher here."

She said this to Brian, the older paramedic, who'd finished a conversation with Henri telling him in no uncertain terms that he was to stay put and he could get his girlfriend a glass of water and sit in the hallway. The paramedic then lowered himself to the floor to speak to Andrea, who was still crying, but had released her grip on Nina.

Maddie spoke down to him. "I think I should call Peter St. Claire, he's the owner of the studio. If that's okay with you?"

Brian looked up at Maddie. "That's a good idea." He smiled faintly at her. "The police will be here any minute and this will all be cleared up. I'm sure you folks can go home soon."

He then turned his attention back to Andrea and asked her to let go of the epi-pen still clutched in her hand. He began to examine it as he asked her questions. "Do you know what her specific allergies were?" Maddie was out of the door before she could hear if Andrea had answered the question.

She moved down the hall to the office where she found Frank sitting on the visitor's chair in front of Laura's desk. He held his hands in fists on his knees and looked as if he was unsuccessfully trying to stop them from shaking.

"Are you all right, Frank?" Maddie asked though she could see he was not.

"Sorry. Sorry, Maddie. That's just the way my wife died. Just like that. One moment she was there, the next, she was dead. I'm sorry. Sorry..."

"Oh, Frank, I'm sorry too." Maddie hesitated. She wanted to console Frank but knew Peter had to be called. "Frank, did you call Peter?"

Frank looked at Maddie as if he had no idea what she was talking about. "I must have forgot."

"It's okay, Frank. I'll do it now."

Maddie kept a surreptitious eye on Frank as she continued on to her handbag, pulled out her mobile phone and called Peter at home. She heard the sirens outside the studio, then the quiet as they were turned off. Peter almost started hyperventilating when she told him what was happening, but said he'd be down immediately. Maddie hung up and wished more than anything that she didn't have to go back down to the classroom and face Nina's dead body. But with both Ricky and Frank out of commission, she knew she was the most senior person at the studio until Peter showed up. She knew what she had to do, and after she gave Frank what she hoped was a sympathetic glance, she headed back to the group.

Outside the classroom, she found Henri and Alice sitting on the bench. Henri, contradicting his brutish behavior towards Alice during the entirety of the class, held her as he crooned softly in her ear. She had her eyes closed and a smile on her lips as she lay against his chest. *It was said that tragedy brings people together,*

Maddie thought in disgust, as she skirted by them. As she crossed the lobby, she saw the female paramedic with Jesse and Robyn. Robyn lay on a stretcher with her head wrapped in a bandage. Jesse held her hand as the paramedic spoke to them, nodding periodically in response to the questions from the paramedic. Maddie held her breath and turned back to the classroom.

There were several other people in the room now, two uniformed officers, one male and one female. The female officer spoke to Ricky, or tried to. Ricky, for the most part, kept his head in his hands and only periodically lowered them from his face to respond to the officer. The male officer was speaking to another man in a suit who was crouched over Nina. While Maddie had been on the phone with Peter, Andrea hadn't moved an inch.

Maddie watched the back of the man in the suit with a feeling of unease rising in her stomach. With his back still to the door, he turned away from Nina's body and spoke to Andrea. She responded in a clear voice for the first time since Nina had stopped breathing. Maddie smirked as she watched Andrea bat her eyelids as the man gently helped Andrea to her feet and motioned to the male officer to take her to a chair. It was easy to see that Andrea was going to recover.

Then the man turned to survey the rest of the room and Maddie's vision blurred. She knew who it was, had known it would be him from the second she heard the first siren. Her stomach floated up to her throat and landed again with a thud that made her think she might vomit. The man in the suit faced her and their eyes met.

"Joe," Maddie managed to squeak out. She cleared her throat and tried again with more success. "Joe. Hi. I'm surprised to see you."

Joe held his mouth shut, then spoke calmly. "Maddie. Hello. I heard you were back in the area. I'm sorry to see you here tonight in this situation." He let his eyes flicker to Nina and back again.

Maddie internally chastised herself. Of course, Joe would be here. A woman was dead and he was a police detective. What she knew was that Joe, the first boy she'd loved, the first boy she'd made love to, the first boy she'd married, even if it was annulled after two weeks, was standing between her and a dead woman.

Chapter Six

Joe watched Maddie as her eyes rolled up into her head and without hesitating, took two steps toward her, caught her in his arms and brought her gently to the floor. The only person who caught the whole three-second maneuver was Andrea and she knew she was going to remember it forever as the most romantic thing she'd ever seen. Maddie revived almost immediately, but in that time, a paramedic had a blood pressure cuff around her arm and Joe had turned his attention towards the rest of the room.

"Can I have everyone's attention? My name is Detective Joe Clancy. I'd like to get everyone out of here as soon as possible, but I'll need to speak to each one of you briefly tonight. Hopefully, there will be nothing further I need from you, but if there is, I'll need your contact details so that someone from my office can get back to you."

Joe had the room's attention. He said something softly to the female officer, after which she left the room. "Please give my officers your attention. Officer Rodriguez will gather your details, starting with the people outside, while Officer Dinhop," he said motioning to the other man, "will begin taking statements in here."

Joe turned back to Andrea and spoke closely to her ear. Maddie sat where she was with the blood pressure cuff around her arm and a thermometer in her ear. She didn't know what she'd expected, but it was more than what Joe had just given her and it made her cringe in embarrassment. He was here to investigate a death and she'd assumed he'd take time out now to have a sappy reunion with her. She was feeling exceptionally sorry for herself when Peter came into the room with a flourish of his arms and a theatrical moan.

"Oh, Maddie, I'm so..." He spotted Nina and blanched. "Oh, Maddie, I really am sorry. You're going to hate me for this, aren't you?" He flopped down next to Maddie and wrapped his arms around her, much to the annoyance of the paramedic who was disengaging the blood pressure cuff. She was satisfied to see that Joe had winced when Peter entered the room and wrapped her up in his arms.

"Peter, I'm absolutely fine. I think Ricky needs more help. He hasn't moved from that position in twenty minutes."

"Well, of course not. They were dating. He must be devastated."

Ah, Maddie thought. *Ricky and Nina's affair was common knowledge at the studio, then.* Peter gave Maddie a quick squeeze, then moved over to Ricky and drew him into his arms. Maddie expected resistance from Ricky and was surprised that he didn't fight the show of emotion. Instead, he collapsed onto Peter's shoulder mumbling about being stung.

Still under the ministrations of the paramedic, Maddie looked around the room to see who was still there. Renée was pacing the length of the mirror, clearly agitated as she glanced at her watch. Her face looked more ugly, if that was possible, the stress of the previous twenty minutes causing it to pucker and twitch uncontrollably. Toby listened to his iPod while sitting again in that ramrod position she'd found him in before his tango class. It was hard for her to accept that it had only been hours since that class. It felt like days.

Finally, given the okay to get up, Maddie walked over to Toby. This time he was aware of her arrival and took the iPod buds out of his ear before Maddie spoke.

"Toby." Maddie was mystified. She felt that she should say she was sorry, but didn't know what she was sorry about. She felt self-conscious for this guy, who obviously felt ill at ease. He was probably wondering how the hell he'd ended up here.

"I'm sorry all this happened. Wasn't what you were expecting from a dance class, was it?"

"Oh... That's fine. I mean, it's not fine at all. She seemed like a nice woman and it's terrible."

Maddie thought that calling her a nice woman was stretching it a little, but she understood. The two sat next to one another in a strained silence before Officer Dinhop approached them.

"Sir, thank you for being patient. May I have your details, then hopefully you will be able to head off home." Officer Dinhop nodded towards Maddie, indicating, she supposed, that he would get to her next. He then sat next to Toby with his notebook and pen ready. Toby sat with his iPod still clutched in both hands.

After jotting down Toby's personal information, Officer Dinhop coughed into a cloth handkerchief before he replaced it neatly in his shirt pocket. He was a middle-aged man with a trim body and no hair. He spoke with an accent that sounded like it came from up North, maybe New Hampshire or Maine.

"I just have a couple of routine questions before you can go. Mr. Downs, were you in the room when Ms. LePore died?"

"What? I mean, should I not be here?" Maddie watched as Toby nearly fell off his chair. "Sorry, I just mean, I wasn't in the room. I was out in the hall."

"And why was that?" Officer Dinhop asked the question in what Maddie read to be a neutral tone, just trying to get facts, but Toby seemed nervous.

"I just wasn't."

"Mr. Downs, I'm just trying to ascertain who was inside the classroom when Ms. LePore died and who was outside it. It's not a trick question."

"Oh, sorry. I'm just a little freaked out. I was outside in the hall." Officer Dinhop didn't say anything, but continued to look at Toby.

"I had been in the class but then the teacher..." At this point, his glance fell on Ricky. "Well, he...Well, it was just uncomfortable and so I left. I'd gone to the toilet and then I was just waiting."

Dinhop looked annoyed. It seemed to Maddie that they all had places they'd rather be. "And what were you waiting for?"

"Does it matter?" Toby started to visibly sweat.

"I was just wondering." Now Officer Dinhop looked a little more interested in Toby's answers.

"I was..." Toby looked towards Maddie and his face turned beet red.

Instantaneously, both Maddie and Officer Dinhop understood and all three looked in different directions.

Officer Dinhop used his handkerchief again. "And so, you were in the hallway waiting. When did you come into the classroom?"

Toby turned to face Officer Dinhop, appearing to be on firmer ground. "That would be when Maddie called down the hall to the man in the office. She told him to call an ambulance."

Officer Dinhop raised his eyes from his notebook and looked at Maddie.

"That's Frank. He's the custodian here." The police officer nodded and continued writing.

"Then, Mr. Downs, what happened when you came inside the classroom?"

"Well, I went over to her, the woman, and felt for a pulse. There wasn't one."

Officer Dinhop raised an eyebrow. "And then?"

Toby shrugged his shoulders. "And then, that other woman started screaming at me and I guess I just sat down here.

Officer Dinhop spent several minutes writing, during which time Toby squeezed his iPod compulsively. "All right, then, Mr. Downs, thank you. That's all. If we need anything else, we'll call you."

In that instant, Maddie realized how exhausted she was. Even the somewhat interesting idea that Toby had been waiting around to see her after class didn't hold her interest for long. She wished someone would cover Nina's body and as that thought darted across her fatigued brain, two more police officers entered the room. Both were women, one exceedingly tall and the other wide, and both wore what looked like jump suits with the Pembroke Police Department logo on the chest. Across each back read the words FORENSICS.

She was up next with Officer Dinhop and after the basic questions were covered, she described what she'd seen in the classroom. He took down her description of Nina dancing around with the box of chocolates and then falling down against the mirrors, unable to breathe, and then explaining how people had tried to help her.

"Ms. Fitzpatrick, you said that she was dancing around the room in a giddy fashion. This was after she had eaten the chocolates, but before she had difficulty breathing?"

"Yes. It was fast, maybe two minutes in total, but she was definitely breathing all right after the first chocolate."

"Then you said that you emptied her bag onto the floor after she'd collapsed and that you found her epi-pen and brought it to her." Maddie confirmed this information with a nod. "And that there was no medication in the epi-pen. Did you see another cartridge in the bag?"

Maddie paused before answering. The longer she sat with Officer Dinhop, the more confused the evening's events became. She tried to clear her head by digging her fingernails into her palm.

"No, there was nothing else that looked like a epi-pen in the bag. After Andrea said the one I gave her was empty, I ran back to look in the bag." Officer Dinhop continued writing notes, so he wasn't looking at her as she furtively glanced in Joe's direction.

"And the chocolate, that was in the bag too?" Officer Dinhop had stopped writing and seemed to be studying Maddie's eyebrows.

"What? No. No, I don't think so. She'd gone out in the hall and had come back in with the chocolates." Maddie's eyes darted around the room searching for something safe to settle on. She didn't know why these questions were making her nervous, but they were. Dinhop gently placed his hand on Maddie's knee and patted it twice lightly before taking it away.

"Relax. I know you're exhausted. We're just about done. You said that she'd gone out into the hall. You mean where Mr. Downs was waiting?"

Maddie sucked her breath in. She didn't like what that implied. "Well, she did go out, but I don't know if Toby was there. She'd been upset with Ricky and left the room. When she came back, she had the chocolates and she said something like 'thank you, darling'. I assumed it was Ricky she was talking to."

"And Ricky never left the classroom?"

"No. Definitely not."

"And the chocolates?"

"I saw her take her handbag with her when she left the room and the chocolates could have been in there. I only saw the box when she came back in. She, was, well, she was pretty much showing them off to everyone."

After Officer Dinhop gave her the same speech about calling if they needed more information, she retrieved her dance bag and prepared to leave. She inched her way across the room and then silently berated her behavior when she realized she was hovering because she hoped Joe would stop and say something. However, Joe was preoccupied with the contents of Nina's handbag and she watched as he picked up various articles and brought them to his nose. At one point, he called Officer Rodriguez over and spoke to her in a hushed tone. Maddie was next to the sound system when Peter motioned to her from the door.

In the hall, they found Officer Dinhop and Henri in a heated discussion. Henri sat in an attitude that broadcast that he was not happy to be there, and Dinhop, who'd proceeded through the interviews in the classroom with gentleness and concern, had switched to something harder and colder. Maddie could see Dinhop's temper boiling as hot as Henri's.

"And just what is it you do for a living?"

"What the hell does that have to do with that broad dying, I'd like to know?" Henri's eyes met Maddie's and, for a moment, she couldn't breathe. The venom coming out of them staggered her and she actually grabbed Peter's arm for support.

"You can make this easy or you can come down to the station." Dinhop stood up as if he'd like nothing better than the second option.

"Yah, I'll answer your questions but don't go thinking I don't know this has nothing to do with her. I didn't kill her."

"No one said you did, Mr. Levitt, we're just taking statements. Now, where is it you work?"

"I work for myself." He averted his eyes from the twitch of Dinhop's hand resting near his gun before he continued. "Mergers and acquisitions."

Maddie and Peter walked out of the front door and joined Frank on the stoop before she could hear Dinhop's response.

Peter ran his left hand through his hair while he let out a long whistle. "Well, if that doesn't happen again in my lifetime, I will be pleased." Then, turning to Maddie and Frank, he continued. "I'll lock up after they've gone. You two go on home now and get some rest."

Maddie thanked Peter, then turned her attention to Frank. From Frank's behavior in the office, she thought he might appreciate an escort home. "Frank, how about if I follow you home?"

"Oh, no, Maddie, I'll be just fine. You get yourself home and into bed." Frank held the railing carefully as he descended the stairs and made his way to his car. Maddie watched him for a moment just to make sure he got there safely and only then remembered that her handbag was still in the office. She ran back up the steps hoping to catch Peter before he locked up. She passed Officer Dinhop and Henri in the hall, still in conversation, but thankfully in calmer voices. Before she got to the office, the restroom door opened and Maddie found Alice hovering on the threshold, looking like a lost lamb.

"Alice, are you okay?"

Though Maddie stood directly in front of her, it seemed Alice didn't see her. She nearly jumped out of her skin and let out a squeal that ended in a gasp.

"Oh, I just think this is the most awful thing that could have happened."

Maddie watched as Alice looked furtively down the hallway. When she caught sight of Henri with Officer Dinhop, she drew herself back against the wall of the restroom in what Maddie could only describe as terror. Maddie already didn't like Henri and she didn't want to leave Alice in such obvious distress. She walked into the room after Alice and closed the door.

"Alice, can I help in any way?"

Alice shook her head, but kept eyeing the door as if she expected a monster to break it down.

"Would you like me to walk out with you or…"

Alice lifted her hand to her mouth and spoke through her fingers.

"I don't know what to do. I think he knew her."

Alice spoke so softly, Maddie had to come within inches of Alice's face to hear her.

"What do you mean, Alice? You think Henri knew Nina?"

Alice gave a curt nod to the door. "Oh, my God, he had something to do with her."

Maddie didn't have time to respond before there was a voice on the other side of the door.

"Alice, baby, you still in there?" It was Henri, both the French accent he'd used in class and the Bayonne bully he'd become with Officer Dinhop, gone. Now the voice was just Jersey syrup. Maddie looked at Alice and her heart sank as she watched the woman in front of her creep towards the door. Just before she turned the handle, she looked sideways and whispered, not to Maddie but to the wall.

"What if he had something to do with it?"

"With what, Alice?"

"With her dying."

"It was an accident, Alice. Nina didn't have the medication she needed, medicine that could have saved her life." But Alice slipped out of the restroom without a response.

Maddie roused herself from the depressing sight of Alice and continued on to the office. Peter was still there and on the telephone. From what Maddie could hear, he was speaking with his distraught wife, Kristy. He waved to Maddie as she grabbed her handbag and retraced her steps down the now empty corridor.

Outside, there was less disorder. The ambulances were gone, so she assumed Nina's body was gone too. A small group of locals who'd come to see what all the commotion was about, slowly moved away. Maddie put her head down as she unlocked her bicycle. She didn't want to be asked any questions by the curious onlookers. When she looked up again and aimed her bicycle in the direction of home, she noticed Frank's car still parked on the far side of the parking lot. She walked her bicycle over and rapped on the window, afraid for a moment that something had happened to Frank as he sat stooped over his steering wheel. At her knock, however, he jumped. Maddie let out a sigh of relief as he rolled down the window.

"Frank, you feeling all right?"

"What happened?"

Maddie stood in front of the open window wondering if something was actually wrong with Frank. "Maybe I should drive you home."

"No, Maddie. Tell me what happened. How did she die? Was it quick? Did she feel pain?"

Oh, God, Maddie thought. *He's having a break down.* Maddie looked desperately around the parking lot for someone to help her, but jumped her attention back to Frank when he pounded his fist into the steering wheel.

"Just tell me how it happened, Maddie. I need to know. Then I'll go home and I'll be fine."

Maddie was unsure and looked towards the studio one more time, in the hopes that Peter would emerge. When she looked down at Frank again, his face looked peaceful yet expectant.

"She was upset when she left the classroom but when she came back she had a smile on her face and she had a box of chocolates that she, well, ate rather suggestively. Then she started to choke." Maddie wanted to stop, but the look on Frank's face made her go on.

"It was like someone was squeezing her neck and she couldn't get any air in. She had her hands up around her neck. Then she started jerking, like she couldn't control the way her body was moving. And she kept looking wildly around the room."

"Did anyone move to help her?"

"Well, first Renée tried to help, then Ricky ran up to her with a bottle of water. I don't know why it took us so long to realize what was happening. It sounds so pathetic now, but we didn't know she was having an allergic reaction; it happened so quickly. She ate the chocolate and then two minutes later, she was dead."

Frank nodded his head as if everything Maddie had said was correct. "Thank you, Maddie. I'll see you tomorrow. I'm sorry Nina LePore had to die." Then he started his car and drove off leaving Maddie hoping that all would be well in the morning.

Joe sat behind the wheel of his car again, staring at Maddie as she watched the janitor's car roll straight through a stop sign. There was a faint smile on her face as he saw her forehead furrow and could almost hear her wondering whether she should follow him to make sure he got home. His breath involuntarily caught in his throat as he waited to see if she'd roll her bicycle over to where he sat. He hadn't spoken to her after his initial greeting and though he was tired enough to sleep right there in his car, the pull he felt from Maddie was too strong to resist. He finally turned the ignition of his car and drove slowly toward her.

"Do you need a ride?"

Maddie looked down at her bicycle and then back at Joe.

"No, thanks, it's just down the road."

Joe was momentarily startled. Joe remained still but kept his eyes fixed on Maddie's. He knew where her parents lived, but he'd been jolted by a memory of Maddie in her old house. Maddie and Joe, seventeen years old and necking in the wood-paneled basement. That's where he'd first felt her breasts. He remembered them under his fingers and stifled a moan as he brought himself back to the present moment.

"I haven't kept in contact with your parents." Joe hadn't thought it possible, but he could actually feel his heart skip a beat.

"No, I guess you wouldn't have."

Joe turned and looked out towards the lights of Main Street. Each of the street lamps had a glowing pumpkin tied around its neck and a scarecrow propped up against its feet. He couldn't attribute the nausea he felt to Maddie, most of it came from his three-beer supper. Luckily, he'd fallen asleep before he'd consumed the entire six-pack. He remembered the potato bake his sister had made and wondered if he'd be welcome to have some now. He looked at his watch.

"Well, good night, Maddie." He pulled away from the dance studio, leaving Maddie straddling her bicycle and wondering if life could get any more bizarre.

Her parents' house was only three blocks away, though most of the ride was uphill. Panting slightly, she pulled into the driveway and parked her bicycle behind the Toyota Camry. Maddie let herself into her parents' house, and without doing anything more than brush her teeth and take her clothes off, fell into bed. Just before falling asleep, the last words Frank had spoken repeated themselves in her head and she wondered why he'd said it like that. *Nina LePore had to die.*

Chapter Seven

The next morning came too soon for Maddie. It was 1 am before she'd fallen into bed and though she set the alarm for the latest she could get away with, she still felt she hadn't gotten enough sleep.

After a shower and breakfast, she dressed and grabbed her dance bag. She was still using her summer bag and at the last moment decided she couldn't deal with its lime green and pink cheeriness. At the risk of being late, she decided to swap it for a more somber autumn affair, a leather satchel a friend from California had given her as a farewell present. She pulled out the contents of her current bag and placed it all on the table before relocating items one by one into their new home. Some things she was not going to transfer, like the extra heavy-duty deodorant she carried in the summer months. She also left the seven extra hair ties that she continually added to her bag 'just in case.'

She put all the things she used on a daily basis into the new bag: foot powder, shoe brush, hairbrush and lip goo. Then she noticed an envelope she didn't recognize. It had been sealed and opened from the top but the front had no name or address indicating ownership. On the top left-hand corner, it read Pembroke College School of Sciences, PO Box 44002, Pembroke, NJ 07803. Before they retired, both Maddie's parents had worked at Pembroke College but her father had worked in the Anthropology Department and her mother in the Foreign Student Affairs Office. She reached inside the ripped opening and unfolded the single sheet of paper inside. One side of the paper was covered in type and read:

Nina, Nina, pretty ballerina. We make mistakes for love and money. You've made a mistake this time.

There was no signature or name under the message. She flipped over the piece of paper to find it blank and sat dumbfounded. She thought back to the previous evening, easily conjuring the nightmarish quality it had held.

At the risk of running even later, she brought the letter over to a bright light and looked again. Then she spotted the letters *SynTech* on the bottom of the back of the page. Faded, but visible under the bright light. Above the words *SynTech* were numbers in columns that ran off the page, as if someone had photocopied them, but had placed the original into the machine at an angle. Appreciating instinctively that it could have something to do with Nina's death—though how, she had no idea—she folded the note back up and put it carefully into the envelope, already wondering if she had ruined any fingerprints that may have been on it. She'd take it to the police station when she had a break later in the morning.

After the commotion of the evening before, the studio was comparatively quiet. As she parked and locked her bicycle, the thought occurred to Maddie that Peter could have cancelled classes, though surely he would have called her if that had been the case. Her worries were abated by the time she reached the doors. She could hear a cacophony of voices coming from the direction of the office, the loudest she recognized as Peter, reliving the evening with theatrical vigor. Frank interjected with a word here and there, but nothing longer than two syllables.

Maddie entered the room and all eyes turned to her. Frank sat in the corner in the same position Maddie had found him in the night before. This time, thankfully, looking a little more alive. Peter stood with his back to the door, his arms in mid-gesticulation. The audience was comprised of Laura at her desk, Cathwrynn who sat primly next to Frank, and Philip, the Lindi-Hop teacher, who leant against the filing cabinet. Peter and Laura welcomed her—Peter, the loudest but with a sigh of relief, as if he'd thought maybe she was going to quit and head back to California. Laura emitted her name with a satisfaction Maddie read as, *ah good, I'll get the female perspective now.* Cathwrynn only tilted her head as if listening to voices, which Maddie realized, might be exactly what she was doing. Philip tapped his foot against the filing cabinet, his dreadlocks bouncing to a rhythm that no one else in the room could hear.

Peter filled her in on everything he'd told his audience so far, but said that they were just waiting for her to get in because, of course, he hadn't been there when it actually happened. At that, he let a quick glance slide over Frank, who still sat against the wall staring somewhere into the middle distance, a glance that said clearly that Frank had not been able to contribute any detail to the conversation. Peter also let it be known that Ricky wasn't that much help, as he was practically catatonic by the time they'd reached his home.

"He just mumbled and said he needed to take something to sleep so I went up to his medicine cabinet and found some codeine. He was out like a light."

Maddie related her side of the previous night, without enough detail for the likes of Laura, but she wanted to get some answers out of Peter. He'd spent more time with Ricky. She was particularly aware of the envelope in her bag and wondered if Ricky had anything to do with it.

"Did Ricky say anything to Joe while you were with him?"

"Nothing. Nothing interesting, that is. He answered the detective's questions, but it was all monosyllables."

Maddie paused and glanced at Peter, aware that he'd called the police officer in question *detective,* while Maddie had called him *Joe,* and wondered if he'd noticed. He appeared not to have.

"It was more interesting later at his house but I can't say that I understood anything. He kept mumbling *how could I have let it happen?* And *now I'm in trouble.* Then the codeine took effect and I left him."

Maddie thought about it. Maybe he typed the letter and felt guilty after he'd bullied her.

"Does anyone know where Nina works?"

Philip moved closer to the group and perched himself on the edge of Laura's desk. He swung a leg back and forth as he spoke, as if they were recapping their night's dates.

"You mean worked?"

Cathwrynn's eyes flew open and everyone one else in the room marveled at his callousness. Laura pushed him off her desk and brushed the area his rear had touched. But before anyone could admonish him, Philip put his hands up in supplication and looked at the group.

"Sorry. It's just that... this is the way I deal with it. You know...death. Everyone has his way of doing it and mine is just trying to make it a bit light because otherwise it gets way too scary. Didn't mean to offend anyone."

Cathwrynn gave him a feathery smile and Laura patted his back as he came next to the desk again.

"Oh, Philip, you're a good boy." He sat back on the edge of the desk and tapped his foot again.

"Oh, and maybe just don't mention her dying to Claire when she gets in. She'll just totally freak." Then Philip took a donut from the box that had been sitting on the desk, untouched since Peter had put it there that morning. Maddie realized she was hungry too and grabbed the only plain one in the box. Between bites, she continued her line of thought.

"Frank, last night, before Nina came back into the class, did she come down here and into the office?"

As if walking through a fog and trying to figure out who she was, Frank peered up at Maddie. Laura and Peter exchanged concerned looks but waited for Frank's answer. Cathwrynn sat next to Frank with her eyes closed and her hands hovering just above her thighs. Philip added a soft tap on the filing cabinet.

"Well...you know, I was busy in here." For ten seconds, Frank thought that was answer enough. Then he jumped, as if he'd received an electric shock and continued. "Yes, I was busy but I did see her. She came running in here, all flustered and searching for something. Then she shot out again." He paused again but this time not for long and when he came back, he came back strong.

"That's right. I don't think she even saw me because I was laying a trap behind the door. I only saw her from the side." He shook his head again and slapped his thigh. "I don't think she even saw me." He looked at the five faces staring intently at him and raised his eyebrows, as if questioning whether that was what they had wanted to hear.

"So, you didn't see her after that?"

Frank rubbed his head, then his stomach before answering. *Good*, Maddie thought, *that's more like the Frank I know*.

"Nope, but I did hear her, of course. She was crying and I wasn't sure she wanted anyone to see her."

Laura huffed melodramatically. "So, the poor dear was sad before she died. I knew her mother, such a sad creature herself. Oh, to be doing so well and then to die like that."

"What do you mean *well*? You mean here at the dance studio?"

"Oh, my no. I mean, maybe she was doing well in the dancing, but what I meant was that she had pulled herself so far up. Their family was from the other side of the tracks, if you know what I mean, and she got herself a job out of high school and then a scholarship to college. Then she got herself a job at one of those drug companies."

"So she didn't work at the College?" Maddie had wondered if maybe the envelope had come from someplace Nina's worked. People often took envelopes and pens and she didn't need any imagination to think of Nina taking supplies.

"Oh, no. One of the drug places down the road. She had quite a good job, from what I remember."

In Pembroke, *down the road* actually meant about twenty minutes down Rt. 78, a large tract of land that had been bought by several pharmaceutical companies in the time that Maddie had been away. Another reason the area remained so prosperous.

"Frank, did you look in on Nina after she left the room, just to make sure she was all right?" Frank looked a little put off for a moment and Maddie realized she'd all but accused him of being insensitive to a woman in distress.

"I most certainly was going to go out and see if she needed anything. I got down the ladder. And remember I'm an old man and I don't move all that fast anymore."

Unsure whether she'd insulted him so much he wasn't going to continue, Maddie smiled and nodded encouragingly. "Of course."

Frank looked somewhat appeased. "Yes, I was heading out the door, but I heard voices in the hall and I realized someone was already with her, so I left them alone." He paused but for a moment. "I mean, it could have been a delicate moment, a lover's spat, so of course, I wanted to give them space."

"So, it was a male voice you heard her with?" Maddie knew it wasn't Ricky, because he was in the classroom the whole time.

"Oh, definitely." He paused and looked somewhere near the ceiling as if looking for the answer up there. "Actually, it was really her voice I heard but maybe I just assumed it was a man. I guess it sounded like that to me."

Maddie really had to teach but she couldn't pull herself away from Frank. "What do you mean?"

"Oh, you know. The way some women's voices get when they talk to a man." Peter and Phillip both nodded in agreement, but Maddie, Laura and Cathwrynn remained silent. Frank looked exasperated and continued.

"You know, her voice got girlish and she talked like she had to convince the person to do something for her. You know, sweet talk."

Maddie couldn't imagine Nina talking that way to anyone but Ricky. "But you didn't hear anyone else say anything?"

"No, not words but whatever he said, it calmed her down."

"You didn't see who it was?"

"No, like I said, I had a lot of work to do in here." Frank had taken on a wounded animal look and Maddie didn't want him to feel any worse than he did. Besides, she knew it had to have been Toby. There was no one else outside the classroom and Toby had all but said that he'd waited around to see her after class. However, when Officer Dinhop had questioned Toby last night, he hadn't mentioned that he'd talked to Nina and that piece of information bothered Maddie.

She looked at the time on the clock above Laura's desk. "I have to get into the classroom."

Laura pouted with a classic huff as her hand made a move for the box of cigarettes in her pocket, then stopped in mid-air as she thought better of it, wagging her finger at Maddie instead.

"Maddie, I expect full disclosure just as soon as you get out."

Peter regretfully rose from his chair. "Okay, people of my dance studio, let's get back to work. The police said they'll let us know when the autopsy is done but they seem certain it was an allergic reaction to the chocolates she ate." At the word 'autopsy,' Cathwrynn, who'd been rising gracefully from her perch, fell back against the seat and started humming.

"But why? What was in them?"

"The other woman, Andrea," Peter said with a look that indicated there could be no other woman. "She said that Nina was allergic to nuts and that she always had an epi-pen with her to avoid anaphylaxis. This time, it seemed, she didn't."

Phillip was swinging his legs with a bit more force, every couple of kicks hitting Laura's desk and making her jump. "Then why did she eat them? That's the stupidest thing I've ever heard."

Maddie made a sound before she could stop herself and everyone turned expectantly towards where she stood near the door.

"Um, I was just going to say that it looked like she thanked Ricky for giving her the chocolates."

Peter slammed his fist down on the desk, causing Laura to shriek. "That's outrageous. I know Ricky wasn't well-liked but he would never give her something she was allergic to."

"If he even knew she was allergic to them." Frank pointed out in a wobbly voice.

Everyone was silent again. Maddie didn't know which idea was worse; that Ricky Russo could have unintentionally killed his girlfriend, or ex-girlfriend (Maddie still wasn't clear about that), or that someone else connected to a letter that may or may not have had anything to do with Nina, wanted to scare her and had ended up killing her.

Chapter Eight

Maddie mumbled something about being really late and ran towards the classroom. She had a group class with four couples from Shadylawn Retirement Village. A mini-van brought them to the studio and took them back, and apart from the fact that she had to repeat everything she said at least three times, they were a delightful class to teach. This was the third class and while she moved more slowly than she normally worked, the class didn't know that and didn't seem to mind.

All of the retirees were easily over seventy. They had signed up for the course, thinking that it was a ballroom tango class and were surprised when Maddie explained that Argentine Tango was different. They seemed to have gotten over the shock of the intimate embrace and were now having a ball. Maddie was glad. It was a happy class to teach for an hour and she was able to let her mind focus on something other than the events of the previous evening.

"Maddie, Maddie?" An octogenarian with the requisite blue hair and arms covered in bangles, waved to Maddie from the other side of the room. She and her partner, Sam, stood face to face, both now with their hands on their hips.

"Maddie, tell us again which way we are supposed to be going," Dorothea asked, not because she needed to know which way line-of-dance flowed but because Sam needed to hear it again.

"Now, now, Dottie, I know just which way I'm going. Why don't you just relax and follow me? That's right, isn't it, Maddie? She's supposed to be following me." Sam emphasized the word *me* as he nodded his head and looked knowingly between Maddie and Dorothea.

"I cannot just relax and follow you, because you keep running me into people, and chairs and just about anything else that gets in your way. And when you're not doing that, you're moving backwards. The amount of money I have to spend on nylons to keep dancing with you, Sam, is just not worth it." Dorothea moved to sit down, her face set in a scowl that looked like it was there to stay.

Maddie smiled. She had heard a virtually identical conversation last week and was sure she'd hear it again next week.

"How about if we try something a little different for the two of you?" Maddie continued conspiratorially. "Just don't tell the other students."

Dorothea brightened at the idea of getting to do something special and different from the other retirees and looked furtively towards the rest of the group. Sam looked less impressed and mumbled something about trying it again.

"Don't worry, Sam, it's just a subtle change. No one will be able to tell the difference."

Dorothea had wiped the scowl off her face and was now coaxing Sam back into dance position.

"All right, Sam, you're going to have to move in line-of-dance but we can do it backwards. You lead Dorothea as you walk. However, Dorothea, you're going to control the direction. Sam, you start by walking." The two dancers started moving deliberately along the mirror.

"Now, Dorothea, because you can see where you're going, when you see an obstacle, like this chair, you signal to Sam with your hand just slightly, that he needs to move into that direction to avoid a collision."

The two dancers' stressed faces slowly relaxed as they worked out a rhythm.

"By gum, Dottie, it works." Sam grinned for the first time in class, showing a noteworthy set of white dentures.

"I knew you could do it." Dorothea happily hummed out of tune to the music with a smirk on her face, as Sam walked backwards and she directed him forwards. Maddie watched as, by gum, it did work.

After lunch, Maddie assisted Peter with a fox-trot class. Before the class, she changed her shoes, this time putting on a pair of flesh-colored two-inch heels. While it brought her height to 5'11", she was still able to look up to Peter at six feet. While she assisted Peter, she felt less in charge of the process and could play around with the follower's role. The shoes she slipped on had been made for a performance she'd danced in L.A. two years earlier. *It feels like another world*, Maddie thought, before a welcome distraction interrupted her reminisces.

"Oh, good, I've got you." Laura produced a squeal and huff simultaneously and ended up frightening both of them. After the mandatory pat on the cigarettes in her pocket, Laura peered down the corridor over her glasses and shut the door.

"So, now I want to know what really happened." Laura settled herself in her chair as if she expected to be entertained for the next hour.

"But, Laura, I've told you everything I know."

Laura didn't give her a chance to continue. "Oh, come on, with the secrecy of that class and now a death. I'm sure there's something else and you just didn't want to say anything while Philip and Cathwrynn were here. They're so young." Maddie was disappointed to see that Laura looked hopeful, as if there was a juicy tidbit that Maddie had kept in order to have a later, gossipy session with the secretary.

"Really, Laura, there's nothing more I can add." Maddie stood to leave. "If I think of anything, I'll be sure to tell you."

"Well, I'm sure you will." Laura opened the desk drawer and rifled through it without taking anything out. "Imagine that poor boy, Toby. He wanted to be in that class more than anything, just so he could see more of you, and then look what's happened. I'll bet he's not so happy now."

"What do you mean, he wanted to see me?" Maddie hoped Toby hadn't said anything to Laura about her.

"Oh, it was plain as day. I heard Peter tell him he could sit in on the samba class and his face just lit up like, well, like he'd just been given something he was really hoping for."

"Well, he didn't say anything to me." Maddie wanted to leave it at that and get out of the path of Laura's insatiable propensity for gossip.

"You know," Laura paused for dramatic effect. "I just don't know about Frank."

Maddie stopped in her tracks and sighed. "What do you mean?"

"Oh, just that he's been strange lately and I don't mean only last night. It's been weeks now and I just haven't said anything." Laura looked around the room as if she thought someone might be listening. Maddie had only arrived at the studio two weeks ago, so Frank just seemed like Frank to her.

"What was he like before?"

"Oh, it's not his personality that's changed. Not really anyway. It's like he's more forgetful." She looked conspiratorially at Maddie. "Do you think it could be Alzheimer's?"

"Um, I'm not sure. I don't know much about the disease. Have you mentioned this to Peter?"

"Oh no, I'm not going to bother him. He already worries too much. I'll just do a little research myself. And you let me know if anything funny goes on."

Laura dropped the subject and went into a filing cabinet to collect something. Maddie left the room thinking that any more funny incidents, and she might just quit.

After the fox-trot class, Maddie and Peter agreed to meet on the front steps to take a walk. Maddie quickly changed her shoes and made sure that the note she'd found that morning was in her handbag so that she could drop it off at the police station. They met on the steps and walked south toward the center of town. Without warning, Peter spoke as if Maddie had asked him a question.

"I just feel responsible. I know that's idiotic, isn't it? It's all this Catholic guilt, I think. My studio. I should have done something. And now Ricky. I don't know if he's going to make it."

"What do you mean? I know he was in shock last night, but I'd thought he would have..." Maddie didn't complete the sentence. She recognized her prejudice and felt ridiculous. Just because she thought he was a fool didn't mean he had no feelings. "Did you see him this morning?"

"I went by before coming in. I had to check. I can't say that I've ever really liked the man. That is, he worked for me, but we were never friends. But this...he looked so lost." Maddie allowed Peter to brood silently for a few moments.

"You know, the strangest thing about tonight..." Maddie found herself pausing when she realized that there were several strange events whizzing around her brain. Alice's reaction in the restroom had been strange and scary, while Frank's behavior in the parking lot had been odd and worrying. For no apparent reason, she dismissed both those incidents and continued. "It's that Andrea really seemed upset, but up until the moment Nina died, they were practically spitting at each other, there was so much hate in the room. I wonder what the story is behind the two of them. And how did she know that Nina suffered from allergies?"

They continued east on Main Street, passing the frozen yoghurt shop and a CVS pharmacy. At Rose Drive, Maddie spotted a shop on their left. Peter had walked several steps ahead before he realized that Maddie wasn't with him and had to turn to see what she had found. What he saw was Maddie with her nose pressed against the window of a florist shop.

"What? Oh, speak of the devil." Peter started and stopped, recognizing Andrea within the shop. "I'd forgotten she owned this place. I always use Carey's on Woodland. It's right around the corner from us." Peter watched Maddie open the door and walk into the shop and, after hesitating, followed her.

The shop was warm and slightly humid, reminding Maddie of her grandparents' conservatory. While she didn't remember much of her grandfather before he retired, after that milestone, he became one of Maddie's favorite people. His fondest hobby was gardening, but he had a specific interest in orchids and it was orchids that grew in her grandparents' conservatory. Against the far wall of Andrea's shop, several beautiful orchid specimens sat in splendor.

Against the other wall, was a counter with workspace on one end and a cash register on the other. Andrea stood behind the counter. She appeared annoyed to see them in her shop and made no attempt to hide it. Though her face was immaculately made up, as it had been the night before, she had dark circles under her eyes betraying the fact that she had not slept well. Andrea hovered behind her counter and reluctantly gave them a toothy smile as she flipped a blonde curl away from her mouth.

"So what can I do for you? You're not here to buy flowers, are you?" Again, Maddie felt an intense dislike for this woman.

"We were just walking by and I saw you." Andrea raised her eyebrow and smirked toward them. Peter was barely over the threshold and he looked as if it wouldn't take much provocation to get him to walk back out again.

Annoyed that she had to defend herself, Maddie changed tactics halfway through her sentence. While the polite thing to do would be to ask if Andrea had recovered from last night, Maddie was a lot more interested in her change of attitude towards Nina as she lay dying in her arms.

"Actually, I have a couple of questions."

"What about?" Andrea asked, folding her arms around her body, her blouse bunching in the middle and revealing an additional inch of cleavage.

"About you and Nina. It was apparent in class that the two of you didn't get on. But you seemed to know a lot about her."

Andrea waved her hands, as if to shoo Maddie away. "Yes, well, I can know someone all my life and not like her." Neither Maddie nor Peter spoke. "Look, we grew up next door to one another. She was my best friend all through school. She only turned into a bitch as an adult." Andrea absent-mindedly pulled wilting stems out of a display vase. "Actually, she was a bitch in school, but I didn't mind then. Let's just say, we grew apart as adults." While Andrea was not becoming a kind person exactly, Maddie did detect a softening in her when she spoke about Nina and it encouraged her to prompt Andrea.

"It looked like what had come between the two of you was Ricky Russo."

"Look, what's it to you? Are you doing a little investigative reporting on your own? Does that luscious cop from last night know you're here bugging me?"

Maddie gasped, then covered her outburst with a cough when she caught the curious look Peter sent her. He'd been silent up to that point and now spoke in a soothing voice.

"No, it's just all been such a shock. I, for one, have never seen a dead body and I sure as hell don't want to again."

Andrea didn't say anything, but stared at Peter and her face softened, a different golden lock falling in front of her eye, giving her the opportunity to push it back in what Maddie assumed to be the beginning of a flirtation. "You know, you look a lot like John Lennon. I always liked him." Peter colored, but Andrea had already turned back to her flowers.

"It's just that Nina and I have always been a bit, shall we say, competitive.

It's always been hard, especially for her." At that statement she paused and looked out the window.

"Nina always liked the same guys I liked. I don't know if it was just because I liked them. The problem was, they always liked me more than they liked her. It was the same story with Ricky. We'd been going out for a year when we decided to take a break a couple of months ago." Andrea turned away from them, opened a refrigerator and reached for fresh greens. "Let me tell you, Nina didn't waste any time getting in there. She started flirting with him, and he's a man, of course, so he spent some time with her. He broke up with her a month ago and that's why she was so upset."

"How do you know he'd broken up with her?"

"Because he told me." Andrea spoke as if that should have been obvious. "We're going out again. I don't know why she was making such a big deal of it all of sudden. I mean, when it happened, she just kind of slunk off for a couple of weeks and nobody saw much of her."

"Did you see a lot of her?"

"Only at dance class." Andrea rushed on. "She didn't even show up for those for two weeks." She flipped her hair off her shoulder. "The best samba classes, if you ask me."

"But maybe he didn't break up with her. Maybe he was seeing you both."

Andrea looked directly at Maddie. "I doubt that." She turned around again and put the vase down on the display counter with more force than was needed and water splashed over her blouse.

"If he wasn't seeing her again, why did he give her those chocolates?"

The expression on Andrea's face would have been comical under any other circumstances. The surprise her expression showed was truly that.

"What do you mean? He didn't give her those chocolates. If she thought that, she was delusional."

"Who did then?"

"I have no idea and if you think I did, you're also delusional."

"No, I didn't think you had. You may not like her, but you didn't want to kill her, I'm sure." Maddie watched as Andrea's face crumpled and a tear escaped her left eye.

"What's that supposed to mean?"

"The chocolates had nuts in them. Someone gave her the chocolates."

Andrea shook her head, slowly at first, but speeded up to a point where Maddie thought she might unhinge herself.

"That's impossible. She could smell a nut ten feet away. You couldn't even open a jar of peanut butter in her presence. Her throat would start to close up and she'd be out of there before you even knew a sandwich was about to be made."

Maddie read true feeling from Andrea and didn't think she wanted to put her through any more. What was she thinking anyway, coming in and questioning her like that? Andrea dried her eyes in the time that Maddie had waffled about and hooked Maddie with a glare.

"If you'll excuse me, I've got to deal with some aphids on my roses."

It was clear to Maddie that Peter's resemblance to John Lennon had gotten them through the door and the answers to a couple of questions, but that was about as far as they were going to get with Andrea.

As she disappeared into a back room, Maddie and Peter exited back out into the autumn afternoon. The wind had picked up and Maddie held her skirt down as the air rushed through the closing door.

"Well, that was kind of stupid, wasn't it? I should be glad I'm not a police officer because I'm terrible at getting information."

"Ah, don't worry yourself, darling. Most people are more agreeable than that one. I don't understand something though." Peter hooked his arm through Maddie's so that she was effectively supporting him while they walked down the street. "What was it you thought you were going to get out of her?"

"Oh, Peter, I don't know. I saw her and decided to take action. I guess I don't trust her and I felt weird about last night."

"Don't we all, darling."

"No, I mean ... Oh. I don't know what I mean."

"Look, why don't we call the police department when we get back? See what they have to say. I have a card from Detective Joe Clancy and he did say to call if we needed to." Peter eyed Maddie from beneath his sunglasses. "Speaking of which, what was that about, young lady?"

Maddie laughed. "Peter, you are probably the only person I know who could get away with that."

"With what?"

"With calling me a young lady and be the same age. Why is it that you seem older than I am?"

"Ah, ancient wisdom. That, and I get all my good lines from my wife. So, don't evade the question. What was all that about?"

"What was what about?"

"Oh, darling, spill. I'll get it out of you eventually." Maddie chuckled, thinking he was probably right. She wasn't sure she wanted to be taken under his wing as another social project but Peter was proving a true source of comfort and amusement in her short time back home.

"I used to know Joe in high school."

"Well, obviously you used to know him and obviously it was in high school. What I was searching for, just for future reference so you never give me a bologna-filled answer like that again, are the juicy details."

Maddie laughed. It was hard not to. "He was my first love. Okay?"

"What do you mean, like you held hands and stared googly-eyed at one another or do you mean you had hot, animal sex?"

Still laughing, Maddie divulged. "Yes, he was my first. I can't quite say it was animal sex but it was beautiful. We only made love twice before our parents made us ...well, stopped us."

Peter looked outraged. "What is this, Medieval Europe? How old were you? How could they stop you?" Peter had dropped his arm from Maddie's and placed himself in the middle of the sidewalk.

"Be fair to my parents." Fifteen years ago, Maddie would have found it impossible to say those words, but she'd grown up a lot since then and come to accept her parents' actions. She continued, holding up her hands, palms up to face Peter. "We were eighteen but we were still living with our families. But that wasn't the main problem." Peter stood with his hands on his hips, now staring over the tops of his sunglasses at Maddie. She lowered her voice.

"The real problem was that we'd gotten married without them knowing." That was the bombshell Peter was waiting for and after he looked appropriately shocked for three or four seconds, he broke out in a Cheshire cat grin.

"Well, well, Maddie Fitzpatrick. You do have some life in you. Tell all."

"I have to call it elope really. We didn't tell anyone, not even my best friend Linda. We had two people at the town hall sign the register and that was that."

"So? So what happened?"

"My mother found us in bed together and completely freaked. In order to calm her down we told her we were married and that freaked her out even more. She immediately called his family. My father came home. There was a big pow-wow. The end result was that they convinced us that if we were meant to be together, waiting until after college wasn't going to stop that. They added to it the fact that we'd snuck off to do it secretly and that meant that we knew that it was the wrong thing to do."

They were both silent for a moment, each thinking of the implications of that statement.

"So, I'm in the presence of a divorced woman?"

"No." Peter looked truly shocked for a moment and Maddie let the silence roll over them just to enjoy him trying to work that one out. With a sigh, she let him off the hook.

"It was annulled." Maddie paused and noticed Peter's raised eyebrows. "My parents got a good lawyer to argue that it had all been a joke." Maddie breathed in the autumn air. "That was the hardest part."

They continued in companionable silence for a while. "Anyway, the long and short of it is that we wrote for a couple of years. He blamed me for running away and moving across the country and I blamed him for not fighting hard enough for me and then for not coming to get me. And then....well, then life just went on and I haven't seen or heard from him since. The only information I get about him is through my sister and even that's sporadic. So you can imagine what it was like to see him last night." Peter stopped and hugged Maddie. She could tell he could imagine.

The two of them had come around Main and up Prospect and had arrived at the dance studio, when Maddie let out a groan.

"Damn! I forgot I was supposed to drop something off downtown." She still didn't feel like talking about the letter, although she couldn't come up with a good reason for her reluctance. She didn't need to come up with an excuse as Peter had spotted several squirrels clinging to a bird feeder and had taken three running steps towards them, shouting obscenities.

Chapter Nine

Maddie had ten minutes before Alice arrived for her lesson, not enough time to get to the police station and back. It occurred to her that maybe Alice wouldn't come at all today. Maybe she'd been so freaked out by Nina's death that she'd stop classes altogether. Certainly, her behavior in the restroom was disturbing enough for Maddie to wonder if she was going to show. She needn't have worried though as, right on time, Alice walked into the studio. Unfortunately, she was trailed by Henri.

Henri's appearance didn't impress Maddie but she put on a smile and greeted them. Before she could say three words, Henri came up behind Alice and put his arm around her protectively.

"I'm staying the hell here with Alice," Henri barked out. "There's no way I'm going to leave her here alone. No knowing what could happen to her." For Alice's part, she smiled sweetly, but her eyes darted around the room, unable to find a place to rest. She then gazed at Henri with the mixture of dread and worship that Maddie had come to recognize. The image of the vulnerable woman from the restroom the night before faded as Maddie realized that Alice didn't need her help. She shrugged. Alice was a grown woman and unless she also suffered from a severe allergy to nuts, what Henri had said made absolutely no sense. As if he could read Maddie's thoughts, Henri shook his upper body, as if ridding himself of the thug persona, and glided in Maddie's direction.

"We wouldn't want anything to 'appen to my belle woman." He looked for a moment as if he was going to take hold of Maddie and she felt herself back up involuntarily. However, Henri was falling deeper into character and didn't seem to notice Maddie's discomfort. While staring at Maddie, he flicked his hand behind him, motioning to Alice. She scooted right up to his side, reading his gesture as a command to heel.

Maddie thought it prudent to simply start the class with the both of them and allow for as little talking as possible. Unfortunately, Henri had a different idea.

"So, what do you think 'appened last night?" He continued to mask what Maddie thought to be his true accent with the inflection of a fictionalized French poet. Maddie chose her words carefully, because she didn't want to hear Henri speak anymore.

"I think Nina died of anaphylactic shock. Peter called the police and they said they'd call us later when they had results from her autopsy." Keeping her distance from Henri, Maddie directed her attention to Alice.

"Remember, keep the ball of your foot on the floor, even if that means I hear your steps. I'd rather that than have your legs swinging around like a door."

At Maddie's words, Henri raised his hands and pushed the air around Maddie's face as if shooing flies. "No, she has to let her legs leave the ground. She shuffles through everything. I want her to be able to kick." He uttered the last remark while making a jabbing motion with his arm for emphasis.

Oh, God, Maddie thought. *This is going to be bad.* She had to nip this one in the bud.

"Henri," Maddie spoke his name with a dripping French accent. "Alice is just beginning. She needs to find her balance, work through her centre and control her weight. She has to attend to all these things before we can introduce..." *Hmmm...how to put this politely?* Maddie pondered. "Before we focus on those more challenging steps." In order to stop a running commentary on Alice's performance, Maddie brought the conversation back to Nina.

"What did you mean by what happened last night? It seemed clear to me."

"Hey, look, I don't know." His thug roots materialized again. "It was all so sudden." He looked towards Alice, who held onto the wall for support as she practiced a backward *ocho* and his voice fell into what Maddie supposed was the sound of a concerned citizen. "It was all 'orrible, wasn't it? People sneaking in and out and all of a sudden, a woman, dead."

"What do you mean people sneaking in and out? Of what? The classroom?"

"Yes, of course." Now Henri started to act evasively again, his eyes shifting uncomfortably between the mirror, the windows and Alice. "You know, that woman, the one with the tight face? She kept sneaking along the sides of the room and then she left and then came back. It was all a little weird, don't you think, 'specially as that other woman died?"

Maddie didn't think it was weird at all. She was sure he was speaking about Renée and thought that Renée had most likely been trying to avoid Henri. Maddie hadn't noticed her sneaking about any more than anyone else. Henri was just gross.

"Well, I didn't notice that and even if it did happen, it had nothing to do with Nina's death." Maddie continued teaching Alice with Henri hovering in the background.

The remainder of the class progressed more smoothly than she'd hoped until she asked Henri to dance with Alice and he refused. He said he was tired after all the traveling he'd to do and he had to conserve his energy. Alice smiled weakly at him. While Maddie couldn't say that Alice was the most interesting conversationalist at the best of times, the zombie-like creature who danced in the presence of Henri was both astonishing and depressing.

She turned the light off as she left the room and headed back to the office to say goodnight to whoever might still be there. Hopefully, Peter, so she could find out if the police had called back. Indeed, Peter was there and next to him sat Joe Clancy.

Maddie's stomach tensed involuntarily. It was one thing to see him during a crisis but another to see him sitting in a chair opposite her boss, looking for all the world like he'd walked in to inquire about dance classes. Peter looked up as Maddie entered the room and waved at her. Joe turned around and pinned Maddie with a stare that made her wonder if he knew she had an unpaid parking fine.

"Hi," Maddie said brightly, in order to fill the space. Joe stood up too quickly, unfolding his lanky body from the seat. Maddie noted the shadows under his eyes, the black hair curling over the collar of his shirt and the way his tongue darted out to lick his lower lip, all in an instant. She breathed in slowly and touched the wall next to her for reassurance. It was as if fifteen years had vanished and she was looking at him in her living room, their parents surrounding them with their anger and anxiety.

Joe cleared his throat. "Hi, Maddie. I was just finishing up with Peter. I wanted to come by and let you know that while all the tests have not come back yet, it looks like Nina LePore died of an anaphylactic episode resulting from a toxin in her body. I don't want anyone worrying about it any longer." Joe spoke slowly, as if he was warning her, nicely maybe, but warning nonetheless and the implication made her bristle.

"What do you mean, worry?"

"We've had several students from the school call our office and some of them have been overly distraught. I've asked Peter to convey the message that Ms. LePore's death was an accident and that there is no need to worry excessively."

"What do you mean 'overly distraught'? Is there a particular level of emotion the police department expects when someone has died?" Maddie heard the sarcasm in her voice but couldn't help sharing her thoughts.

Joe read it clearly as well. As if a wall had sprung up instantly between them, he turned back towards Peter who sat, mouth hanging open like a moonstruck goldfish. But Maddie wasn't done.

"Could it have been anything else? Like poisoning?"

Joe tilted his head a moment and looked at her questioningly but with no visible emotion. "Why would you ask that?"

"Oh, nothing. I just mean, she worked for a chemical company. I wondered if something from there could have caused the reaction?" Her voice fizzled out. She sounded lame even to herself.

Joe nodded slowly, never taking his eyes off her. "You're right, she worked at SynTech. However, she was a secretary in a small department that had nothing to do with the chemicals. There's no reason to believe she would have been in contact with something that would have caused that reaction." Joe rubbed a spot on his left forearm. "I read your statement last night. You said that you didn't do anything to help Nina LePore until she'd collapsed, but that she'd been acting strangely for several minutes. Any reason for that?"

Maddie stood silently but she was seething inside, knowing that she wasn't going to answer Joe. She wasn't going to admit that she enjoyed Nina's display. Nina was not a likeable person and watching her make a fool of herself was a guilty pleasure, at least until she died. Joe turned back to Peter.

"As I said, we'll keep you informed but the outcome will likely be an accidental death, which means that the studio should have no further involvement in the case." He turned so that he could see them both and spoke as if the exchange between them had never happened. "I'm very sorry for your loss. Even if you didn't know her well, I understand that it must have been quite a shock."

Joe spoke with a detachment that Maddie didn't recognize but she instantly regretted her childish outburst that Joe was so successfully ignoring. If he could rise above her inappropriate remarks, so could she.

"I'll walk you out," she said, moving into the hallway. Joe looked like he was going to speak, but didn't and nodded instead. Peter watched them leave with a pensive expression on his own face.

The two moved down the hallway and didn't speak until they'd reached the front door. Maddie turned to face Joe, unsure of what she was going to say but knowing that she couldn't let him walk out without at least recognizing what they once meant to one another.

"I just wanted to say that it's nice to see you. Even in these circumstances."

Joe looked directly at Maddie. There was no shuffling or darting eyes or hemming and hawing. He simply stared at her, making her wonder what he was thinking.

"Nice? Yes, it's nice. I really am sorry this all happened here. It's rough."

Maddie looked away. "I know. I've been walking around in a daze the whole day, not really believing what happened." Again the silence between them was complete, but somehow not completely wrong. Joe spoke first.

"Was there anything else you wanted to say?"

"Oh, yes. I would love to see you again. I mean when you're not busy."

Joe looked embarrassed. "I meant about the case. Anything about Nina."

Now it was Maddie's turn to redden. "Oh, silly me. No, everything's fine. If I think of anything, I guess I can call you."

"Yes, any time." As Joe pulled a card out of his pocket, Maddie marveled at the realization that he'd nipped her attempt to reconnect in the bud with astonishing talent. He handed her the card and walked out the door. It was the second time someone she'd known from her youth had handed her a business card. She was obviously doing something wrong.

Joe climbed into his car, absently rubbing his temple to try to ease the throbbing that had commenced the second he left the building. The image of Maddie staring at the card he'd handed to her so ridiculously, confirmed his status as a complete jerk. He pounded his hand into the steering wheel, the reverberations making the thudding in his head more pronounced. He stretched his neck to either side and reached into the glove compartment for a bottle of Advil. It wasn't a beer-induced headache, the three bottles he'd had last night were normal for him though you'd never tell from his physique. At 6'2," his body could take that kind of abuse and spread it out over his lean limbs. Since he also ran ten miles a day, he stayed in excellent shape.

Joe swallowed two Advil dry and hammered the wheel again. While not the hardest thing he'd ever had to do in his life—watching Maddie get on a plane fifteen years ago took that prize—saying the words he just did while handing her his business card, was up there with the worst of them.

While Joe'd had other relationships, a couple of very good ones, Maddie had taken up a lot of space in his heart. Joe accepted that, because he never thought he would see her again. But now, she was here and perversely, she was sticking her nose into a situation that he was responsible for and one that could get her hurt. While he wasn't going to let that happen, he also wasn't going to give the dance studio the full details of Nina LePore's toxicology report.

Chapter Ten

Maddie was in the lobby, carefully folding the card Joe had given her into the smallest square she could manage, when Peter arrived carrying a box and several bags. "Come on, sugar-pie, I'm leaving. Take your bags from me before I expire." Maddie absently took her bags and opened the door for Peter, still laden with objects.

"Can I help you take some of those to your car?"

He thanked her as he handed one of the boxes to her. "They're the new brochures, complete with my newest addition to the dance team," he smiled winsomely at her. "Everything okay here?"

"Yeah, fine. Just a bit of a reality check," she replied quickly, unwilling to dwell on her disappointment. What irritated her most was that she didn't understand why she was disappointed. It wasn't as if she'd expected a reunion, or even wanted one.

"I'm surprised the police have written this off as an accidental death so quickly. I thought things like this took ages to look into and, I don't know, investigate."

"I wouldn't know. Can't stand those police procedural things on TV. Kristy and I try to watch movies made before 1939. After *Gone With the Wind,* everything changed." They'd arrived at Peter's car and as he opened the trunk, Maddie took several brochures out of the top box.

"Do you mind if I take some of these? I know someone who may want to start lessons."

"Certainly, take all you want. I try to casually leave at least ten wherever I go. By the way, what made you ask Detective Clancy about the case?"

Maddie hit her palm against her head. The note. That's what she'd meant to tell Joe about, but she'd clean forgotten during her abortive attempt at conversation.

"Damn; there was something I wanted to show him. I'm going to have to stop over there tomorrow."

"Oh, gee darn. I bet that'll be tough," Peter gave her a quick hug and laughed good-naturedly.

Maddie turned towards her bicycle and heard Peter get into his car and start the engine.

"Oh, and Maddie, don't hate me when you read the brochure." Peter waved as he screeched out of the parking lot.

Oh, no, Maddie thought. *That can only mean one thing.* Maddie knew before she'd opened to the third page that she would be there in full color and that all her accolades would be listed under her image, including *Dance for Your Life.* She scanned the paragraph and came to what she'd dreaded.

Among many honors, Maddie is recognized as being a choreographer on the forefront of Nuevo Tango. Her Emmy award for her Argentine Tango will go down in history as being a once-in-a-lifetime event.

Maddie skipped the rest of the bio. It wasn't as bad as it could've been and, to be fair, to ask Peter not to include her stint as a reality television choreographer would have been unreasonable. It didn't mention the full frontal nudity and maybe some of the people reading the brochure weren't watching television that night.

Cycling home, Maddie tried to enjoy the cooling air, but found herself returning to the middle of the ridiculous confrontation with Joe, equally frustrated by her inability to say what she meant and his disinterest in her. She parked her bicycle in its place, wishing she had a sympathetic ear to moan into. As she entered the house, the telephone rang and she answered it on the cordless phone, so that she could pour herself a glass of wine and rummage in the vegetable bin for some carrots.

"Hello....well, speak of the devil...no, no. I was just thinking about Mom and Dad and you, really. I miss you."

It was Maddie's sister, Sylvie. She lived in Burlington, Vermont, with her husband and daughter. It was good to talk to her, mostly about the family's upcoming trip out East for Christmas, the first Christmas they would be together in New Jersey in fifteen years. As she drank her glass of wine and dipped the carrot sticks into hummus, she considered the ramifications of not telling Sylvie about Nina, but knew they would be too big. Though she wanted to forget last night, at least for a little while, and she knew Joe's involvement would come into it, she also knew Sylvie currently had no other news source in town. She braced herself by filling her glass to the rim before she began her story.

"What? You've got to be kidding. And she was dead? Really?"

After spouting numerous expletives and a series of detailed questions, Sylvie happened upon the one detail Maddie had been anticipating.

"Was Joe there?"

Maddie silently thanked her sister for not pretending to be subtle about the question, a strategy she thought her mother would employ, and responded in kind.

"Yes, and it was awful. I saw him today too, and was able to make a fool of myself a second time." Maddie gulped the remaining liquid in her glass. "He's improved his blow-off skills to an astounding level."

"Oh, Maddie, I'm sorry. Is he still engaged to Tracy Gallini?"

"Tracy Gallini? What do you mean? You never told me that."

"Yes, I did. I told you last year. You just weren't listening. Her husband died a couple of years ago and she has four kids, all under the age of ten."

"You most certainly did not tell me that." Maddie's head started to ache. What a fool she'd made of herself. "You told me about the girlfriend in Maryland and you told me about the engagement to that NBC news reporter but you never told me he was engaged to Tracy Gallini."

Sylvie seemed to be moving furniture around on her end of the phone. "Well, sorry. I meant to. Anyway, did you notice if he had a ring on?"

"No, I wasn't looking."

"Of course, you were. Did he?"

"Fine. No, he wasn't wearing a ring and now I have a headache and I'm going to make some supper."

"Wait a second. Have you told Mom and Dad about this?"

"I sent them an email this morning from the studio so I expect a call any time now. I mean it; I'm hanging up."

"Okay, but keep me posted. I want a word-for-word report of what Mom says when you tell her that you've seen Joe." Maddie knew she would.

The next morning promised the kind of day Maddie had hoped for; crisp with the smell of woodsmoke in the air. As she pedaled away from her parents' house, she saw the smoke rise from the neighbor's chimney. She smiled and knew exactly what she was going to do that night. Her itinerary included a beautiful bottle of red, a good book and a roaring fire. She couldn't wait to get through this day.

Slowing down at the only traffic light between her parents' house and the studio, she found herself parallel to Katy Clemment's cherry red car. Katy had pulled up next to Maddie but seemed oblivious to her surroundings, her attention focused on a pile of paper in her lap. They were moving in the same direction and as Maddie stood next to Katy's closed window, she could see Katy lift and discard several pieces of paper, as she simultaneously yelled into the mobile she held in her other hand. Maddie could see her mouthing words, but couldn't hear what they were. Judging by the look on Katy's face, however, Maddie decided it would be a good idea to just pass by. She was doing exactly that when Katy looked up from what she was doing and instantly recomposed her face. She rolled down her window, motioning to Maddie to stay.

"Wow, hi. I'm glad to see you. I meant to stop back in yesterday to say hi but was completely swamped." Katy was so chirpy and excited to see Maddie that she wondered if she'd imagined the whole tantrum within the car.

"Let's meet up for lunch. Maybe not today, I'm still really busy, but what about in the next couple of days?" Katy's mobile rang and she looked down to see who it was. Her eyes narrowed as she read the caller ID, and then she looked up at Maddie. Clearly feeling the need to explain her reaction, she continued.

"Ex-boyfriend. I've done everything I can to be nice but I am just..." She didn't finish the sentence, but looked back at the phone. She seemed about to toss it onto the floor of the car, but thought better of the idea and instead hung onto it with a grip that made the veins on her arm stand out.

"Sorry, I have to go. Good seeing you." As Katy drove off, Maddie realized that she had not had the chance to open her mouth—it was all one-way traffic—nor had they made a date for lunch. Maddie was probably better off. Katy didn't look as if she'd be good company right then.

Maddie's first class didn't begin until 10:30 so she made her way over to what was becoming her Friday morning ritual; coffee and pastries at Vito's. Today, she decided to have her coffee at the counter, but would bring a box of treats back to the studio to share.

She order her coffee at the deli, along with a box of *cannoli* and *boconnotti* from the person behind the counter, a young woman, possibly a cousin from Italy. Taking her coffee to the window, she sipped her drink as she paged through the local paper, smiling as she read the announcements page, which was virtually unchanged during her fifteen-year absence. The requisite engagements and anniversaries were there, including Pembroke College's centenary celebration. One of the many activities Maddie read about was a lecture given by Dr. Jesse Booth, titled *Environmental Waste: Everyone's Problem*. Maddie shuddered: she couldn't think of a more unappealing topic. Flipping through the rest of the paper, she ordered a refill, although she knew she couldn't put off the inevitable visit to the police station forever.

The municipal buildings were new to Maddie, modern brick and glass structures built in the last decade that were more spacious than the mock colonial buildings they replaced. And they were well sign-posted. She followed the boards to the police department and then those for the administrative services where she found Joe's office with a secretary sitting at her desk in front of his door. When the secretary looked up and smiled, Maddie squealed.

"Maureen! Wow, I didn't expect to see you! How are you?"

Maureen came around the desk with her arms outstretched and drew Maddie to her ample bosom. She laughed as she spoke, and her voice was exactly as Maddie remembered it.

"Well, well. Madeleine Fitzpatrick! It's so damn good to see you. Joe told me he saw you. Me, I'm absolutely great. But you! Tell me, how are you?"

Maddie laughed as she tried to get a word in edgewise. Maureen's personality was infectious like that. Maureen Clancy was Joe's little sister. She was five years younger and only thirteen when Maddie had left for the West Coast, yet for all the time passed, she was as familiar to Maddie as if she'd seen her yesterday. Maureen and Joe shared an uncanny resemblance, the same long, straight nose, with a smattering of the mandatory Irish freckles across the tip, full mouth and intense, cat-like green eyes. Their hair color was the extreme opposite though—Joe's hair so dark and brown it was almost black and Maureen's a dirty blonde whose ends looked like they had been dipped in a can of purple paint. Maddie wondered how Maureen got away with that working for a police department.

"I'm well, Maureen. Actually, maybe that's stretching it a bit far. You obviously know what happened at Peter's studio two nights ago."

"Of course, you're not fine. Why would you be? How many people have died right there in front of you, gasping for breath?" Obviously, Maureen had heard all the details. While she didn't show disrespect for the situation, she exhibited the light-hearted approach to life that Maddie remembered and it looked as though she'd even extended this perspective to police procedural work.

Maureen took the moment to gaze significantly at Maddie and squeeze her arm. Why, Maddie was unsure. She then spotted the box Maddie held and laughed.

"You brought him some donuts?" Maddie looked at the box and instantly remembered an experience of all the thousands that she'd faced since she'd left Pembroke.

The day before Maddie left for college, Maureen had come by to say goodbye and bring her a plant for her dorm room. Needless to say, it wouldn't have made the trip to Northern California, so Maddie'd had to leave it. However, the thought behind it touched Maddie in a way that she never told Maureen. What Maddie remembered was the thirteen-year-old Maureen pulling her into a hug and saying to Maddie, *Don't worry, you'll be my sister-in-law yet.* Up to that point, Maddie was unsure whether Joe's mother and step-father had included Maureen in the family discussions about Joe's short-lived marriage.

Knowing she had to drop the letter and get back to work, she tried to make light of her memory. "Actually, no. The pastries are for the studio. I have, however, brought something I think Joe ought to see. I guess he's not here?"

"Course he is. Just inside. Why'd you think that?"

"Well, because…" Maddie looked toward Joe's door, the uncomfortable realization that Joe had likely heard her voice and had not come out to say hello.

"So, what is it you have to give him? Or is it personal?" The comment was accompanied by a sneaky smile.

"No. It's not personal, Maureen. Here." She handed the envelope to Maureen. Maybe it would just be better if she dropped the letter off and left. "It's a letter I found in my dance bag."

When Maureen looked at her questioningly, Maddie added, "I found it in the bag I keep my dance shoes and brush and things in." Maureen nodded. "Well, I didn't know it was there that night and anyway, it's for Nina LePore. Well, I think it is anyway." Now Maureen didn't look confused, but eager.

"I'll give that to him straight away but I'm sure he's going to have to talk to you about it."

Picking up the pastries she'd placed on Maureen's desk, she turned to go. "Sorry, I have to run. I have a class to teach in a couple of minutes. He has my details if he needs to speak with me."

As Maddie said a final good-bye, Joe's office door opened. Maddie jumped, nearly upending the box she held, and let out an involuntary squeak when she caught sight of Renée Lambert, her bun as tight as ever. Joe followed behind her, his hand on her lower back, guiding her out of the room. When he caught site of Maddie, he slipped his hand away from Renée and he took a step backwards into his office.

"Thank you for coming in, Ms. Lambert. We'll be in touch when we have more information. And remember, there's no need to worry." He then looked at Maddie. "Did you need to speak to me, Maddie?"

Maddie had to step aside as Renée careened out of the room without even a glance in her direction. She swallowed a short response to Joe's brusque manner and shook her head. "No, I have to get back to the studio. I gave Maureen a letter you should see." Maddie waved vaguely over to Maureen who held the letter in her hand. A look of disgust passed over Joe's face and Maddie grinned when she realized that Maureen was going to make Joe cross the room to get the letter. Sibling rivalry was alive and well in the Clancy family.

Joe stomped over to Maureen and snatched the offending letter as Maddie left the room. She turned in the hallway to find Maureen hustling out the door behind her with a grin on her own face.

"Look, Maddie, I know that this can be awkward and I don't want it to be. I'd love it if you could stop by for drinks sometime," Maddie paused.

"I'd really like that, Maureen."

"Oh, goody. Tim and I, that's my husband, just got a trampoline and it's the most fun."

Maddie continued to smile as she left the building and climbed back on her bicycle. The thought of Maureen's breasts on a trampoline made her laugh out loud as she pedaled back to the studio and her next class.

Upstairs, Joe Clancy's office was quiet. Maureen hadn't returned from delivering Maddie out the front door, but if she had, she would have heard a groan from behind the door followed by a low chant meant to calm him. He took several large swallows of water, then sat back in his chair and wiped the sweat from his forehead. Maureen was right, he was going to have to get a grip on this situation.

On top of all his awards for police work, Joe had graduated at the top of his class at Johns Hopkins, majoring in psychology and then again at the New Jersey Police Academy. It had been years since anyone had called him Mad Joe Clancy, a name derived from the fact that his father had been institutionalized at a psychiatric hospital and then committed suicide when Joe was 12. His parents had already divorced by that time, and his mother had married his stepfather, but once the news got around Pembroke Junior High, it would seem that the sins of the father would indeed be visited upon the son.

Joe didn't hold it against the kids in his class; he'd done the same; Fat Johnny was a skinny kid whose father was the only morbidly obese man in town; Scratch was what they called a girl named Sue because her mother had scratched her husband so badly when he left her for another woman, he needed 29 stitches across his face. Joe knew children were cruel, but he'd risen out of that adolescent battleground to become an asset to his community.

Everything was under control he told himself as he counted his breaths, ten seconds in and ten seconds out. First off, he had to read the letter Maddie'd brought in. Getting into this case, as well as the numerous others he was dealing with, would take his mind off the issue of Maddie.

Joe opened the envelope that he'd ungraciously taken from his sister, read it and placed it on the desk next to the file that read 'Nina LePore.' Since his college days, he'd disciplined himself to continuously focus on whatever work he had in front of him from beginning to end. This constant repetition, earned him the reputation of being meticulous to the point of over cautiousness. In Pembroke, where the politics and lifestyles were fairly conservative, this habit had served him well.

Maddie. His stomach flipped again. There were already enough anomalies in this case to warrant a closer look and he didn't want Maddie's involvement to cloud his judgment. He was finishing the file when Maureen came back into the room and immediately pointed a well-polished nail at him.

"Jesus, Mary and Joseph! You're going to have to get a grip on this situation if you plan..." Joe didn't let her continue or if she did, he couldn't hear her reprimands, because he'd firmly closed the door between their offices. As he gathered papers from his desk and prepared to make a phone call to the morgue, he could hear Maureen raise her voice enough to be heard through the barrier.

"...and don't think that just because you don't want to talk about it now it means it's not an issue. It's bloody well been an issue for fifteen years." Joe could hear the phone ring at Maureen's desk, followed by silence as she answered it.

An issue that has lain dormant for fifteen years and can do so for another fifteen, Joe thought. He saw the light blink on his internal phone, indicating that the call was for him. Because Maureen hadn't announced the caller, he knew it was the call he'd been expecting.

Five minutes later, he opened his door and moved toward the fax machine. Maureen was typing but took a few seconds to look over her glasses at Joe with an affectionate yet exasperated look in her eyes.

"And what was that about guiding Renée Lambert out so solicitously?"

Joe appeared not to have heard Maureen, as he picked up the fax that had arrived and read it. He'd already heard the news over the phone but devoured it word for word anyway. Without looking up again, Joe spoke.

"I don't know what you're talking about."

"Oh, yes, you do and don't deny it. It only proves how much Maddie has gotten to you."

Joe's nose remained stuck in the faxed report. Maureen pursed her lips and debated whether to push it. She sighed. And let it go.

"Toxicology for LePore?"

Continuing to scan the document, Joe grunted an affirmative.

"Interesting?"

It seemed Joe was only going to offer another grunt in response, but at the last moment he lifted his face and gazed out the window.

"Yes. Interesting."

Chapter Eleven

Maddie arrived back at the studio with just enough time to pass out some pastries and use the restroom. She warned on pain of death that there had better be a *cannoli* left when she finished teaching. Frank promised he'd protect the honor of the *cannoli* from the likes of Peter. Everyone laughed as Peter took on the look of a wounded puppy. He had a habit of forgetting how many he'd eaten as soon as the first one hit his mouth.

"It's not my fault my mother never let us have sugar growing up. I'm just making up for lost time," he said as he reached for the box.

Maddie's first class of the day was made up of three couples in their late-twenties. The female half of each couple seemed a whole lot more enthusiastic to be taking an Argentine Tango class than the male half. It was soul-destroying to listen to jibes like *hey, why can't we learn the horizontal tango?* peppered throughout the class but she had to get through it. Thank goodness they hadn't seen the new brochure or made the connection between Maddie and the *Dance for Your Life* fiasco. They were already a little too enthusiastic about anything to do with dancing and naked bodies.

Maddie had to repeat the most recent instruction three times because every time she said pelvic, one or the other of the boys—and she did think of them as boys—would gyrate frantically and all three would break off into loud guffaws, while their girlfriends shook their heads and slapped them affectionately.

"Okay, I have an idea." Maddie figured if they were going to act like children, she might as well give them a child's game to play. She handed each boy a balloon.

"Okay, blow it up, and tie it." They each did it with the requisite release of air to make farting noises.

"Now take your places with your partner in the A-frame position we've been talking about, but this time place the balloon between the two of you at chest level." A bit of scuffling ensued, but, all in all, they did as she asked.

"Now I want you to walk with your partner. Wait. Leave your arms down at your sides. I want you to walk with your partner and make sure the balloon stays in place. The object of the exercise is to keep the connection between you and your partner at the chest level," before she could continue, there was an explosion that interrupted Maddie's instructions.

"Brad, you idiot, you blew it up too much." His partner, Carla, had her hands on her hips and though she spoke the words in irritation, there was a smile on her lips.

"Sorry, babe. Guess I just got too much air in me."

"You can say that again. Here, let me do this one." Carla took the balloon Maddie held out.

"Okay, everyone keep going. Slowly. The connection comes when you slow down enough to listen to each other. I want you to hear what your partner's body is saying to you."

Mark, the grumpiest of the boys, started to speak but his partner Sue, slapped him on the arm.

"Don't even think about it." Sue looked to Maddie apologetically.

The class was up and Maddie was pleased. Their improvement today was more than she'd expected. Even Mark seemed satisfied. As he slipped through the door, he turned back to say over his shoulder.

"Thanks, Teach. That was pretty good."

Peter was shaking his head when Maddie spotted him from across the room.

"Hmm. Should I be worried?"

"Oh, no, Peter, please. If he remains that enthusiastic about the class, I'll be ecstatic. Last week he sat down halfway through the class and wouldn't get up."

Peter snickered. "Imagine turning down an opportunity to dance with you."

"Believe me, with this group, I'd rather they knew as little about me as possible."

"I can't believe you don't want to play it to the max. You know the publicity it could drum up won't be around forever. By next month, they'll have a group of Highland dancers all doing their unison jig, all going commando. Then you'll be old news and you'll have to rely on your extreme talent alone."

Maddie choked on a mouthful of water and coughed several times before she could speak. "Well, if you put it like that Peter, I don't know why I haven't written an op-ed for the Pembroke Eagle to announce my arrival."

"Oh, that's a good idea. I could…"

"Peter, don't you dare."

"So, who was she and why did she do it?" Peter sat next to Maddie with his own bottle of water. Maddie sighed. She'd already told Peter part of the story when he offered her a job but hadn't divulged her relationship with the now infamous Morgan LeRoux.

"I was her dance history teacher at UCLA."

After a moment of expectant silence, Peter realized that she'd said all she planned to say. He slapped his knees and got up to leave.

"Oh, that's explains everything." Dramatic eye-roll. "Thanks."

"Okay, I was her teacher for a senior year thesis course and I failed her."

"Now that really does do more to explain it. Ouch."

"Hmm...funny thing is, her behavior in class that warranted the fail and her behavior in the competition ended up being the same. The difference between being famous and infamous was lost on her. She'd written her thesis on a contemporary performer that it turns out she slept with. Baring the affair to the department was the total substance of the paper. I told her it was unprofessional and not worthy of being called scholarship, and, that she had to rewrite the paper to pass. She didn't. I failed her which means she didn't graduate, and now you've seen how she got back at me."

"Maddie, you're proving to be a deep well and I'll remind myself to not be surprised the next time you tell me a story," Peter looked sideways at her, an expectant look on his face. "You don't have anything else you want to tell me do you?"

Maddie laughed, in spite of herself. "No, I don't and I hope to keep it like that for a long time to come." She looked at her watch, "I have ten minutes before my next class."

Maddie used the restroom, then stretched a bit before class. She thought about the last year and knew she did have several more sordid stories but she didn't want to divulge any more to Peter. She'd already told him more than she'd imagined herself doing. With just a minute or two before her class arrived, she was surprised to see Alice shuffle through the door.

"Um, sorry, Maddie. Sorry, do you have a minute?"

"Hi, Alice, yes, just a couple though; I have a class."

"Oh, it won't take long. I just wanted to say that I was being stupid. I mean, don't worry about anything I said the other night when...um...she died. I was just scared." Alice spoke as if she was going to run out of air. Maddie walked closer to her, as she hovered at the door, unwilling or unable to enter the room.

"Alice, I was worried. Are you sure everything's okay? Is there anything you want to tell me?" Alice began shaking her head passionately. "I may be able to help, Alice."

"Well, maybe there's one thing." Alice had brought her chin almost to her chest and whispered, so that Maddie had to step closer. "It's just, I know Henri knew her, even though he won't admit it."

Maddie waited for more but didn't get it. "How do you know, Alice?"

Alice swung her head around at the sound of a door opening behind her, and as she continued to scan the hallway, she whispered. "He's buying the riverside place and she has something to do with it."

Maddie tried to make sense of what Alice had said. She knew Nina worked for SynTech but unless SynTech was buying the property, she didn't know why Nina would be involved. Before Maddie could think of something to say, the door opened again and her class noisily piled into the building. Alice scurried along the wall until she was out the door. Maddie hoped Alice would show up for class the next week, this time without Henri.

The arriving class had quickly become Maddie's favorite class to teach. It consisted of eleven people from a single family, varying in age from eighteen to seventy-nine. They had signed up en-masse for a six-week course to prepare for a family wedding. The class was the loudest one she taught, as it seemed that the whole family were required to respond to a single utterance from any other member. Her favorite was Tia Angela, seventy-four years old, who, with her seventy-nine year-old husband, Danny, glided across the dance floor as if they were teenagers again.

"Oh, Maddie, this is what we all used to do. If you didn't know how to dance, then you never would have found a husband."

Danny maneuvered Angela around a corner as she elegantly rested in his arms, her eyes closed and a serene smile on her face.

"Lucky for you, I was there to save you from all those young boys who thought they knew how to dance," Danny remained alert to possible collisions with some of the younger and less accomplished members of his family.

Still with her eyes closed, Angela chirped. "Me, lucky? Hah. The day you saw me dancing was the luckiest day of your life." Danny grunted a reply as Maddie bit back a giggle. Then Angela continued. "And, it must be said, it was the luckiest day of my life." Danny nodded as if he'd just won the point, but his wife wasn't done. "Because it was the day that you finally became man enough to ask me to dance and not just watch me from behind your Mamma's bosom."

At those words, Danny stopped dancing but from the thrust of Angela's face, Maddie could tell she was not surprised. The whole room had become unnaturally quiet as Danny pursed his lips and raised his arm, as if about to make a point. Angela simply looked at him, her hands now on her wide hips. With a glance that combined defeat and love, Danny lifted his arms to invite his wife into an embrace again.

"My Mamma did have a big bosom."

Normalcy returned, as the family began chattering about the dance classes they'd taken. Maddie watched the class and offered advice when needed, but then she saw something that took her breath away. The *fish wiggle*. That wasn't the step's name, in fact it wasn't even a step, just the end of a step that only sometimes worked so eloquently.

"Okay, can I have everyone's attention? Tia Angela, Danny, will you dance again? Just repeat the step you just did."

The couple hadn't stopped dancing, but Danny lifted his shoulders slightly. "What step? I don't do steps. I just move."

Maddie nodded. "I know. You two are a great example of the improvisational qualities of the Argentine Tango. However, what you just did was what we call a walking turn. Can you do that again?"

Danny looked suspiciously at Maddie.

"Just carry on in the line-of-dance and walk Angela in a complete circle before continuing in the same direction."

Danny shrugged again, but followed Maddie's instructions and rewarded her with the example she'd been hoping for.

"Watch your grandmother's...ahem...rear, as your grandfather turns her around—here—just now as she straightens back into line-of-dance. Do you see?"

Maddie looked around the room at the family members who'd stopped to watch and saw recognition of the same beauty mirrored on their faces. Several spoke at the same time.

"Nana, you're so beautiful."

"Mama, you've still got it in you."

"Am I going to be able to do that?"

Angela basked in the admiration and Danny seemed to take it all as a compliment to his skill as a lead. Maddie laughed loudly.

"Yes, you'll be able to do that to. What they are doing is a natural movement that comes out of the walking turn that we've been working on. As the follow moves around the lead and naturally corrects her relationship to him, the beautiful fish tail you're watching is produced. Your grandparents do it so well partly because they're listening to the way the other is moving and they can do that because they've been dancing together for years."

Class was over and she'd walked Tia Angela and Danny and the rest of the family out of the door, where they piled into one of two gigantic Oldsmobiles and tooted the horn as she waved good-bye. Maddie stood pensively as they turned the corner and drove out of sight. Angela and Danny had been dancing for what, maybe fifty years together? Even if she met someone today, it was unlikely he would be able to dance, and they would have to dance together for more than a few years to reach that special place where they could anticipate each other's movements. Maddie cursed silently, aware that she was as angry with herself for being so naïve as to want to have a partner to dance with into old age, as she was with Craig for breaking up with her and ending her romantic notions.

In the office, true to Frank's word, there was not one, but two *cannoli*. There was also a note from Peter. The first part of the note said that Toby had called while she was in class and asked if she could squeeze in another private lesson that afternoon. Maddie thought it would be good, both for her wallet and Toby's dancing. She was pleased that he was enjoying Argentine Tango after trying so many dances and being ready to give up. She had to admit she was also pleased that she was going to see him again so soon.

The second part of the note said something about *cannoli* and 'ye of little faith.' Maddie chuckled, then found Toby's mobile number and texted him to confirm that she'd see him in an hour and a half for a class. She then wolfed down her pastries, followed by her lunch and was heading out the door to run a few errands when Ricky barged into the room and ran straight into her. Several folders plummeted to the ground, as they collided. Maddie immediately bent to help Ricky pick up the stray papers that had escaped a folder, but Ricky snatched them away from her before she could be of much help.

"Ricky, I'm so sorry..." She'd hardly gotten those words out when Ricky pushed her aside.

"I have work to do. And don't be sorry, we'd broken up. She was no longer anything to me." At that, Ricky walked away, leaving Maddie dumbstruck.

Had he really just uttered those gross, tactless words? Maddie had witnessed Ricky behaving insensitively in class two nights earlier, but she'd also watched as he showed genuine shock at Nina's death. His coarseness aside, what bothered her more was that she recognized the papers he was carrying. The letterhead and printout were identical to the back of the note she'd found in her dance bag the day before. She continued down the hall, vowing to keep her distance from Ricky Russo from now on.

As she passed the smallest of the classrooms, Maddie heard the raised voices of both Ricky and Peter. Ricky sounded irate, so much so, that for a moment Maddie thought Peter might be in danger.

"I need the time off. That's it. I'm taking it and if you think you can stop me, I'll flippin' show you." Maddie's heart caught in her throat. From behind the closed door, Ricky's anger was palpable. Yet, Peter responded in much the same tone and the two seemed at a stalemate.

"Ricky, you can't keep rescheduling your classes. I don't have enough time slots left to give you. If you take off more time now, that's it. Just leave. Look, I'm sorry that this is a bad time..."

Peter was interrupted by the sound of something hitting the ground making Maddie jump from her position in the hallway. Frank had also appeared behind her and stood, unashamedly listening.

"It's got nothing to do with anything. Not anything here. It isn't about Nina. That woman was a bitch."

Maddie could hear Peter gasp. "You can't mean that. The poor woman's dead."

At that, Ricky guffawed. "Poor woman. That's right. I'm back together with Andrea and we're going away and that's that. That pretty little tart can take my classes, I don't give a crap."

Maddie realized her mouth was hanging open in the wake of the tart comment. She wondered again what Ricky had over Peter that allowed him to remain even one more second in the building, let alone on Peter's payroll. Frank looked at her, pursing his lips and shaking his head. They were waiting for more sounds from the room, when Claire walked up all bright and bouncy.

"Hey, what are you two up to?" Maddie and Frank both whipped around and prepared to motion her to be quiet but before they could, the classroom door was yanked almost from its hinges and Ricky flew out the door nearly colliding into Maddie again. This time he didn't even bother greeting any of them but growled as he stomped past them and into the men's room.

"Did he just growl?" Claire asked in a puzzled, but light manner. "It's so funny." Neither Maddie nor Frank thought Ricky's behavior was funny and both looked perplexedly at Claire.

"I mean, it's funny the way that different people react to death, isn't it? He's just pushing people away to hide his pain." When neither Maddie nor Frank responded, she went on a little less sure of herself.

"Don't you think? I read a lot about it in psychology class and when my grandmother died, well, I remember I just laughed. I mean at first. I was really sad."

Maddie smiled briefly in Claire's direction and watched as Philip approached the threesome. Claire and Philip made an unusual sight in that Philip's dreadlocks hung almost to his waist while Claire used clippers without a guard on her virtually bald head.

"Come on, Babe, gotta boogie." Frank and Maddie watched as Philip wrapped his arms around Claire and the two danced off.

Peter came out of the room next and shook himself as if to rid Ricky from his skin and promptly went into an explanation.

"I know. He's cruel. He's gross. He does not deserve the respect of any person in this establishment. He pays me to use the studio. Just so you know."

Maddie realized that Peter was a mastermind at getting information out of people but for all of that, she knew very little about him.

He frowned before continuing. "I'm barely making ends meet at the moment and his fee to me has really made a difference. To tell you the truth, I would wipe Ricky Russo from my memory banks if I could. Good riddance to bad rubbish, as Grandma Georgiana used to say."

"Sounds like my grandmother too. Mine also used to say *where a window closes, a door opens.*"

Peter grinned. "Thank you, Maddie. A misquote from *The Sound of Music* was exactly what I needed. What are you saying? That I need to have a little faith?"

"Yep, I guess that's what I'm saying." Maddie was glad Peter was smiling again, but her heart felt heavy. At the sound of money problems at the studio, her stomach clenched.

Peter picked up Maddie's hand and placed it snugly in the crook of his arm as they walked down the hall together. "And now, it's time to dance."

Together, they walked to the largest classroom. Maddie knew after only a short time working with Peter, that it meant only one thing, and that was that he wanted to polka. With a minimum of practiced movements, Peter had turned on the sound system and set Johann Strauss playing. The ridiculous sounds of the tuba and the accordion blasted out the speakers, as he grabbed Maddie around the waist. The polka, while a somewhat laughable dance today—Maddie often reverted to dancing the polka with her friends after they'd consumed several bottles of wine—was the rage in Europe in the 1830s.

Peter's innate skill and discipline in dance was the only thing that kept a polka with him from dissolving into a carnival act. He attacked the dance with passion, literally lifting Maddie off her feet. Luckily Maddie was in her sneakers, making the jumps and turns easier. Peter made up for anything Maddie was lacking, however, as he danced out his demons.

After the third polka, both dancers were in a lighter mood, but Peter declared he wanted to be even higher, so he walked downtown to get a Red Bull before his next class. Maddie had caught her breath and was heading toward the office, when she heard Ricky's voice from behind the closed door of the men's room.

"....and don't think you'll get away with it. Just what I mean. Yeah right, you're threatening me? You bitch. Just remember, I go down, you go down."

Maddie could hear what sounded distinctly like a door being kicked and she knew better than to be waiting outside the door again when Ricky appeared. She scooted into the office to find Laura at her desk, plastering her errant grey hairs into submission with gel. Wrinkling her nose, Maddie asked. "Is everything okay in here?"

"Oh, I know. I'm just about at my wits end. This product says it's suppose to infuse aging hair with the glow and manageability of youth. That is, of course, a quote." Maddie nodded when Laura looked at her expectantly. "Would you say it's working?"

"Hmm…yes."

"Oh, I don't think it's worth it; it's too sticky. And the smell; enough to make me gag." Laura threw the offending bottle of hair gel in the garbage can.

"Oh, and Toby is coming back in this afternoon." Laura clapped her hands together, huffing happily. "I'm so pleased he's finally found a dance style that suits him. Although," this time a conspiratorial huff, "I think it might actually be the teacher that suits him."

"Oh, well, yes. No. I'm not dating. I'm not ready yet." Maddie retreated as quickly as she could, while trying to remain calm. She didn't know why Laura's saucy comment had flustered her so much. Obviously she was just joking, but Maddie had grown quite nervous at the idea of Toby having a crush on her. Maybe because she thought that she might consider having a crush on him, too, and the very idea felt alien.

Maddie aimed for her favorite spot at the back of the museum garden and had been lost in her own thoughts so she didn't notice another person already occupying it until she was practically on top of her. Andrea sat with her hands clasped in front of her, looking to Maddie as if she was waiting for her. *But that's ridiculous*, Maddie thought. *How would she know where I take my break?* Anyway, the last time they'd spoken had not been pleasant.

Maddie stopped in her tracks, deciding that ignoring Andrea was probably the best course of action, when Andrea broke from her reverie and gave Maddie a slight nod.

"Hi, Andrea." Maddie spoke tentatively, not believing that the woman in front of her could utter a pleasant word. However, Andrea surprised her again.

"I'm a bitch. I know it." Maddie coughed politely as Andrea smiled a toothy grin.

"You don't have to pretend I didn't say it. That was the thing that held Nina and me together. We were both bitches." She paused and didn't say anything for thirty seconds, time during which Maddie mulled over several things to say, but couldn't decide on any one of them, so kept silent. She was glad when Andrea spoke again.

"That's what kept us together and I guess what drove us apart." She took a roll of Life Savers from her handbag, took one out, then offered one to Maddie.

"You know we were best friends our entire lives?" Maddie shook her head again, both to say no to the Life Saver and to Andrea's question.

"We were, though I guess you'd find that unbelievable, having met us in these circumstances. We lived next door to one another as children, went to all the same schools, including college. We never lived more than five miles from each other, both when we married, and then divorced. Then I met Ricky," Andrea paused in her story but looked as if the story continued in her head.

"I loved him. At least I think I did. Whether she loved him too, that I'll never know." She popped another Life Saver in her mouth and sucked hard. "What happened was that once he set eyes on Nina, his feelings for me changed and I couldn't stand that. I don't know why. We've always had guys, sometimes the same one."

Maddie had raised her eyebrows, only mildly questioning—she'd lived in San Francisco for years, after all, where unconventional relationships were the norm.

"I don't mean at the same time. We were never into that. I mean that one of us would date a guy, then break up with him and the other would try him out. None of it was serious. Not back then anyway. Then we both married. Can't say either was a really great match but in the end I was the lucky one. My husband died and left me a small fortune. Hers divorced her and she got nothing. Not even a house. That's what it really came down to."

Maddie was feeling pretty stupid at this point. She wasn't really sure what it all came down to. Not having anything better to say, she just mumbled a sincere sorry.

"Oh, for pity's sake, you don't have to be sorry. I'm the one who's sorry. I messed up with my best friend. We hadn't spoken in over a year."

Again, Maddie was starting to feel like she was a wind-up toy. "But I don't understand what you meant by 'that's what it came down to.' What?"

"Money. It's always money, isn't it?" Maddie shrugged in response.

"I said that I loved Ricky. I think Nina did love Ricky. But Ricky? Ricky only loves money. He may have loved Nina more than he loved me. But the fact is, he loves money more than anything, even Nina."

"I'm sorry to hear that." Maddie was thinking about the conversation she'd had with Peter and how Ricky threw money at him in order to be able to teach at the studio. "It's strange that he'd be so consumed by money when he throws it around like he does."

Andrea practically fell off the bench, she jumped so high. "What do you mean? He has nothing!"

"Oh, well, I guess I mean that he had enough not to seem worried about it."

"What?" Andrea looked like she was going to spit. "I supported the bastard. I did since the day we met.

He'd had his eyes on Nina for ages, I knew that. But she didn't have any money, so there was no way he was going to leave me to go live in a poor house. I promise you, he knew on which side his bread was buttered."

Andrea was breathing hard, but had unclenched her fists and was stuffing another Life Saver in her mouth. She didn't offer Maddie another one.

"Then why did he go to her, I mean, eventually?"

"She was coming into some money or had come into it. I don't know for sure. We hadn't stopped talking completely, but by that time but it wasn't like it used to be."

"When was that?"

"This time last year."

"How had she come into money?"

"No idea. She may have won it or something. All I know is that one minute I was paying for every single article of clothing that man wore, every piece of food that went into his mouth, his car, his damn vacations with me. Everything! The next minute, he's over there with her and she's doing the same."

"Are you sure she was? I mean, if you weren't talking, how do you know?" Maddie thought that maybe he'd loved Nina enough to live with her and struggle through their money problems. She knew enough not to say that though, and risk breaking the very tentative link strung between them.

"No, you're right. I can't be sure," Andrea sighed. "But I knew. Until you live with him, you don't get it. It wasn't all him. I read the situation from her too. She spoke it loud and clear without ever having to say a word. She said it in everything she didn't say, just the same way that I kept the fact that I was supporting him from everyone."

Maddie got that. It would have been far more embarrassing for Nina to have everyone know that she supported her lover and then assume that the only reason he was with her was that she had enough money to keep him happy. The conversation with Andrea sat uncomfortably close to the anxieties that still woke her in the night. Maddie knew what people could do for money. She knew what she'd done. Maddie nodded absent-mindedly, her brain struggling with Nina's death and Ricky and his money problems. Maybe she was trying to make connections where there weren't any.

"Anyway, I'm breaking up with him. That's why I'm here," Maddie must have looked surprised, though she was trying hard to remain neutral.

"I was telling the truth yesterday when I told you we were back together." She looked at Maddie in a look that said *don't pretend we didn't have a conversation* and Maddie signaled that she remembered.

"He broke up with her last month and came back to me. And I took him in. But that was last month and now she's dead and I'm not putting up with his crap any longer."

Andrea spoke these last statements as if she were preparing for battle. She stood up fast and Maddie expected to see her punch the air as she continued to rally the troops.

"So, I expect that's why she was so upset at class." Andrea didn't respond at first.

"Hmm…yes. I expect so." She was lost in thought and had begun to walk away, before spinning back to face Maddie.

"Why are you doing this?"

"Doing what?"

"This. Caring about Nina and what happened to her. Asking these questions."

"I don't know." She wasn't going to admit anything else but then she recognized the expression of pain on Andrea's face. "It's not just Nina; it's Peter and the whole studio. I guess moving back, I expected Pembroke to be like it used to be and it isn't. But I still want to make it work. I don't want it to fall apart."

Andrea didn't move and kept her eyes glued to Maddie's.

"I could ask the same about you. Why are you telling me these things?"

A tear rolled down Andrea's face. "Because I can't believe I let this happen." After several seconds, she wiped it away and popped another Life Saver.

"Look, obviously I'm not going to take Ricky's salsa class any more, but you teach Argentine Tango, right? Can I join your class?" Maddie was surprised and she wasn't sure if it was a good kind of surprised. She thought about telling Andrea about Ricky's conversation with Peter but chose not to. She'll know about his plans anyway.

"Well, I'm in the middle of a course. I can let you know when the new one is starting up."

"Oh, I'll just take some private lessons to catch up. I have the money." She lifted her handbag off one shoulder and swung it to her other arm. "Or maybe I'll just take classes with the John Lennon look-alike. What does he teach?"

"Um…"

Andrea cackled, "Don't worry. I know he's married."

Chapter Twelve

The new perspective Andrea supplied, combined with the letter and Ricky's shocking attitude, led Maddie to feel even more strongly that Nina's death was not a straightforward case of anaphylactic shock. How did her sudden financial windfall tie in with her death? And if Ricky dropping her so suddenly had something to do with her not being able to support him any longer, does that mean she'd lost the money as suddenly as she got it?

Maddie pondered these thoughts as she made her way back into the studio to teach a followers' technique class. While Argentine Tango was a partner dance, Maddie felt that individual work in the technique of walking was as essential to dancing tango as throwing innumerable baskets was to basketball players. She held the class on Friday afternoons and found that it quickly filled when she advertised it as an exercise class, as much as a technique class. She'd consistently had ten women the past two weeks, sweating and thinking about dance in ways they never had before.

Maddie waited in the classroom, hoping that Robyn would show up early. She hadn't forgotten that Jesse worked at the College and that the envelope she found in her bag had the college address on it. He worked in a different department, but it was all Maddie had to go on.

She entered the classroom but was disappointed to see that Robyn hadn't arrived early, and even more so to see that Renée Lambert had. Maddie stiffened, the image of Renée leaving Joe's office that morning, his hand on her back, uncomfortably close. She didn't seriously think that Joe would be interested in someone who looked like she'd just swallowed a raw egg, but the unreasonable jealousy still sat heavily in her stomach.

Renée turned abruptly from Maddie as she entered and went to a chair on the other side of the room where she sat down hard and began to search in the bottom of her bag.

As Maddie considered waiting in the hall to avoid the tension surrounding Renée, Robyn and Jesse walked in.

Maddie smiled broadly. "I'm glad to see you both. Are you all right?"

The exuberance the couple showed two evenings previous was diminished but not completely absent.

"We'll survive. We're bred from South Carolina stock."

From across the room, a laugh escaped from Renée before she clamped her lips shut and attended to the shoe she was brushing. Neither Jesse nor Robyn reacted, so Maddie also let the outburst pass.

"Can I ask you a question?" They nodded in unison. "I got the impression that you knew Nina outside the class." Maddie noticed the distressed look on Robyn's face and put it down to memories of the night. Jesse spoke.

"I'd only met her once at the College. The company she worked for had to provide information for an environmental enquiry and I lead." Robyn sat down to change her shoes as she took up the conversation.

"When we started taking this class we always greeted her, but really, we weren't the same kind of people." She turned a bit pink as she said this.

"Do you know what department she worked for?"

"She was a secretary in the shipping department, that's why I met her."

"How so?"

"I provided guidelines for a management system for waste removal the governor is trying to pass through the state legislature. Something tougher than exists today. That's why Nina was there: as a representative for SynTech. Imagine that? Sending a secretary. They don't even have the balls to send someone in authority." Jesse stopped short, realizing what he'd just said.

"I'm sorry. I don't usually speak like that. They just get me so angry. They go ruining our environment and then send a secretary to take the brunt of criticism."

"Do you think that if she worked in shipping, she could have gained access to the chemicals?"

"Do you mean something that could have killed her on Wednesday night?" Robyn looked horrified, but Jesse simply shook his head. "I don't think so. Any time there are dangerous chemicals present, there's a huge amount of paperwork, not to mention all the safety measures in the way things are packed and moved. We're pushing for tougher laws, but it wasn't like SynTech had a problem."

Maddie thought about it and almost instantly chastised herself for letting her mind jump to wild conclusions. Robyn looked thoughtfully at Maddie.

"Do you think it was just a terrible accident that she died?"

Maddie knew better than to stress Robyn out more than she was already.

"Yes." Maddie forced herself to smile. "I do think it was a terrible accident." However, she couldn't shake a feeling.

It wasn't until after Jesse had left and Maddie had gathered the class into the centre of the room to start warming up that she noticed that Renée had disappeared.

Her private with Toby was immediately after the technique class so at the end of class she said quick good-byes and made her way to the small studio. As she'd expected, Toby was waiting for her when she poked her head through the studio door.

"Hi, Toby."

This time he wasn't listening to his iPod but seemed to have been waiting for her arrival with trepidation. She felt a couple of nervous flutters in her stomach and chastised herself for listening to Laura's gossip. All but tripping over his own feet as he rushed to greet her, Maddie felt an urge to reach out and steady him as he walked. She controlled the urge and took the hand he had stretched out in front of him.

"Hi, Maddie. It's good to see you." Toby pumped her hand up and down with an enthusiasm she hoped he didn't use when they started to dance. "How is everything here?" He didn't wait for an answer. "And with…" Toby let his voice trail off, but motioned with a quick jerk of his head towards the studio down the hall. Maddie understood his meaning.

"As well as can be expected. I, for one, can't wait for the weekend."

"Well, yes, of course. But do they know anything? Anything more about what exactly killed her?"

Maddie was about to open her mouth and tell him that she'd been to the police station earlier that day, but stopped herself short. Something about his nervous energy made her equally nervous and she decided that she'd better leave the police to do their own communications work and keep her inquiries to herself.

"As far as I know, it was pretty much an allergic reaction and she didn't have her medication with her."

Toby's nervousness went up a notch at that information. He looked as if he was having an internal conversation, alternating rubbing his hands together in front of his chest and shaking them out at his sides. Maddie went from thinking he was being a bit eccentric to being seriously worried about him.

"Toby, are you okay? Do you want to sit down?" She motioned to the chairs against the wall as they started towards them.

"No. I mean, no thank you. It's just that I have allergies too. Serious ones and I just want to know what it was so that I can make sure..." His voice trailed off again. Maddie wondered why, if he was so keenly aware of the danger of his allergies, would he come back into the building before he knew it was safe.

"Well, as far as I know, it was just a straightforward allergy to nuts." Toby interrupted Maddie with a howl that made her jump away from him, then held his hands together as if in prayer.

"You have no idea what it means to be so allergic to something that it could kill you, do you?" he asked as Maddie shook her head, taking a deep breath and smiling as apologetically as she could.

"You have to watch every single step you take, every single thing you put in your mouth. Hell, once I had a cup of coffee at Dunkin Donuts and they hadn't washed out the thermos. Turns out it had some nut coffee in it before. Let me tell you, I could have told them that after the first sip. They almost killed me." Toby collapsed in a heap on one of the chairs.

"I'm sorry; I just lost my cool. My parents died when I was little and I have this severe allergy. I've had to look after myself for a long time. I feel like some days I can't think of anything else but death."

Maddie took a step away from the man now deflating in the chair in front of her. Toby had recovered from his outburst as fast as he'd gone into it but she wasn't going to take a chance. She was also relieved to know that Toby had allergies, too. Officer Dinhop's questioning the night of Nina's death had left her wondering, even if she wasn't going to admit it to anyone else, whether Toby had anything to do with the box of chocolates. She had the uneasy feeling that Toby's brief death monologue had been orchestrated. Maddie looked up to find Toby staring into her eyes, his turquoise irises surrounded by lashes so dark they looked like they were coated with mascara. Looking into them made her squirm.

"You look like you had an interesting conversation going on in your head."

Maddie coughed and could feel the heat of a blush stealing across her face. She knew her reaction was partly due to the embarrassment of her thoughts, but mostly due to the intensity of his stare and her response to it.

Toby looked at Maddie with interest, then leaned in closer and gave her a lopsided smile that was unexpectedly charming. *Uh-oh,* Maddie thought.

"Do you want to go out this weekend?"

Maddie would have fallen over if she hadn't been sitting in a chair.

"I, uh..." Toby didn't let her finish, but got up shaking his head.

"Sorry, I shouldn't have asked you that. Being my teacher and all, right? Is it like that? Do you have to sign something saying that you won't date the students?"

"Uh, no, not at all. It's fine, I guess."

Maddie thought about Ricky Russo and Nina and Andrea, but didn't say anything. "I'm sorry if I looked confused. I was just surprised. I've only just come back to town and I haven't really..." Maddie wasn't sure how she wanted to put her next thoughts into words. What she was thinking was that she hadn't been on a date in ten years but knew she wasn't going to say that to him. "I haven't been out much yet."

"So, tomorrow night?"

"Sure, that would be great."

"Right. Earlyish, say six? Then we can see if we want to do something after." Maddie stared at him, wondering where this man had come from. His personality had changed so radically, she wondered whether maybe he was bipolar.

"That sounds great. Shall we meet here?"

"Don't trust me knowing where you live?" he asked with a sly grin.

"No, not at all. I just thought it would be easier."

His face clouded over for a moment. "Well, okay then. See you here tomorrow at six."

"Wait, what about your dance class? We still have time."

"Oh, I'll take a rain check. I'm not in the mood now. Besides, I have some business to take care of."

And with that, Toby was out the door. Maddie listened as he greeted someone in the hallway and then heard the outer door open and close. She had a date and while she was surprisingly excited at the thought, she was equally as nervous when she thought about being alone with him. She'd have to make sure she shaved her legs tomorrow.

Now that she didn't have to teach, she could take off early and get on with her Friday night. It was only 4:30 pm and while she didn't have anything further than the bottle of wine, book and a blazing fire planned, she still felt a thrill at the thought of playing hooky. After closing up the room, she went to say goodnight to Laura. When she got to the office, it was empty and the phone was ringing. She picked it up.

"St. Claire's Dance Studio, this is Maddie. How can I help you?" The other end of the line was silent and Maddie was about to hang up, when she heard a manly cough. It was Joe. She recognized the sound of him as if he was seventeen and calling her at 10:00 at night, an hour after her parents had said they didn't want any of her friends calling. Especially him.

"Hi, Joe." She didn't say anything else, but then neither did he. "Is there something I can do for you?"

Joe cleared his throat before speaking. He actually had to clear it two or three more times before words came out.

"Hello, Maddie. Yes, I was calling to speak to you actually. I understand you found a letter in your" he paused, "dance bag this morning." Maddie wasn't sure whether he was asking her or telling her. "I need to know whether you showed this to anyone. Did anyone else touch it?"

"No, I didn't show it to anyone and I don't think anyone but me touched it, but then again, I don't know who put it in my bag, so someone else could have touched it." Maddie was feeling defensive, so before Joe could get another word in, she asked him a question. "So, do you think there could be something more to her death than just an allergic reaction?" When he didn't answer, she spluttered out a frustrated cluster of run-on sentences.

"And just so you know, Ricky Russo doesn't have money of his own and he sponges off women like Nina and Andrea. And did you know that Nina came into money a year ago and that's why Ricky was going out with her?"

Spent, she waited in silence for Joe to say something. The silence continued for so long, Maddie wondered if Joe had hung up, or at least removed the phone from his ear until she'd finally shut up. Biting her lower lip, she realized that she wouldn't have blamed him. Then he did speak and Maddie could feel the chill in Joe's words.

"As I already told you, Maddie, she died of anaphylactic distress. In other words, she couldn't breathe. She couldn't breathe, because her throat had closed up. Her throat had closed up in reaction to a chemical in her body that she would normally have fought with the use of her medication. Her medication syringe was empty. At this point, it's all a tragic accident. I'll let you know if anything changes in this investigation, if you need to know. Otherwise, please leave me to do my job."

After he hung up, Maddie stood with the receiver still in her hand, her face burning. The weight in her stomach had risen to her chest and sat so heavily she thought her heart would burst. "Did I really just say that?"

"What did you say? Are you talking to me?" Laura walked up behind Maddie, one hand unsuccessfully trying to flatten her wayward hair as she put the watering can in the closet.

"I…" Maddie found it hard to go back over the conversation that had just taken place. It must have lasted a total of one minute, but it seemed like hours of her life had passed. "I just spoke with Joe." Laura looked at her with interest. "He just wanted to give us an update on Nina." Laura raised her eyebrows. "He said the investigation is progressing. And, well, that's that." Maddie finally hung up her end of the phone and made to leave the room.

"Well, seems Joe wasn't really calling to tell us about that poor dead girl. Seems maybe he had ulterior motives for calling," Laura huffed in a suggestive manner while stacking several files on her desk containing what looked like competition applications.

"No, Laura, trust me. He didn't have any ulterior motives."

"All right, honey. You just have a good weekend. Oh, I almost forgot. Peter said he'll call you tomorrow to explain, but he won't need you in the afternoon, so just have a relaxing weekend and try to forget about everything. Those were pretty much his words." Laura turned off her console and made preparations to leave herself.

Maddie headed out and found Claire and Philip making out in the hallway, Philip's hair cascading over the two of them. When she discreetly coughed, the couple sprang apart, bumping into Maddie and causing all three of them to ricochet in different directions. Their energy seemed incapable of slow movement.

"Maddie! Sorry! You going home?" Maddie nodded rubbing her head after it had grazed the wall and avoided a hanging shelf by an inch.

"Oh, Maddie!" Every time Claire spoke it was as if she was going to pronounce the most exciting news her young life had witnessed. "Is Toby your student?"

"Yes, why?"

"His sister was here looking for him. I think she was expecting to drive him somewhere." Claire looked at Philip nodding. The two of them nodded at each other, confirming that yes, she looked as if she wanted to drive him somewhere. Maddie didn't think they could nod any more without risk of their heads falling off or his dreads poking an eye out. Their vigorous head-bobbing routine finally over, they turned to leave. Maddie walked out with them.

"Well, thanks. He's not here anymore. He left early. What did she look like?"

"Old," they chorused, but only after they looked at one another to confirm their assessment.

"Old?" Maddie realized that *old* could mean anything to these two.

"Yeah, you know. Probably about your age." From behind her, she heard Philip add, "Um, not that you're old, Maddie."

Yeah right.

The sun was streaming in the lobby at a glaring angle and, as Maddie reached into her bag for her sunglasses, the lobby door opened and a whiff of Chanel #5 came in on the breeze. Hillary, Maddie's mother, wore only Chanel #5 and for a nano-second, Maddie's heart stopped, thinking that maybe her parents had returned early.

"Oh, great. I'm glad I caught you. I keep meaning to stop by and get your number, but I'm so swamped!"

It wasn't her mother, Maddie sighed. It was Katy Clemments.

Without giving Maddie time to respond, Katy came into the lobby and looked around as if she'd never been in a building before. "Wow, I haven't been in this place since it was a men's club. Remember?" Maddie nodded, even though she didn't remember. Katy continued her visual exploration enthusiastically.

"My grandfather used to take us here once a month for sundaes on the club's family days. Only time females were allowed in the building." She wrinkled her nose at the last comment as if trying to smell out the gentlemen who'd make such archaic rules. "Mind if I look around?"

"No, of course not." Maddie did mind; she wanted to go home, and mentally chastised herself for not saying so. Instead, she followed Katy down the corridor as she touched the wooden shelves that held photographs of dancers in competition dress and Christmas parties. Shelves that probably once held photos of old men smoking cigars, reading newspapers and maybe a stuffed bear head or two.

"I just love old buildings. Not that this is all that old, of course, but it still has such a feeling of history, doesn't it? An essence, I like to say." She continued her tour into the largest of the studios.

"I just love the feeling of something coming into use again. Think of all the people who've come through here. First, those old men having their cognacs and reading their newspapers; now young lovers coming to dance together."

Maddie smiled at the thought that she and Katy had held the same picture of the men's club clientele, although young lovers dancing together was stretching it a bit.

Katy left the room and walked towards the office, all the while touching the walls and cocking her head as if she could here them speak. Maybe Katy was under the misguided impression that Peter wanted to sell the building, Maddie thought uncharitably. As if reading Maddie's thoughts, Katy laughed.

"Oh, sorry. You'll have to excuse me. It's just that I'm in such a good mood." Then she grabbed Maddie's arm and whispered as if sharing a secret. "I love my work."

They entered the office to find Laura turning off her lamp and stuffing her hair into a baseball cap. When Laura caught sight of Katy, she stopped short and looked as if she was going to say something but then thought better of it. A little more brightly than Maddie thought necessary, Laura greeted Katy and told both women she wanted to lock up. Ignoring the tension, Katy swung around to Maddie.

"Are you done for the day? How about a drink? In fact, let's go to the Grass & Toad, my treat." Then she swung back to Laura, and much to Laura's horror, popped herself on the edge of the desk. "I know you from somewhere. Was it an apartment? On Rosemead?"

Laura regained some of her composure when Katy slid off the desk.

"Yes, my husband and I were looking at one. We ended up taking a place near Central Avenue School."

Katy nodded absentmindedly. "Ah, yes, the Brookman house. It's been divided into three separate apartments." Maddie didn't know why, but it made her uncomfortable knowing that Katy had this kind of information at her fingertips. Laura, she noticed, looked equally bothered.

Katy pivoted back to face Laura and Maddie. "Well, no worries, I sold it to a lovely lady, Elizabeth, and her two poodles." Turning back to Maddie, she smiled. "Well, shall we go?"

Why not? Maddie thought. *Maybe a night out on the town, or at least an adult dinner and conversation is just what I need.*

Maddie nodded. "Oh, and here, take the brochure for your mother." Maddie handed the new brochure to Katy, who took it and put it in her handbag. "Great, let's boogie."

The two younger women left the room and then the building, leaving Laura tapping the cigarettes in her pocket as she locked up the building.

Chapter Thirteen

The Grass & Toad was five minutes from the studio the way Katy drove, barely stopping at stop signs and cutting through parking lots with familiar ease. Maddie surreptitiously eyed Katy. She was almost exactly Maddie's height, which at 5'9" had taken both of them over the heads of many of the boys they'd gone to school with. Katy was still very fair, a highlight job every couple of weeks by the looks of it, but a very classy one. She looked like she'd taken care of herself in the last fifteen years and rather than thinking back to the excruciating days of high school and feeling resentful, Maddie realized she'd been missing a social life and that maybe Katy was exactly the person she needed to lead her back into one.

The Grass & Toad, a faux British pub/restaurant, had opened while Maddie was out West and had become a respectable favorite for local families. The clock had only just struck five, but already there was a happy crowd at the bar and many of the tables were filled with an assortment of elderly couples and young families. Maddie and Katy made for the bar and ordered two Magic Hat #9s.

"So, let's not make this into one of those reminisces about high school things, because I'm sure neither of us want to go back to those days." Maddie remembered not liking Katy much in high school. Why, she couldn't recall, but she liked this newly discovered direct Katy, and agreed she didn't want to go too far down memory lane.

"All right. I agree, however I have to add to that that I don't want this to become a 'what have you done for the past fifteen years thing' either. Agreed?"

"Excellent. A girl after my own heart." The two women clinked beer bottles and drank to that.

"So that leaves us with: what are your plans? Are you here to stay or just passing through?" Katy looked completely relaxed in this element, turning periodically to wave or smile at someone coming through the door. Maddie craved the ease with which Katy greeted people, the feeling that she'd missed out on some happy-go-lucky time of her life, while Katy had it in spades. Katy must have seen the envy on Maddie's face, because she smiled and told her that she'd sold homes to at least ten of the people in the room.

"I've done really well here in Pembroke. It has that quality that doesn't seem to go out of style."

"Do you live in town?"

Katy looked at her scandalously. "Of course! I sell based on the fact that I'd never live anywhere else. Here's my card." Katy handed Maddie another card, apparently oblivious to the fact that she'd done the exact same thing, and said almost the same words, when they'd first met outside the dance studio. Maddie looked at the card again, pretending she hadn't seen it, and read it again. Kind of hokey, but it obviously seemed to work.

"I'm sure I don't need to say that if you're looking to buy, you must come to me. There's a really sweet two-bedroom house on Elm: just perfect for one person. So, are you dating anyone?" Katy asked draining her beer.

Maddie had a mouthful of beer and lost some of it when she coughed. She motioned to the bartender for a napkin and shook her head.

"Sleeping with anyone, then?"

Maddie laughed at that. It had been a long time since she'd just slept with someone. Light years.

"That's not really where my head's been since getting back, but you're making me think that I should get off my rear and get out there." She also thought it was downing a beer in a bar for the first time since her return, that was urging her to get back out there.

"Is that the way they say ass out West? Rear?" Both women laughed good-naturedly. "And why not? You're still gorgeous and you need something to get that sad look out of your eyes." Maddie spluttered an incoherent denial. Katy, however, kept right on talking.

"I've got friends. If you're just interested in a little hook-up, I can help in that department." She took a swig from the new beer placed in front of her.

"In fact, if you want something more, I can probably help too. It seems that we've reached the age where all the people who married young are getting divorced and now are looking for someone they can take into the second half of their lives." Maddie sucked in her breath a second time. She liked Katy's direct approach, but that comment had cut a little close to home. Katy didn't seem to notice Maddie's silence. "I was married, did you know that?"

Maddie was probably told in one of her mother's gossipy letters or phone calls but she couldn't remember. If she had, she didn't recall the details, so she indicated that she hadn't, to get the story from Katy. Contrary to what they'd agreed on at the beginning of the evening, Maddie did want to hear some about what Katy had been up to.

"Five years, to Bob Raitt." Katy looked at Maddie with a huge grin, waiting for a reaction. She wasn't disappointed.

"What? Bob Raitt? Wow, how did that happen?" Maddie had definitely not heard that news, because she would have remembered. Bob Raitt was the most openly gay person in all of Pembroke when they were growing up, and for a long time, the only openly gay person in their high school. He single-handedly started the Gay Alliance and was so charismatic that he got a group of straight kids to join the club in solidarity. Katy was still grinning, enjoying Maddie's reaction.

"Well, it's not as interesting a story as you might think; that is, no sex involved." Maddie had to admit this was the first thing she'd considered.

"I studied advertising at Seton Hall and would come back here every month or so. Bob was at Princeton. He came home a lot too, because he was working with the club he started at school, remember?" Maddie nodded. "That club was really important to him. It helped some kids know that there were people who understood what they were going through, and know that they had a place to be. Anyway, we saw quite a bit of each other during those years, so when the proverbial doo-doo hit the fan after graduation, I was someone he turned to."

"Okay, I want to hear about the proverbial doo-doo hitting the fan but we have to order food or I'll fall off this stool." They both ordered food and opted to stay and eat at the bar.

Katy continued. "Well, you know his immediate family knew he was gay and it was all fine, at least on the surface." Katy took a swig and rolled her eyes. "But he had these grandparents who one, didn't know and two, would not have approved, and three, were incredibly rich and had given all of their grandchildren vast amounts of money when they turned 25. So, long story short, he decided to tell them he was gay, because he wasn't ashamed, but they wouldn't budge in their idiotic philosophy that being gay was a crime against God. That simple. There was yelling and cursing and all sorts but the end result was that he had to get married—

to a woman—to prove he wasn't gay and then they would give him five million dollars."

Maddie's mouth hung open. Katy nodded at her in a conspiratorial way. "So, just like they do in the movies, the gorgeous girl steps in, marries the gay guy and is paid half a million for her efforts."

"No kidding?"

"No kidding."

"Where is Bob now?"

"Vancouver. We still exchange Christmas cards. No hard feelings. I got the money to start buying property. His grandfather was ignorant and creepy, but I have to give it to him that he had connections. He was into real estate, not like me but big, industrial stuff. I was able to get some properties I could never have dreamed of if I hadn't been a Raitt for five years. I'd buy cheap, fix it up and sell expensive. I liked it so much that I decided to get a realty license as well." She winked at the bartender as he placed their starters in front of them. "Saves me having to pay a percentage of my earnings to another realtor."

As the two women bent to their plates, someone came and sat heavily on the barstool next to Maddie. Maddie swallowed a bite of clams casino and turned to find Renée Lambert wobbling on the stool, her hair pulled back in a bun as tight as ever. Maddie nodded a hello and drained the remainder of her beer, hoping that Renée would always wear her hair in a bun, otherwise she might not recognize her.

"Hi, Renée. I'm sorry I missed you leaving class today."

Renée took a sip from a Martini glass, then dropped it in front of her, causing it to spill half the contents on the bar. Maddie managed to pull her handbag away from the liquid in time.

"Oh, everything is fine. I don't have problems the way some people do." Renée looked around the bar as she spoke, as if people with problems were lurking around, ready to spread them on her. She wore more make-up than she had that morning, not that it softened the harshness of her features. Her eyes were heavily lined in black and her lids covered in purple. It wasn't a particularly attractive look on her.

Maddie glanced at Katy, who'd stuck her face back into her starter and was unsuccessfully stifling a giggle. Renée reached into her bag and brought out a pack of cigarettes, then extracted one from the box using only her mouth. With the cigarette still in her mouth, she continued speaking.

"So, what's happening with the dead woman and do you have a light?"

Maddie looked at Katy, who shrugged and continued eating her starter. Maddie eyed her own starter growing cold and shook her head towards Renée.

"Nothing more than they knew earlier. It was an accident. And...um, I don't think you can smoke in here."

Renée didn't hear Maddie about the smoking, but reached for Maddie's bag, apparently looking for a light. "Of course, it was an accident. What idiot would think it was anything else?"

"Renée, that's my bag. I don't have a light. Maybe they have one behind the bar."

Renée looked down at Maddie's bag in her hands and threw it onto the bar in disgust.

"You could have just told me so."

With that, Renée slipped off the bar stool and wove through the tables toward the exit. Maddie and Katy looked at one another and simultaneously burst into laughter. Katy had almost finished her coconut shrimp as Maddie took another bite of clams.

"Wow, she was in rare form tonight," Katy said as she motioned to the bartender.

Maddie asked questions between mouthfuls as Katy ordered wine for them both.

"Do you know Renée?"

"No, not really. I've seen her around, in here and at the Y but I've never had more than a brief conversation with her. She used to date Guy Robertson, you know, the doctor who lost his license when he was found selling drugs to high school students."

Maddie had heard that story. Her mother, staunchly anti-drugs, was mortified to have that kind of news coming out of Pembroke, but she read the newspaper chronicle of the situation word for word to Maddie in California.

"Oh!" Katy yelped and jumped off the barstool. "I think I just got my period. You don't have a tampon, do you?"

Maddie did and reached into a zippered pocket in the side of her bag to get at it. Katy reached forward to grab the tampon before Maddie had even taken it out of her bag. She didn't have time to tell Katy not to worry, that it was in a discrete pouch, before Katy fled to the restroom. She'd only just finished her starter, when the bartender brought their main meal and Katy returned, a sheepish grin on her face and a sweater tied around her waist.

"I have no idea how that crept up on me. I'm usually like clockwork."

They'd chosen to share a Caesar salad and each ordered burgers that they quickly tucked into. Between mouthfuls, Katy asked Maddie what she'd been up to, apologizing for backing out of their deal but since she'd already ponied up her story of Bob, Maddie had to deliver the goods. Maddie knew she had to divulge and with two beers inside her and a glass of wine in process, she found she didn't mind all that much.

"Well, I haven't been married, but I was with my ex-boyfriend for ten years." Maddie laughed out loud, not a happy one but one of bitter-sweetness that Katy read immediately and because her mouth was stuffed with burger, questioned with a raised eyebrow.

Maddie sighed and figured she would have to get it over with. The gay connection did not go amiss and she wondered if everyone had a gay story in the closet.

"I'm laughing because I wouldn't have thought this would have been one of the things we had in common." Katy looked perplexed. "My ex-boyfriend is gay, too." This time it was Katy's turn to look incredulous. "Only, I didn't know." Katy looked appropriately shocked.

"I had thought we were on the path to being married and was rudely awakened when he told me that, actually, he didn't imagine spending the rest of his life with me and having kids, because he was going to a therapist and was dealing with that fact that he'd never been comfortable in a heterosexual relationship." Katy's mouth formed the shape of an *O*. Telling her had been surprisingly easy, but now Maddie wanted more wine.

Katy finally closed her mouth. Her eyes darted over Maddie's face, appearing to try to read something in there. "Wow. I thought I had a good story, but that takes the cake."

"Hmm…well, I'd just as well not tell that too many times. I can't really see the funny side yet."

Katy quickly took the lead with a laugh. "Of course, I won't say a word. My story is quite humorous, but then my heart wasn't invested in it." She swallowed the last drops of wine from her glass and summoned the barman, who promptly brought out the bottle of Pinotage they'd been drinking. "And, of course, I did end up with a half a million dollars in my bank account."

Maddie giggled, pleasantly drunk for the first time since returning to Pembroke. "Hell, I wish I could have landed that deal."

"Well, there's plenty of money around here and no end to the number of men who'd fancy the pants off you."

Katy was laughing as she looked around the bar, which in the last hour had filled almost to capacity but the humor of the conversation had been lost for Maddie and, all of a sudden, she just felt really sad. She wanted to end this part of the conversation. It was one thing to talk about it as if it were a movie, but when Maddie started delving too deep into the words she was saying, the raw pain of rejection was too much for a Friday night getting drunk in her home town.

"So if you're all into the real estate thing in this town, what's happening down at the waterfront? I was there a couple of days ago and there was a bit of a scene, complete with flashing police lights."

Katy started nodding, as if she were agreeing with Maddie's explanation. "Oh, that thing has gotten totally out of hand. The place is worth so much money and did you know that one of the prospective buyers wants to build a mall?"

"Yeah, I'd heard that. Disgusting." Maddie was feeling drunk, but even so, realized she was talking too loudly.

"Why's it disgusting? It's just the way of the world, isn't it? If people want KFC, then people are going to get KFC. You can't stop progress." Maddie heard the irritation in Katy's voice and wondered why Katy didn't seem the least bit drunk.

"You know, I'm so sick of people going on about how we can help the environment at the expense of our economy. How do you expect people to prosper if they don't have the economic incentives to do so? Tell me that."

Maddie was feeling distinctly drunk and she didn't want to have an argument in her current state so she changed the subject abruptly.

"Actually, I have a date this weekend."

Katy looked inordinately pleased. "Do tell."

She was glad that she'd avoided a confrontation with Katy, no matter how benign.

"Nothing serious. A guy named Toby. I met him at the studio." Katy took a long gulp of wine before speaking again.

"So, what's he like?"

"Taller than I am, which is a plus." Katy nodded knowingly. "And quite good-looking. But really, it's nothing. I think he just asked me today because he was feeling sorry for me. I think he's also probably a bit young."

Katy brightened. "A boy toy! I'm all into that!" Katy's eyes flickered somewhere over Maddie's head. "So, speaking of dating, didn't you date Joe Clancy back in high school?"

Maddie dropped her fork and as she tried to catch it falling off the bar, managed to splatter salad dressing on her shirt. The question made Maddie uncomfortable. You couldn't have missed the couple back in high school, but as far as she knew, no one outside their families knew about their brief nuptial union.

"Yes, why?"

"Oh, he's just sitting over there with his sister and Tracy."

Maddie swung her head to look, then regretted it and dropped her gaze to the stain on her shirt. "Katy, sorry, I'll be right back. Just going to use the restroom." Katy replied with a wave of her hand and immediately pulled out her phone.

After using the toilet, she splashed cold water on her face, thinking that it had been fun, but it was time to end her evening. Feeling more clear-headed, she walked out but came to an abrupt stop when she heard a voice outside the opened emergency door.

"I swear to God, I'll kill you if you even think about it." Maddie was paralyzed. It was a male voice and it sounded angry. She wanted to move, but her legs wouldn't react. She heard a feminine sound, something between a whimper and a sniff. Then the male voice again. "You'd better think hard before you threaten me again."

It was Ricky, Maddie was certain of that. Finally her legs obeyed and moved down the hallway and back out to the bar.

Chapter Fourteen

Entering the bar again, Maddie apologized to a waitress she nearly collided with, as she tried to casually glance back in the direction she'd come from. She breathed a sigh of relief; no one was there. She allowed herself to believe she had imagined the conversation she had overheard as she made her way back to Katy. Before she got there though, a sharp movement from the corner of the room caught her eye. She glanced in that direction and found Maureen sitting at a full table. Joe was there, but Maddie couldn't take her eyes off the other woman at the table—one child on her lap and another one pulling on her braid.

She looked young, sweet in a Laura Ingalls sort of way. Her hair was long and braided in a thick cord pulled over her left shoulder. The child on her lap pulled hard on the braid as the woman gently removed the hand and tried to steer the girl to the chair next to hers. Then another head appeared from under the table and a fourth jumped up and onto Joe's lap. This was Tracy and her four children under the age of ten. In an instant she would soon regret, Maddie strode over to the table.

Maureen looked up and smiled openly, but Maddie caught the look she gave Joe before his head sunk into his soup bowl. "Hi, Maddie. I'd like you to meet my charming husband, Tim."

Tim smiled and stood up, as he shook her hand. "Maddie, good to meet you. Would you like to sit?" Tim made moves to look for an extra chair.

"No, thank you. I'm here with someone." At that, Joe twitched as if pinched, but didn't look up.

"And Maddie, do you remember Tracy? She was in school a couple of years behind you." Tracy smiled up at Maddie but was quickly distracted by the youngest of her children who'd started to cry. Maddie gave what she hoped was a pleasant smile in return but she was feeling distinctly light-headed.

"It's nice to see you Tracy. Actually, Joe, I wanted a word. If you don't mind."

Maureen looked stricken as she watched her brother, but Joe simply stood up, placing the child in the now vacant chair and made his way out to the lobby. Maddie could do nothing but follow although what she wanted to do was take a baseball bat to his head. She didn't know what percentage of her anger was due to the alcohol, Joe's silence or Tracy's presence.

When they arrived in the lobby, Joe turned slowly, never taking his eyes off Maddie. It was a full minute before she realized that he was waiting for her to speak.

"Okay, I told you earlier on the phone that Ricky Russo has no money and lives off of these women." Joe didn't make a sound but Maddie could see his nostrils begin to flare. "And I told you that Nina recently came into some money." Still not a peep from Joe but he was listening. "Well, I just heard Russo, at least I'm almost positive it was him, in the hallway, threaten someone and I think that someone was Andrea. I think she wants to break up with him and he won't let her." She nodded her head slightly at her own succinct analysis of what she thought had happened. She felt less pleased with herself when Joe's eyes dilated and a sound like a muffled whine escaped from his mouth. Maddie took a step back.

When he spoke, every word was pronounced in a monotone, every syllable drawn out to last twice as long as needed, thus her name lasted four seconds and sounded like it was coming from the mouth of a venomous snake.

"Maddie, I will say this one time only. Do not get involved. You have no idea what you're getting into."

"All I'm doing is telling you what I just heard."

The words had come out of her mouth before she could stop them and now her heart was racing. She tried to justify her response to Joe; he was a police detective, but he was also her high school boyfriend and she deserved the respect of what they once were together. She averted her eyes while taking another substantial step away from Joe.

"And, by the way, it probably wasn't an allergy to nuts that killed her."

This time, Joe couldn't hold back a glimmer of surprise and Maddie didn't miss it.

"Toby is also fiercely allergic to nuts. He can't even go into a room if there are nuts in it and he didn't have a reaction at all."

Joe pursed his lips and made several attempts at speech before whispering "And who's Toby?"

Joe's question didn't register for a few seconds as she came up with her own ideas of what could have happened to Nina. *Maybe she'd accidently eaten some of the poison that Frank was using to kill mice or maybe she'd unintentionally come into contact with something at SynTech.* Maddie raised her eyes to Joe's.

"Oh, he's just one of the students at the studio. He's a private student. He was there that night and your police interviewed him. But listen, Joe. Nina had a bandage on her neck and she kept going on about how Ricky had helped her. I think she was stung by a bee or something earlier in the day and that's why she didn't have an epi-pen."

"That's right, Maddie. It was an accident."

"But, Joe, what if it wasn't? What if Ricky was with her, which is what she implied? And what if he knew that she might not have any more medication?"

"So you're saying that Ricky wanted to kill Nina because she didn't have any money to support him and that he gambled on the fact that she'd been stung by a bee and wouldn't have replenished her medication?"

"Yes, that's exactly what I am saying. He could have..."

Before she'd even finished her sentence, Joe had turned away, forcing Maddie to wonder if he was actually speaking to her.

"I'm warning you. I cannot protect you all the time. If you get hurt, we'll all be sorry." He rejoined his table without looking back.

Maddie sucked in her breath as she turned toward the window and the outside world. Who'd asked him to protect her? He obviously had his hands full with Tracy and her ready-made family. What Maddie was trying to tell him was that Andrea could be in danger and, yet again, she'd been unable to get Joe to listen to her.

Oh forget it. She mentally kicked herself, angry that she'd once again made a fool of herself and vowed to forget Nina and go home to bed.

When Maddie had returned to the bar, she found Katy wasn't sitting where they'd eaten their burgers, but was a couple of stools over talking with a tall, very blond man. She leaned into him in a suggestive manner that said she either knew him or was about to.

Maddie smiled. *Good for her,* she thought but her smile instantly melted as she saw two people reflected in the mirror behind the bar. Ricky and Andrea.

She hadn't imagined it. It was Ricky and he'd been talking to Andrea. She grabbed onto the edge of the stool. *He's going to hurt her. Did he kill Nina? Is that what this was about?* She had to calm down. *Breathe,* she thought. *Just breath. Whatever the situation is, Joe is right. It's his job to handle it.*

Maddie tried to catch Andrea's eye in the mirror but peroxide blonde woman seemed completely oblivious to her surroundings. Maddie watched as the two made their way across the bar. They looked as if they were going to head out the door, but at the last moment, Ricky veered to the right and took a seat at a table near the small stage. Maddie looked closely at Andrea. She didn't look happy, but she didn't look scared either: bored more than anything. She continued to watch the couple as Ricky tried to take Andrea's hand across the table but it was whipped out of his reach before he could. Andrea then grabbed something deep inside her bag and Maddie smirked as she saw Andrea take a roll of Life Saver's out and pop one into her mouth. She didn't offer one to Ricky.

Maddie couldn't watch them any more. Ricky was making her feel sick. She wandered back over to Katy, who was still chest-to-chest with the tall, blonde man. They made a very good-looking couple.

"Oh, there you are. Come meet Lance. Lance, this is my old, old friend, Maddie. We went to high school together."

Katy was now clearly intoxicated and Lance had that bleary look that told Maddie he was too. He smiled genially though, and stuck out his hand toward Maddie, hitting her in the left breast. Both Katy and Lance started laughing.

"How do you do, old, old friend Maddie?"

Maddie took his hand and said she did very well, then said her good-byes and told Katy that she had to get home She reached for her wallet, then let out a yelp.

"Damnit, where's my bag?"

Katy was wobbling on her barstool but she grinned and reached under it, producing Maddie's bag with a flourish.

"I think you just may be a little drunk, girlfriend. Lucky I grabbed it," Katy hiccupped. "Not that I think anything would have happened to it. After all, there's a police detective in the room." Katy lifted her eyebrows suggestively and broke out in giggles. Lance added an insincere laugh to hers. Maddie just wanted to get out now so she mumbled something and pulled her wallet out, but Katy waved her away loudly saying again that it was her treat and that they should do it again real soon.

She thought about going over to say good-bye to Maureen, but even with Joe's back to her, she could feel his hostile energy and she couldn't bear looking at Tracy's angelic smile and all her children. As she left the building, her phone rang. It was Peter.

"Sorry to call so late. Just wanted to make sure you got my message."

"Yeah, absolutely fine. I just had another disastrous conversation with Joe. And I'm drunk. I just want to go home."

"What did you have a conversation with Joe about? I hope you're going to say it was about a date and not Nina LePore."

"It's just that, well, you don't deserve this. Not to you or me or any of the other teachers. I want this job. Well, to be frank, I need this job. I want to be here and if Ricky screws it up for us, we'll all suffer and that's not fair."

"Maddie, please don't get involved. I'm sure the police can take care of it."

"I'm not getting involved. Not really. Like I said, I'm just interested in making sure the studio doesn't get more bad publicity. Trust me, I know what it feels like."

"The studio will be fine. Nina's death was an accident. Implying that Ricky had anything to do with her death is wrong, and could be libelous."

Maddie swallowed hard, wondering why Peter was laying into her so hard. Her ears rang and from the heat radiating from her face she knew she was bright red. This was not the conversation she'd thought she was going to have, the one where Peter thanked her for coming to the studio's defense. Maddie stifled a bitter rebuke and said good night.

She let herself into her parent's house and noticed a message waiting on the answering machine. Momentarily wary, she pushed the play button and was pleasantly surprised when she heard her mother's voice come out of the machine.

"Maddie, darling...just calling to check in...Hope everything is all right, darling. We're in Knysna and we've just eaten the biggest oysters you've ever seen. You think they're big at Live Bait but these are enormous. Okay, your father wants to say hello...No, dear, it's the machine...Hello, Maddie, how's everything going? Remember to turn the thermostat slowly or else you'll get water from the furnace all over the kitchen floor...Okay? Okay...we love you. Take care."

Maddie smiled as she climbed the stairs and prepared for bed. Not only did her father remind her to take great care with their twenty-year-old furnace every time they spoke but he also wrote a fifteen-page treatise on the subject before he left and all but stapled it to her forehead. Just as she'd reached the second floor the phone rang. She ran into her parent's room to pick up the extension there.

"Hello, Fitzpatrick residence, this is Maddie." Maddie waited but there was nothing on the other end. Not even the heavy breathing Maddie had gotten used to living with in California. This utter silence frightened her more. She looked at the caller ID and saw it read *Unlisted*. Then she heard a click. She didn't hang up herself until the sound of the solid dial tone rang in her ear.

Hours later, Maddie woke with a start and looked at the digital clock. It was three in the morning. Something had woken her and she listened for anything out of the ordinary. Her heart racing, she turned on the light. Her mobile was on the table next to her bed and she picked it up, feeling safer with it in her hand. With two steady breaths, she calmed down enough to realize that it was not a sound that had awakened her, but her dream. It was already fading but the image of Toby remained. She thought they were on a date and he'd had an allergic reaction. In the dream, he was trying to breathe and Maddie couldn't do anything to help him. Maddie took a sip of water and turned off the light, telling herself to relax, that it was all the anxiety of the past couple of days. But something troubled her. Just as she was drifting off, her eyes flew open. She remembered what was bothering her. If Toby had severe allergies, why wasn't he carrying adrenaline the night Nina died and why hadn't he helped her? Maddie could only think of two answers to that question. Either he was lying about his condition, or he'd wanted Nina to die.

Chapter Fifteen

Maddie woke with a headache at nine. She tried some yoga stretches to ease the tightness in her neck, to no avail. Then she ran a bath, hoping it would relax both her muscles and the confusing thoughts about Toby. Maybe she was being melodramatic about the whole thing. Maybe Toby had a perfectly good explanation for why he didn't have adrenaline on him or why he didn't offer it to Nina. In the middle of the night, she'd contemplated cancelling the date, but in the light of day she convinced herself that she was being ridiculous.

After eating breakfast, Maddie locked the door and took off downtown. First, she was going to get strong coffee at Vito's and then she was going to do her shopping. On the way home, she'd stop at the studio to pick up her bicycle.

Vito's was full of Saturday morning customers. From behind the counter, he waved a cheery hello to Maddie as she waited in line. As she waited, she felt a tap on her shoulder and turned her head slowly to avoid the feeling of a bag of marbles ricocheting against her eyes. Maureen stood immediately behind her, the tips of her hair now black instead of purple.

"Hey there, stranger. You took off last night. I didn't even get a chance to say good-bye." Maureen seemed to be her natural chipper self, leading Maddie to believe that she was going to ignore the obvious discomfort that existed between her and Joe.

"Hi. Sorry about that. I think I had too much to drink, too fast."

Maureen grinned at her. "I'm damn glad to hear that, Maddie. Just what the psyche needs every once in a while." Maddie had reached the front of the line, placed her order then turned back to Maureen. She took a deep breath.

"I have to admit it was awkward, seeing Tracy there and, um, all the kids." Maureen tilted her head to the side, her brow furrowed.

"Why?"

"Uh..." Maddie felt ridiculous. Maureen probably hadn't thought about Joe and Maddie's relationship in years and obviously assumed Maddie was way over it, as any normal person would be. In fact, she was over it. It wasn't like she had pined away for fifteen years. The only reason Joe was on her mind these days was because they were both living in the same town again.

Having grown tired of waiting for Maddie to say anything more, Maureen pulled something out of her bag. "Here's an invitation to my birthday. And I don't want to hear you say that you can't come because of my brother. We've got a big back yard; I'll keep you separated."

Maddie said that she'd love to come, inwardly wincing.

After finishing her coffee, Maddie walked over to Whole Foods, a welcome addition in Pembroke in her absence, and shopped with pleasure, the headache finally abating. With a bag of groceries in each hand, she left the store and walked slowly to the studio to fetch her bicycle; fretting, now that her shopping was complete, over whether it was going to be there. Maybe she should have picked it up first and not risked some high school delinquent stealing it. She let out the breath she'd been unintentionally holding when she turned the corner of Spruce and saw that her bicycle was still chained to the rack at the far side of the parking lot.

She'd placed her groceries in the baskets either side of her back wheel when she heard the sound of a door slamming and looked up. She saw that the front door to the studio was open and blowing in the wind, so that with each gust it slammed against the doorframe, then bounced back several inches and hovered before beginning the cycle again with the next gust. She'd assumed that Peter wasn't coming in that morning, but she could have been wrong. She walked toward the door, looking around the corner of the building to see if Peter's car was there, but the lot was empty. *He could have parked in the back*, Maddie thought, *but why was the front door open? Logically, he'd have entered through the rear of the building.*

Sticking her head through the door, she called out to Peter. When there was no reply, she walked into the lobby, peering into the studios as she walked toward the office. All the studios were empty.

"Peter? Frank? Laura?" At the end of the hallway, Maddie found the outer door to the office open and went through. Laura's watering can sat in the middle of her desk, which was unusual because Maddie remembered her storing it in the closet yesterday. Otherwise, everything looked normal. Peter's office was locked and she poked her head into both the men and women's restrooms, just in case, as she headed back outside. Pulling out her mobile phone, she took one last look at the building before dialing Peter's number, added to her speed dial since Nina's death. She felt uneasy in the pit of her stomach and it didn't abate when he answered.

"Hey, babe. You having a nice lie-in?"

"No, actually, Peter, I'm at the studio. You're not here, are you?"

"No, I'm currently thigh-deep in cot assembly. Care to join me?"

Maddie laughed, some of her queasiness fleeing at the sound of Peter's loopy life. "I think I'll pass on that one and, no, I don't want to know. Listen, though, the studio is open."

"What do you mean?"

Maddie had another queasy moment when she remembered that Laura had worried about Frank forgetting things. Maybe he'd forgotten to lock up.

"Exactly that. I found the front door open and no one inside." Maddie looked around the parking lot again, hoping that a reasonable explanation would present itself. "Hey, wait a second." On the other side of her bicycle, partially covered in leaves, she saw something she recognized. "My keys."

"What? Maddie, what are you talking about?"

Maddie was trying to reconstruct her evening. Had she been at her bicycle when Katy arrived and invited her out? No. She was inside. They had a whole conversation with Laura before they both left together and Laura locked up. Or, at least she thought Laura locked up. She never went near her bicycle but rode in Katy's car. She picked up the keys on the ground. They were not her house keys but the keys to the studio. It was a simple chain with the figure of a dancer on the ring with four keys, one each for the front and back doors, one to the office, and one that opened the closets in each studio where the sound systems were stored. *Oh damn,* she thought desperately.

"Um, Peter, I'm sorry. I just found my keys in the parking lot. I must have dropped them when I was leaving. I'm so sorry; I hope it wasn't my keys that someone used to get in."

"But what would they take? Was the computer still in the office?" *Peter*, Maddie thought, *didn't sound annoyed, more incredulous.*

"I think so; I'll just go check."

"Look, I have to clean up but I'll be down in about 20 minutes."

"Okay. I'll wait till you get here. And Peter, I am sorry."

"It's okay, kiddo," Peter reassured her, and she laughed at yet another nickname he'd come up with for her.

Back inside, she turned on the lights. This time she went into each of the studios as well, to make sure that everything looked as it should. The sound systems for each room were locked into closets, but she also looked in each one. Nothing seemed out of place. If it was a burglar, maybe they hadn't thought to look in the closets. As she walked back into the office, she took a deep breath, but let it out when she saw the computer sitting on Laura's desk just where it should have been. Then she remembered that Laura would've had a petty cash box and that if it were teenagers taking advantage of an opportunity, that's what they would have gone for. She opened one drawer after another, but didn't find a box.

She was about to give up when she thought to look in the filing cabinet behind the door. The top two drawers were stuffed to the gills with files but the third drawer opened easily and there, just behind four files, was the cash box. Maddie opened it and saw about $200 in small bills and change. So, possibly these hooligans, if there were any hooligans at all, were not very brave. Maybe they came in and danced about in some of the classrooms. The thought made Maddie smile and she hoped if that were the case, Peter would get some business out of this experience.

As she turned to leave the room, she noticed the coat rack was on its side behind the door, wedged between the wall and the file cabinet. It was one of those old-fashioned coat racks that are circular and have four horn-like appendages jutting out of the top. One of the appendages had been split and was hanging by a few strands of splintered wood. As Maddie righted the coat rack, she stepped into something that caused her foot to slide out from under her and she quickly steadied herself by grabbing the coat rack. When she regained her footing, she looked to see what she'd slipped in.

She bent down and gingerly reached forward until her fingers came into contact with something sticky. Whatever it was, it was clear and as she lifted her fingers to her nose, her brain raced through several options. It didn't have the telltale scent of a cleaning fluid or disinfectant and it wasn't sticky enough to be glue. Thinking she'd wipe whatever it was up so that Laura or Frank wouldn't have to deal with it on Monday, she stood up. Immediately, she staggered back, instantaneously recognizing what an idiot she'd been. It was probably a poison Frank had put down to kill the mice. *Damn, how could I have been so stupid?*

Within seconds, her nose began to tingle, followed by a burning sensation that quickly became so strong she reached up to make sure her nose hadn't been seared.

Feeling completely foolish that she'd stuck an unknown substance into her face, she made her way to the restroom to wash it off but found that whatever it was that was causing the pain in her nose had spread to her eyes. They began watering first but that grew to a sting and within seconds began to burn so badly she couldn't keep them open. Her nose now felt as if it was on fire and she couldn't stifle the moans of pain. Groping for the door, she hauled herself into the hall, praying that Peter was on his way, or that someone would be walking by to help her. As she inched her way along the wall of the hallway she cursed the fact that she'd left her phone in her handbag.

She reached a door and felt for the handle, pulled it open and peered inside. *Damn, she'd gone too far.* It wasn't a restroom, but Frank's closet where he kept cleaning supplies and tools. Maddie stood holding the door, breathing more slowly as she realized that she could see a little, then sucked her breath in so hard she choked on it. Later, she told Peter that it felt like she stood there for an hour, not being able to breathe, but in actuality, within three seconds of seeing what she thought she saw, she screamed louder than she'd ever screamed in her life.

Leaning up against Frank's ladder, looking as if he were about to climb it, was the definitely dead body of Toby Downs.

Chapter Sixteen

She must have fainted. Either that, or her brain had decided that seeing the body of Toby Downs was just too much information. She remembered screaming but she didn't remember Peter arriving or how she left the building. Peter had to tell her that he'd had to carry her out of the building, because she wouldn't, or couldn't, move her legs. He found her crumpled against the wall opposite the janitor's closet, a photograph of Ricky Russo clutched in her left hand. The photograph had been hanging in a spot above the place Maddie sat and judging by the trickle of blood running behind Maddie's left ear, Peter thought she must have whacked into it pretty hard before collapsing into the puddle that he found.

He then told her that he'd heard Maddie's screaming the second he turned his car off and his heart was in his throat as he entered the studio, more scared than he'd ever been in his life. He thought he was going to find Maddie being beaten or raped and he cried in relief the moment the two of them were safely out of the building. He managed to call the police, incoherently trying to explain what was in his closet and within a minute, he could hear sirens, as he sat on the front steps with both arms around Maddie.

The first police car to pull up had its lights and siren blaring and only turned the siren off when it pulled into the parking lot. The lights were left spinning, lending a bizarre carnival atmosphere to the situation. Two officers climbed out of the car, Dinhop and Rodriguez, the same officers who'd arrived just four nights earlier when Nina had died. Officer Dinhop moved warily as he looked around the parking lot, his hand hovering over the gun at his waist. Rodriguez made her way directly to Maddie and Peter. Maddie seemed unaware of her surroundings as she huddled into Peter's chest. Peter nodded towards the door and spoke quietly.

"In the janitor's closet. On the left, just before the restrooms."

Appearing satisfied with the parking lot, Dinhop moved over to Maddie and Peter and asked them to describe what they'd seen. By this time, another police car had turned up, its lights also flashing. The newly arrived officers were speaking into their walkie-talkies and all but ignored Maddie and Peter who were still crouched on the front steps. Maddie had yet to utter a word, so Peter took the opportunity to tell Officer Dinhop what had happened from his perspective.

At that point, Officer Dinhop asked Maddie to explain. More cars were appearing as well as an ambulance. Maddie thought about how useless an ambulance was in this situation. She knew Toby was dead. She couldn't get the wide-eyed stare of his chocolate eyes out of her head and gagged, swallowing vomit as she tried to get oxygen into her body. Her nose and eyes were still burning like crazy, making her want to dunk her head in the sink, but she couldn't face the idea of standing up and going back into the studio. Her throat felt raw and it took her several attempts before she could make herself heard.

"I had a date with him." Both Peter and Dinhop said '*what*?' at the same moment. Peter backed slightly away from Maddie much to her disappointment but then seem to realize what he'd done and reached around to hold her again.

"You were meeting him here, this morning, for a date?"

Maddie shook her head. "No, the date was tonight. I was just here collecting my bicycle." She couldn't see her bicycle, but she motioned to where she thought it might be standing against the rack.

Now that Maddie had removed her face from where it had been buried in Peter's chest, the officer could see the rawness around her eyes and nose, and it took him only a nano-second to bark out an order.

"Get medical attention here immediately." He then spoke into his walkie-talkie as he turned away from the pair. Finishing his conversation, he bent down to Maddie's level. "What did you touch inside?" Receiving no answer, he continued slowly. "Maddie, which rooms did you go into?"

The paramedics had arrived and swarmed around Maddie, separating her from Peter much to her distress.

A rising panic was beginning to surface outside the studio, as members of the 11 am swing class began to arrive. Peter kept a lookout for Philip and Claire as he made his way over to the yoga teacher who rented the space Saturday mornings. He'd been told that classes would have to be cancelled that day and everyone was to go home, but most of the students and teachers stayed around to see what was going to happen. Peter moved from group to group telling everyone that things would be back to normal on Monday.

Maddie was laid down on a stretcher and strapped in, and was lying, her face covered in several layers of bandage, when she heard Joe's voice. The paramedics were lifting her into the ambulance as Joe climbed out of his car and walked towards the stretcher.

Joe nodded to Officer Dinhop and then bent over Maddie before speaking softly. "Are you all right, Maddie?" She couldn't see him, but felt his breath on her neck, and it made her feel dizzy again. She realized that she was not all right. It may have been that a small part of her reacted to the way he said her name, but it was mostly the dead body in the closet and she immediately burst into uncontrollable sobs. Joe slid his arms awkwardly into the small space between the stretcher and her body and she clung to him as best she could while strapped in so tightly.

"Sh...Sh... It's going to be okay. I'm going to take care of everything." Slowly, Joe released his grip.

"I'm tharry." Maddie's voice was barely audible through the gauze and her sniffling.

"Sh... They're taking you to the hospital. I'll see you later."

Joe nodded to Peter then disappeared into the studio as Maddie was lifted into the ambulance.

Chapter Seventeen

"Do you mean from Tuesday?"

"Maddie, it's all right. You're in the hospital." Peter stood next to Maddie's bed, his hand holding hers as she unsuccessfully fought the bedcovers. The nurses had tucked her in well. She'd been talking in her sleep for several minutes as Peter kept watch. He'd spoken to Maddie's parents who were making plans to come home from South Africa early.

"It's all from Wednesday. Why don't they know?"

Maddie had vacillated between crying and yelling incomprehensibly and had become so distraught that Peter had called the nurse to see if they could give her something to help her sleep. The medication had taken effect and allowed Maddie several hours of respite from her ordeal, but now she was waking and her dreams were obviously still there.

"But the milk. I left it. It's going to go bad."

"Shush, there now, Maddie. Everything's fine. The milk has been taken care of. You just sleep now."

Maddie woke again to the sound of people talking nearby and couldn't, for the life of her, remember where she was. Why were there people in her house? She didn't feel in any danger, however, so she lay quietly trying to make sense of the words she was hearing; reality orientation, receptive aphasia, decubitus ulcer.

As she withdrew her arms from the bedding and tried to sit up, she experienced a dull ache behind her eyes. Only then did the horror of the day pin her back onto the pillow. But like a spring, the second her head hit the pillow, it ricocheted back up in a bid for freedom, until a searing pain in her arm stopped any further movement. Reaching across her body with her free arm to try to stop the sting, she saw that that she was connected to several tubes and in her ascent from the bed, had managed to yank one of them partly out. A beeping noise had begun at once and a nurse walked promptly into the room to where Maddie half-lay in bed.

"All right, let's fix that, shall we? You just lay back down and we'll have that sorted. Are you hungry? Shall I get you a cup of tea?"

"What day is it?"

"It's still Saturday, dear. 9 pm. You slept the whole day through so you should feel good and rested."

Maddie didn't feel good and rested and didn't like the fact that this efficient woman was telling her that she should.

"What was it on my face that made it burn? Was it a poison?"

"The doctor will be coming in a short while and he'll be able to tell you more. You just rest here and I'll bring you a snack. I'll tell your friend that you're awake and he can come and see you."

The nurse left after she'd reconnected the dislodged tube and showed Maddie where she could press a button to raise the head of her bed. Maddie pushed the button until she was sitting upright and thought about the friend who was waiting for her. She hoped it would be Joe and hoped she hid the disappointment when Peter walked in. She immediately chastised herself when she saw the looks of concern and relief on his face.

"Maddie, how are you feeling?" Peter lowered himself carefully into the chair next to the bed.

Without any warning, Maddie started coughing and reached to pour a glass of water but she didn't move quickly enough. Peter had already stood up to help her, then patted her leg affectionately as she controlled the cough.

"You just relax now. Is there anything else I can do?"

"Thank you. No, I'm fine, just tired. It sounds idiotic when I think that all I've done is sleep for nearly twelve hours."

"It's not idiotic. If you feel tired, then you are tired. Sleep, Maddie."

And that's what she did.

Maddie woke some time in the early hours of the morning and pushed the button to call a nurse. While the nurse wasn't able to answer any of her questions, she did bring Maddie some tea and a pile of fashion magazines. Her face felt nearly normal, the only reminder of yesterday was a slight sting on either side of her nose. She gingerly touched these delicate areas and felt no difference in the texture of her skin.

Her bed was positioned next to the only window in the room and through it she could see the steeple of the Presbyterian church and the clock tower of the train station. Bored by the magazines provided by the hospital, Maddie thought back to when she and Joe would get on a train, saying that they were going to the library or some other equally inane destination for two seventeen-year-olds in love. They would ride to the end of the line, making out the whole time, then get out at Dover to buy a soda and wait for the train to let passengers on again to take them back to Pembroke.

The train conductors knew them well. One in particular had a soft spot for their young love and would sometimes let them into the first class carriage if there were no other passengers using it.

She pressed the button for the nurse again. The longer she sat alone the more anxious she grew. She felt absolutely fine and yet the nurse had alluded to the fact that they might have to keep her in the hospital under observation for several days. The nurse also relayed a message that Peter had called and said he'd stop by her house to get anything she might need. Maddie asked for her handbag and was told that she hadn't come in with one. Hopefully, Peter would have found it, and taken care of it.

Maddie continued to contemplate her boredom and frustration at being virtually imprisoned while a murderer was loose in the vicinity of Maddie's workplace, when the door to her room opened. There were two beds in the room but the other one was unoccupied. In the doorway, a nurse stood with a chart in her hand. She peered over reading glasses at the page, and then looked around the room, her eyes hovering over the empty bed as if puzzled, then glanced at her clipboard again and, with a click of her pen walked toward Maddie. She was tall and thin, and her hair was pulled back in a tight bun, with a pinched looked that Maddie had come to recognize. Renée Lambert. Again. Maddie would never have guessed that Renée was a nurse in her *real* life and the look of shock on her face must have annoyed Renée, because the nurse glowered before flipping the chart over and sitting herself primly next to Maddie's head.

"Madeleine, I am Renée Lambert. I don't know if you remember me but I was in Ricky Russo's samba class last week." As if rehearsed, she continued in an efficient manner, seemingly unaware, or at the least unwilling to admit that she and Maddie had met many times. "I am a nurse here at County, I'm sure you didn't know that." Here she paused for a breath, allowing Maddie to say something.

"I do remember you, Renée." Maddie had an irrepressible urge to laugh. She felt like a fourth grader being introduced to the Mayor. She didn't know what else to say, but Renée was obviously waiting for something. "I didn't know you were a nurse. We didn't get a chance to talk."

"Well, no, that's understandable, isn't it? It was a shock to see that woman die like that, and I've been surrounded by death since I began nursing at twenty-two."

Not having anything better to say, Maddie mumbled *yes, it had been a shock.* She couldn't get the picture of Toby's body out of her head, however, and didn't know whether she was allowed to say anything about it, so she let her mumble dwindle to a sigh and then shut her mouth.

Renée, however, had other plans for the discussion. "I understand that something else has happened at the studio. Another body?"

"How did you...?"

"How did I know? We are given all the pertinent information." Renée was slighted, Maddie could tell. "When a police officer enters the emergency ward, things get very serious around here. We have the best technologies. Most of our departments rival the best in the country." Maddie couldn't understand why Renée was speaking as if she were trying to sell Maddie on the hospital.

"Regardless, this sort of thing doesn't happen every day at County, so you were big news. And, of course, the location of the incident was on the report so I knew I could be of assistance." Maddie didn't believe that those two thoughts related to one another, but kept quiet. Renée had moved away from the bed and now paced between the window and the door.

"Is it a coincidence that two people died at the same place in the matter of a single week?" Maddie opened her mouth to speak, but Renée barreled on. "No, I think not. What I would like to know…"

Maddie never found out what it was Renée wanted to know as the door opened again and another nurse walked in. Maddie watched as Renée spun around and thrust the clipboard at the other nurse, then she stormed out of the room, neither greeting the other nurse or saying good-bye to Maddie.

The other nurse looked somewhat surprised but not offended. "What did *she* want?" The nurse's badge read 'Cynthia.'

Maddie shrugged her shoulders. "I don't think anything really. I met her last week so I think she was just coming in to say hello." Cynthia continued to look at Maddie's chart and nodded.

"Good. Well, you seem quite fit. How are you feeling?"

"Absolutely fine. Whatever it was only lasted a couple of minutes. I feel perfectly normal now."

Cynthia spoke in a voice that told Maddie that she understood her frustration. "Good, I'm glad to hear that. However, you need to stay here another night. Interaction with a toxic substance that can affect the central nervous system like that is something you have to take seriously. Until the tox guys can tell us exactly what it is, we need to keep you here for your own protection."

Maddie understood but felt useless. She wanted news and wished that Peter would show up. No sooner had she finished that thought than he walked in, arms filled with two grocery bags.

Cynthia finished reading something on the chart and told him that there were only twenty minutes of visiting hours left that morning as she walked out.

Peter's bags were filled with items from her house, including her pajamas and robe and her toiletry bag. He'd also included the two books that were beside her bed. She thanked him profusely, as he made himself comfortable in the chair next to her.

"So, tell me what's happening." Maddie supposed that the nervous feeling in her hands, causing her to squeeze the flesh of her palms, came from the fact that she knew whatever was happening, was not good, and it's worst impact would be on Peter and the studio.

"It seems that Toby Downs was a drug dealer. Peter let the sentence sink in for a moment, as Maddie involuntarily shuddered and then groaned. She should have guessed that he was into drugs. She wasn't naïve and the complete one-eighty in his personality on Friday, should have told her everything she needed to know. She twitched unconsciously in her bed, shocked as she realized that the last time she'd spoken to Toby was less than forty-eight hours ago when she'd accepted a date. Maddie watched as Peter rubbed his knee as if it ached. Like the evening before, he looked older and tired. Then it occurred to her that drugs might mean one thing to her and another to him. She had to be sure that when he said drugs he didn't mean selling a little marijuana.

"What drugs are you talking about? I mean, was it serious?"

"Serious? Yes. It seems that he had a veritable chemistry lab in a back room of his house. He was producing meth-amphetamines on a large scale. The police are still going through and inventorying the room. They want to know who he was working for and who he was connected to."

Peter looked as if he'd swallowed a live fish. "I can't freaking believe this. How is it that someone can do something like that and no one notices?"

"So I assume you never saw him taking or dealing drugs at the studio?"

Peter replied vehemently. "Absolutely not. I would never have condoned that. I've worked too hard..." His voice came to an abrupt stop, as he was overcome by his emotions. He sucked the air between his teeth before speaking again in an effort to control the anger that he felt. "What I mean is that I've worked hard to get what I have and if I were to lose it because of the stupidity of a drug dealer, well, I don't know what I'd do. Lucky he's dead." Peter's head dropped into his hands and he sat quietly, but his shoulders heaved as he took deep breaths. The fact was, Maddie felt a similar anger at the thought of losing her job because of Toby.

Maddie came out of her own reverie. "Do they know anything more about the chocolates Nina ate? Could it have been a drug and not just nuts like the police are saying? " She knew that Toby was out in the hall when Nina left the classroom and could have given her the doctored chocolates. What she couldn't figure out was a reason that he would do that and then end up dead himself. As if hearing her thoughts, Peter raised his head from the position it had been in.

"Maybe he overdosed? Maybe he was on something and then forgot how much he'd had."

"Possibly, yes, but then why was he in the closet? And what reason would he have had to kill Nina? What we need to know is: did Toby and Nina know one another? Remember, Nina was having money problems? Andrea said that was why Ricky broke up with her." Peter looked at Maddie with interest.

"Well, she could have been taking drugs and hadn't paid Toby because of her money problems, and he got angry." Maddie was pleased with her first attempt at solving Nina and Toby's connection, but Peter looked unconvinced.

"I don't know. If Ricky went out with her, then I can't believe she was into drugs. He's in AA and is proud of the fact that he's been clean for eight years now. I don't think he'd be with someone who could jeopardize that."

"Unless she hid it from him." But even as Maddie said that she knew it wasn't true. She'd seen the way that Nina had behaved in class. She was desperate to get Ricky back, and if she'd known that he wouldn't take her back if she took drugs, then Maddie suspected she wouldn't go near them.

"Then maybe she was borrowing money from him and hadn't paid him back," Maddie shook her head.

"I don't think that's likely. What about SynTech?"

"What about it?"

"Nina worked there and Alice said something about SynTech buying that riverfront property and Henri being involved." Peter looked puzzled. "I can't remember what her point was but maybe that's where Nina and Toby could have known each other. Do we know if he worked at SynTech?"

"No idea. But then it could be that he had something to do with the riverfront property and that's how they knew one another."

"We have to find out how Nina was involved in that sale."

"No, Maddie, you have to relax and stay healthy." Maddie slumped back in her pillow. She'd let Peter think what he wanted. She knew what she had to do.

There was a tap on the door and Cynthia poked her head into the room.

188 *Dying to Dance*

"Visiting hours are over. Let's leave the patient to get some rest," Peter rose, promising to return the next day, hopefully to bring her home.

Maddie had thought that she'd never be able to get through the day, but was pleasantly surprised to find that another day in bed was just what she needed. She read through most of it, flipped through some television channels and ate food that was uncharacteristically good for hospital fare. She fell asleep early and was glad, because she had to acknowledge that she was dismayed that Joe hadn't come to see her, even if only to interview her about Toby. At least if she was sleeping she wouldn't have to think about her disappointment.

At some point in the night, a sound woke her. Her eyes popped open and she had the heart-stopping feeling that someone was watching her. She cautiously raised her head to look around the room and in the hospital glow, she saw Joe sitting in a chair pushed into the far corner of the room, watching her, his body tense and ready to jump.

Maddie wasn't positive she was awake but she hoped desperately that it was so. "Joe?" she asked tentatively, afraid that if she spoke too loudly, Joe would prove to be an apparition.

He finally made a movement, just the slight relaxing of his body, as he lifted his hand and caressed the space just inches from his body. If he'd been sitting next to Maddie, it would have been her body. As it was, Joe caressed the air and let his hand drop. He sank back into the chair and whispered.

"Go to sleep, Maddie. I'll take care of you."

Chapter Eighteen

When she woke Monday morning, the chair in the corner of the room was empty. Maddie sighed and leaned over to the window to pull the curtains open. The sky was a clear blue and the sun shone, the kind of day that made Maddie think that anything was possible and allowed her to optimistically wonder if the past forty-eight hours had been a nightmare. The doctor arriving in her room shortly after another surprisingly good breakfast of scrambled egg, toast and coffee, his brow furrowed in worry, confirmed her that it wasn't.

"Our best guess at this point is that it's a derivative of sulfuric acid." When Maddie looked at him blankly, he continued. "A product that might be used in dyes or pesticides," Maddie continued to stare at her doctor in horror. "Don't look so frightened. You were treated initially with oxygen and cortisone and those seem to be doing to trick." Maddie wasn't frightened of the chemical itself, more the idea that Frank could have used something dangerous in the office to kill mice and that he could be fired for that. The doctor sat next to Maddie and spoke in a measured tone that really scared her.

"You're over the worst of it. However, there's a latent period of at least ten hours, maybe more." Maddie felt tears in her eyes and expected the worst but the doctor reached for her hand.

"I said you've turned the corner. We kept you here as a precaution until we were absolutely sure what we were dealing with. For the next couple of days, I want you to take special care."

Maddie nodded, tears of emotion still dribbling from her eyes. The image of Frank laying mousetraps and Frank using a pesticide to kill them filled her mind. She knew that Peter appreciated his custodial efforts, but she wondered if he'd be able to forgive him and allow him to stay at the studio. The doctor didn't know this, though.

"I want you to call me the instant you feel anything out of the ordinary and I want you to come back here in three days, so we can make sure you're one hundred percent recovered."

Her doctor stood from his perch on the chair. "Listen, while the name sulfuric acid is ominous, it's easy enough to get hold of; there doesn't have to be a sinister explanation."

"But there is. Toby's dead. And he was a drug dealer."

The doctor held his hand up, as if warding off Maddie's words. "I have to be honest with you here, Madeleine. I've been asked to direct you to the police for all further questions. The fact is, I don't know anything more about the victim at the dance studio. What I do know, is that you will be all right."

The doctor told her she was free to check herself out and after he'd left the room, a new nurse appeared and asked her if she wanted her to call someone.

"No, it's early. I feel absolutely fine." The nurse nodded and left the room, clearly not interested in how Maddie got home.

She prepared to leave, wondering whether she was being overly dramatic. Could Toby's death and the chemical in the office be coincidence? It didn't seem possible, and that worried her.

She suspected Peter would be annoyed that she hadn't called for a ride, but what she really wanted was fresh air and solitude. In the lobby she inwardly cursed her bad timing when she ran into an exhausted looking Renée and guessed that she must have just completed the night shift.

"So, everything must be fine." Renée held the door open for Maddie.

"Yeah, I actually slept well and I'm feeling fine." Renée kept a brisk pace next to Maddie, looking straight ahead.

"You must have worked a long shift?" Maddie was trying to figure out how long the shift was. She had seen Renée yesterday at 11 am and it was now 8 am. That seemed like a very long shift. Renée waved her hand, propelling Maddie's words into the cool breeze.

"Oh, someone didn't show up and, you know, it's not like being at a store or a restaurant where you can deal with it. Someone doesn't show up at a hospital, people could die." Renée was clearly not pleased that she'd had to cover for what she considered another person's selfishness.

"Do you want a ride?"

"Oh, no thanks. I'm just going to take the bus. They said it comes every fifteen minutes."

"Don't be stupid. I'm going back to Pembroke anyway."

Maddie smarted at being called *stupid*, even if it was just an expression. She supposed Renée should be given the benefit of the doubt, however, as she'd been up all night saving lives.

"Sure, thanks." Renée rolled her eyes, showing her displeasure. At what, Maddie wasn't sure but she vowed not to take it personally. Maddie put her bags into the back seat of Renée's Ford Fiesta and strapped herself into the front passenger seat. Once in the car,

Renée started talking again and seemed to have let off some of her steam, as she managed a half-smile.

"So, what have they found out about the dead boy?"

"His name was Toby. Toby Downs. I didn't know him really, just from the studio." Maddie stopped talking, wondering if she should talk about the drug connection. "I don't think he had family in the area. I guess that's what they're going to be looking at."

"Well, that's all well and good, but what was he doing at the dance studio and have they figured out who did it?" Maddie could hear the rising anxiety in Renée's voice and wished that she hadn't accepted the ride now. Renée continued, her voice growing increasingly loud in the small car as Maddie surreptitiously opened her window.

"What do the police do all day? This should be an open and shut case. It's not like that many people can get into that dance studio, right?" Maddie didn't know which question to answer first, or even whether she was required to answer any of them. Renée's next words made it clear that she didn't expect an answer.

"This whole town is just crap. How could this happen? Do they know who he hung out with? Why wasn't he protected?"

"Protected from who?"

"From whoever the hell did it! What, are you stupid?"

Maddie blanched. Things were spiraling out of control quickly. While she was still half a mile from home, she told Renée to stop.

"Thanks, here is good." Then, feeling that she had to explain herself even though Renée had been totally out of line, she blurted.

"I don't feel like going home so I'm staying with a friend today." She needn't have bothered speaking because Renée was all but ignoring her now. The car screeched to a halt and Renée spoke under her breath, words that Maddie just caught as she pulled her bags out of the back seat.

"You just wait, you'll be next." Before Maddie had even closed the door, Renée had peeled away from the curb, leaving Maddie wondering what had just happened.

She walked the half-mile to her parent's house, and once inside, dropped her bags at the foot of the stairs and then made her way up to the bathroom for a long, hot shower.

Feeling more able to deal with what was on her plate after scalding her body for ten minutes, she made an egg salad sandwich and a strong cup of tea. She was almost finished when the phone rang. She answered it while thinking that the most sensible idea would be for her to ignore it, then turn on the television and drink beers all afternoon, thus simultaneously numbing herself and preparing herself for bed.

"Maddie, you're home. Are you all right? I called the hospital. Should I come over?" Peter was sounding characteristically concerned, but uncharacteristically hyper.

"Hi, Peter, I'm fine. As a matter of fact, I was just thinking about cracking open a beer." Maddie heard a yelp on the other end of the phone. "Are *you* all right, Peter?"

"What? Oh yes, yes. Absolutely. It's just, well, Kristy's gone into labor and she's in the bath and I just wanted to make sure you were all right."

"Peter, that's great. And I'm fine. You go and have yourself a baby and don't worry about me."

"Maddie, you'd tell me the truth, wouldn't you? I could pop by quickly now. Do you need anything?"

Maddie stopped herself from yelling, but the impulse was strong. "Peter, you have done a great job looking after me this past week. In fact, you've done nothing but support me since I moved back. But now it's time for you and Kristy to stop thinking about everyone else."

"Ok, if you're sure. I have to admit I'm a bit freaked out right now. I thought that having a baby would be like opening my studio, but now that it's time...I just don't know how to help Kristy."

"Peter, I know you're helping her. Just being with her is helping her. You've prepared for this. You told me yourself about all the classes and the breathing and the chocolate and that bowling ball thing you wore for a week in commiseration." That got a chuckle out of him. "Now go and have a baby."

She hung up and then smacked her hand against her head. She hadn't even asked Peter if the studio was still closed. *Ah well. I'll find out soon enough.*

She did open a beer, but she couldn't bring herself to turn on the television. Instead, she went into her parents' conservatory and settled herself onto the swing chair. The room faced the south and was sucking up the feeble autumn sun that made the room uncomfortably hot in the summer but created the absolute perfect environment to sit and ruminate on the past couple surreal days.

Most of her thoughts were jumbled. She couldn't get the idea that she had accepted a date with a drug dealer, or manufacturer, or whatever he was, and now he was dead. That thought was stuck there at the front of her brain, lodged and festering, and she wished something else would nudge it out of the way. Then something did. Maddie's keys were outside the studio on Saturday morning. Presumably that was how Toby had gotten in, along with someone else who was responsible for his death. But Maddie was sure she had the keys with her. It's possible she dropped them when she went out with

Katy, but she remembered getting into Katy's car near the front door, nowhere near her bicycle.

Maddie recalled the image of Katy sitting next to her handbag when they were at the Grass & Toad. She could have taken her keys while Maddie was in the restroom, but why? And, for that matter, Renée was there, as well, and she'd been messing about with Maddie's bag when she was looking for a light for her cigarette. Maybe Renée had taken them. But again, why?

Then there was Ricky. He was there that night. Maddie liked the idea of Ricky being guilty but had to admit that he wouldn't have had to steal her keys to get into the studio. In the samba class, Ricky had ignored Toby, but that didn't mean that they didn't know one another. Then again, maybe Toby had gotten her keys, somehow, or even picked a lock, and had gone into the studio on his own.

Then a horrifying thought occurred to Maddie. Maybe Ricky was trying to frame Peter. Why, she had no idea. Maybe she should call Peter and ask him if he'd any altercations with Ricky in the past. She stood up and promptly ran into an iron plant pedestal, and screeching in pain, sat back down with tears in her eyes. What was she thinking, anyway? Peter was having a baby and she was just being ridiculous. She either had to get over herself or else she should get a notebook and like any good detective, take notes and follow trains of thought or else risk sounding like an episode of *Scooby-Doo*. She had the empty beer bottle in her hand and was rolling it between her fingertips, when there was a knock on the front door. She got up, unconsciously rubbing the spot she'd just whacked and opened the door to Frank. Perplexed momentarily at how the studio custodian knew where she lived, she smiled uneasily.

"Hi, Frank. Is everything okay?"

Frank looked down at his feet, then lifted his head and scratched at his chin.

"Maddie, sorry to barge in on you like this." His hands came together in front of his chest, then rested on his belly. "I looked up your address in the files. Hope you don't mind."

Maddie was conscious that she did feel uncomfortable with Frank standing on her front doorstep and awkwardly glanced toward the neighbor's quiet house. Frank must have sensed her unease as he took an embarrassed step back.

"The studio's closed today and I guess you know that Peter's wife is in labor." Frank looked so apologetic, Maddie instantly felt ashamed.

"Frank, I'm sorry I've been rude. Please come in."

"No, no, Maddie. I just wanted to make sure you were all right and..." Frank fumbled to find the right words and after looking around the front steps, seemed to find them. "Maddie, I know I could have called, but I wanted to see you in person. I needed to make sure you were okay." Tears appeared in the corners of Frank's eyes and he quickly wiped them away with his fingertips. Maddie stepped forward into the space Frank had vacated and placed her hand on his arm.

"I'm fine, Frank. Really. Just tired."

Frank's hands trembled as he grabbed the hand Maddie offered.

"It wasn't the pesticide, Maddie. I promise you. I read the bottle. The label said it was okay to use around children and animals." Frank's eyes pleaded with Maddie to believe her and he waited for a sign to indicate that she agreed with him. Maddie bit her lip, unable to respond in words. She couldn't signal such a thing, because she didn't know who or what was responsible for the accident. Frank looked crestfallen as he read Maddie's face.

"I'm so sorry, Maddie."

"Frank, please don't blame yourself. I don't think it was anything you used in the studio. There's something far more sinister happening and we need to find out what it is before we all lose our jobs." Maddie almost added *or our lives*, but stopped herself.

It was now Frank's turn to take a step away from Maddie. He leaned up against the column and looked at his shoes as Maddie continued.

"It must be Ricky. He has to be the connection. That's who the police should be talking to."

Frank continued to look at the ground, as he shook his head in what Maddie read as disbelief.

"You didn't hear what he said to Andrea on Friday night. For all we know, she could be in danger. There's definitely something shady about him. Where did he go on vacation for instance? And why did he say he was leaving town so suddenly?" Her voice had steadily risen to an urgency that now seemed to alarm Frank. He stood straighter and looked as if he was preparing to say something when the phone rang shrilly from behind Maddie. She pivoted to pick it up from a table in the entrance hall.

"Hello, Fitzpatrick residence, this is Maddie speaking...Oh, Mom, it's so good to hear your voice. I'm fine, I'm fine. No really, I have the all-clear from the hospital and Frank from the studio is here with me now." She looked over her shoulder at Frank, to find him in profile to her, looking out over her parent's front yard with his lips pursed and his hands clasped behind his back.

"Oh good, I can't wait to see you. Do you want me to collect you from the airport? Are you sure? Okay, I love you, too. I'll tell you all about it when you get home."

Feeling calmer and needing to apologize for her outburst, Maddie followed Frank to the bottom steps of the porch. "That was my parents. They're at the airport in Cape Town and flying to London tonight. They'll arrive in Newark tomorrow night but have a taxi picking them up."

Frank didn't say anything, but looked up through the trees and squinted at the feeble sunlight as it squeezed a way to their spot on the step.

"It's not Ricky."

"How do you know?"

"People act strangely when they are hiding something. Most often they're hiding something from themselves."

"I know. That's what I mean. What is he hiding? First Nina, then a dead body shows up at the dance studio. He's got to be hiding something. I can't believe he's not a suspect."

"He's hiding pain, Maddie. Hiding it away in some unused part of himself, hoping it doesn't find its way out."

How do you know?"

"I know."

Maddie didn't have the heart to question Frank any longer. The intimate way that he uttered those last two words told her that Frank was not going to be any help if she continued to voice her suspicion. She suddenly felt revived and in need of fresh air, so after saying good-bye and apologizing again for her accusations, she changed into sweatpants, grabbed her helmet and climbed on her bicycle in an attempt to coerce her brain into making sense of Toby's death.

Fifteen minutes into her exercise, she was already feeling better. She pedaled west of town, mostly uphill, so that she could cruise downhill when she finally tired. Out past the municipal park, she came across whole areas of Pembroke she'd never seen. It seemed the whole pharmaceutical industry had up and moved from wherever they used to be to northern New Jersey. She passed several large estates complete with guard gates and twelve-foot fences before she came to SynTech.

If she was honest with herself, she had to admit that she knew exactly where she was headed when she decided to take a ride and this knowledge made her self-conscious in front of the guard gate. She tried to look relaxed, as she gulped several mouthfuls of water and debated going inside. She'd just decided that she could say that she was a friend of Nina and that she wanted to pick up some personal items, and had drawn up the courage to approach the gate, when a car squealed around a bend and almost hit her as it swung into the entrance and came to a screeching halt in front of the booth. The man on duty didn't bat an eyelash, but waved the car through, then turned back to something engrossing him within the small building. Maddie realized she was holding her breath and she let it out slowly before turning her bicycle around and quickly pedaling back to town.

She tried to make sense of what she'd just seen. Ricky Russo was the easy part; she already knew he played a part in this, but the passenger in the car was Jesse Booth. Maddie remembered the last time she'd seen him with his wife. He and Robyn were obviously uncomfortable in the samba class but they'd never given any indication that they knew Ricky outside of class.

Panting, she arrived home and as she unlocked the door, the phone rang. "Hello, Fitz..." She didn't get a chance to finish her rote phone greeting but was interrupted by her sister's exclamation.

"Are you okay? Sue Reeve, remember from high school? She just called and said that there was a murder at the dance studio. Is it true?"

Maddie spent the next ten minutes giving Sylvie a truncated version of the events of the past two days.

"But this is insane. Are you in danger? Is anyone doing anything about it?"

Maddie could hear the genuine concern in her sister's voice but her anxiety sounded a lot like Renée earlier that day and Maddie's stomach couldn't handle it.

"Syl, you know Joe's handling this case."

There was a discreet cough on the other end of the phone and Maddie imagined her sister raising her eyebrows and giving a little smirk.

"So, is the mad Irish boy back in the picture?"

"I didn't say anything about being back in any picture. I just said he's running the case. And, Syl, he's a professional."

There was another silence on the line before Sylvie added, "So, you've seen him."

"Of course, I've seen him. And don't call him mad. You know he hated that."

Sylvie laughed on the other end of the phone. "Well, it sounds like you're going to be all right. But you know you should come here until Mom and Dad get home."

"Stop worrying. They'll be home in two days. I've got to stay. My boss, Peter, is having a baby and I want to be able to help at the studio if he needs it." After reiterating that she'd better take care of herself, and another sly comment about old beaus reappearing, Sylvie said good night.

Maddie hung up and went to the bathroom to brush her teeth, vowing to ignore the phone if it rang again. It didn't and she fell into bed and slept soundly until her alarm went off at 7 am.

Chapter Nineteen

Tuesday morning was sunny, clear and cold. She'd made a call to the studio and spoke to Laura. Classes were resuming as normal from Wednesday, so they had a day to decompress and tidy up. Over her protestations, Maddie told Laura she'd be in to help, but that she had an errand to run first.

She needed to see Jesse Booth. Peter was going to be busy with a new baby and wasn't going to have the time or energy to make sure the studio's best interests were taken into account. Somebody from the studio had to make sure that the police were looking into every aspect of Nina and Toby's deaths and Maddie was certain Ricky wasn't going to volunteer.

She cycled to the college and asked at the guard booth for directions to the environmental science building. Finding it easily, she stopped her bicycle and locked it up to a lamppost along with several others. Jesse's office was on the second floor and the door was open when Maddie arrived. She sighed. She was lucky and he was there, going through a stack of papers on his desk. When he saw her, he jumped up form the desk, closing the file he'd been reading and sliding it under a book.

"Maddie, hello. This is unexpected."

Maddie had thought through what she wanted to ask Jesse and until she arrived in the office had felt confident. While she felt less self-assured as she stood in the doorway, she knew she had to continue.

"Hi, Jesse. I hope you don't mind, I just have a couple of questions."

Jesse's eyes darted around the room and eventually landed on Maddie again as he shrugged his shoulders. "Sure, I guess. How can I help?"

"Well, I was out yesterday and I saw you at SynTech with Ricky. I was wondering what was going on."

Jesse opened and closed his mouth several times before speaking. "Yes, well…Ricky has been helping me with my proposal for the department." Jesse was backing up slowly and came to a stop when he ran into his desk. "You know, he works for SynTech and it's just been hell getting all the documentation together." Jesse turned around and grabbed several books off a shelf and in that time seemed to compose himself.

"I'm just on my way out now. If you don't mind, walk with me." Jesse locked his office and led Maddie back down the stairs. "You know, it's been quite pleasant working with SynTech these past few weeks. All of a sudden, it's like they've grown an environmentally responsible arm. I don't know who to thank, but Ricky has been a real help in sorting out the exact procedures needed to dispose of pharmaceutical waste safely." They arrived at another building. "Well this is where I'm heading. I hope I see you again."

Maddie turned back to where she'd parked her bicycle, wondering why she felt anxious, and then realizing that Jesse was lying.

As she passed Andrea's florist shop on the way to the studio, the door opened and Andrea stood in the frame mid step. Maddie stopped, the impulsive urge to know more getting the better of her.

"Andrea, do you know if Nina was happy working for SynTech?"

"Still playing Nancy Drew?" Maddie waited for an answer. Finally, Andrea shrugged her shoulders, as if she were commenting on nothing further than Nina's taste in shoes. "Who knows? Who the hell likes work?"

Maddie didn't retaliate that she actually liked to teach people to dance.

"Maybe someone came to the class with the intention of killing Toby, and Nina got in the way." Andrea shook her head and rolled her eyes, but Maddie was looking through the window at the orchids inside the shop. "Or maybe they came to kill Nina and Toby saw something, so then they had to kill Toby."

"That's crazy. Why the hell would anyone want to kill Nina? I mean, the only person who really knew her was Ricky and he's an ass, but killing...no way." She stopped all movement and looked as if she was digesting the possibility of Ricky killing Nina. She continued softly.

"Ricky wouldn't do that. I know he makes an act of being all macho, but that's just what it is, an act."

"Don't they always say it's usually about two things; money or love?"

This time, Andrea tossed her highlighted hair and laughed. "You know, you should really move to Hollywood. They'd make an crappy television movie out of this."

But Maddie felt like she was onto something. "When exactly did Nina come into money?"

Andrea placed a hand elaborately on her hip and stared at Maddie. "It wasn't a year ago, I know that. This time last year we were talking about going away. You know, a cruise in the Caribbean. Just us girls. I was with Ricky but it wasn't going anywhere and I felt like I needed a break. I wanted Nina to come with me but she said she couldn't afford it. That's when our bickering grew into fighting." Andrea turned to lock the door to her shop.

"It was my fault, really. I was so angry that I'd been paying for Ricky that when Nina said that, I just exploded. I said things I didn't mean. Like that I already had a boyfriend who sponged off me, I didn't need a friend like that, too."

"It was unfair of me. Nina never asked for anything. She worked hard to get what she had. She just didn't get all the breaks I did."

"So, she didn't have money a year ago, and then what happened?"

"I don't know for sure. Like I said, some distance had come between us. But a couple of months after that, around Christmas, she showed up with a fur coat on and a new car. It was the same time she starting paying more attention to Ricky." Andrea began walking away from her shop, leaving Maddie no alternative but to follow if she wanted to finish the conversation.

"Ricky had been eyeing Nina all along, I knew that. I was getting tired of paying for his lifestyle, Ricky knew that. Funny thing is, I knew he liked Nina but I never worried about it, because she was broke. Hah. The joke was on me."

"Did she say anything about the money?"

"No. Not directly, anyway. Once, in one of our last semi-good moments, she said something about how what goes around comes around. I would have thought she was just talking about us, but she was manically ripping a piece of paper up into little pieces when she said it. She left after that and I don't know why, but I picked up the pieces from the trash can."

Andrea tilted her head to the side and shrugged her shoulders, letting them drop dramatically, so that her breasts wobbled in a ridiculous fashion.

"Anyway, I put some of the pieces together and saw it was just a copy her résumé and old letters of recommendation. I don't know why she was so frustrated. I knew she actually liked working at SynTech, with all the employee benefits and good holidays, plus, she got to work with Ricky."

The two women arrived at CVS and without a farewell, Andrea disappeared into the pharmacy. Maddie rode away, no clearer than she had been. She arrived at the studio and found Frank and Laura's cars in the parking lot, as well as a police cruiser and Joe's unmarked car. She locked up her bicycle and hurried inside.

She wasn't sure what she expected to see, but it wasn't what she found. Nothing looked out of order. The hallway was clean, the door to the janitor's closet open, with the contents of the closet sitting in an organized manner. As she walked down the hallway, she paused to look into the classrooms. The first two were open, sunlight streaming through the windows, empty of anything but the mirrors. The third room had the same sunlight and open windows but Frank was there mopping the floor and humming to himself. He turned to Maddie as she stuck her head through the door.

"Maddie. Good to see you. How're you holding up?" Frank had stopped his mopping and was leaning on the pole looking like he was ready for a long chat.

"Good, Frank, thanks. This place looks great. How long have you been here?"

"Oh, I got here 'bout six. Didn't see why we should wait to clean the place up. I spoke with Peter already." Frank tapped the broom twice with his index finger. "They've got themselves a baby girl. Sounded like he hasn't slept in days."

Frank was interrupted by a discreet cough from the doorway. Maddie turned to find Joe scanning a file in his hands. He lifted his eyes from the page and met hers.

"Maddie, can I have a word?"

Maddie's stomach flipped, but she nodded to Joe first and then to Frank as she followed the detective out of the classroom and into the office. Laura looked up from her kneeling position in front of the filing cabinet, Cathwrynn hovering over her with a perplexed look on her face.

"Oh, good, would one of you give me a hand here? This drawer is stuck."

Joe bent down immediately and maneuvered the drawer so that it opened several inches, but had to admit defeat when the overflowing papers caught in the runners.

"It's going to need some WD40 and reorganization."

Joe stood back up, collected the file he'd put on Laura's desk and disappeared into Peter's office without another word. Maddie offered a consoling look to Laura, but the secretary didn't appear to have digested Joe's patronizing remark. Instead she furtively glanced at Cathwrynn, who was now backing slowly away from the filing cabinet and looking somewhere near the ceiling. Laura followed her gaze and as she stood up and muttered.

"She's been acting strange all morning."

Maddie noticed that the packet of cigarettes habitually in her front pocket was there, but this time it had obviously been opened. Laura noticed Maddie's gaze and straightened her shoulders and continued in a cautious whisper.

"I mean more strange than normal and, yes, I smoked one. With all that's been going on around here, how could I not?"

Maddie nodded enthusiastically and mumbled something about it being completely understandable, then looked at Cathwrynn again and found the petite red head staring directly at her. Her words floated out of her mouth and seemed to disappear as soon as she said them.

"I am relieved we were able to avoid a confrontation."

Maddie looked to Laura for support, but Laura gave another habitual huff and buried her head in her top drawer.

"A confrontation with what?" Maddie didn't want to ask, because she wasn't sure how she would respond if Cathwrynn said she was avoiding a confrontation with the filing cabinet.

"With his spirit. It was here. You know that." Maddie didn't know that and she heard another fake cough coming from Peter's office and knew she had to report to Joe.

"You do know. He came to you in a dream, didn't he?"

Maddie jumped. He had, hadn't he? The night before she found his body she'd dreamed about him and their date. Until that moment, she'd forgotten about it, but Cathwrynn was right. Maddie looked at her with what might not be respect, but was certainly a willingness to take her more seriously. A voice behind her rudely brought her out of this new notion.

"Maddie. If you can spare a moment?" Joe's voice was filled with an irritating mix of sarcasm and patronization. Maddie's smile became brittle as she followed his voice and closed the door behind her.

"So sorry, Joe. We've just had a murder here at the studio and some of us are taking a little time to adjust to the situation." Maddie sensed that Joe had a lot to say and braced for his retort. He surprised her, however, by handing her several pieces of paper held together with a paperclip. He remained seated behind Peter's desk, his face pointedly focused on a notebook in front of him. Standing over him, Maddie could see the silver in his hair reflecting in the overhead lights. For a startling few seconds she felt dizzy, the most improbable vision appearing in front of her eyes. A seventeen-year-old Joe, Maddie standing above him with scissors in her hand, lengths of his black hair lying at her feet. Joe loved his hair. Only at the final threat of suspension did he agree to cut it and he would only let Maddie do it. She'd been so nervous with those scissors, knowing how much he hated the authority the school had over him and suspecting that she was likely to make him look like a clown. She gasped when she remembered that she had collected that hair and put it in her special box. A box that was probably still in her parents' attic.

Joe tapped the papers in front of him impatiently, then picked them up and thrust them towards Maddie as if he thought she wasn't going to look at them. How could Maddie tell him she'd just remembered who Joe was?

"These are the names of people whose fingerprints were found here the morning after Toby Down's death. Please look through them and tell me who you recognize."

Maddie took the papers from Joe's outstretched hands and tried to catch his eye, but he'd turned back to the chair and sat down hard. She scanned the list but saw it as a futile mission.

"Joe, I don't know most of these names. I've only been back a couple of weeks." Joe cut her short.

"I know. Just look through them and tell me who you know."

Maddie started at the top of the list again. She saw several first names of the elderly people she taught with Peter and told Joe she assumed they were the dancers from the fox-trot class. She also pointed out Tia Angela and Danny. "But I don't see any of the other people from that family. Maybe the doors and walls were washed after that class."

Joe sat with his hands making a steeple shape under his chin, his eyes now digesting Maddie. With her concentration on the list in her hands, she had unconsciously sucked her bottom lip into her mouth and was gently chewing on it, a mannerism she'd continued for fifteen years. Joe swallowed audibly before speaking.

"Not everyone has fingerprints on record. Unless you work for a government agency, there's no law yet to require national fingerprinting. And not everyone has a passport."

Maddie bent her head to the list again. "I think these two are in Cathwrynn's class, you'll have to ask her. And Katy Clemments picked me up Friday night. Robyn and Jesse were in Ricky's class. And so was Renée Lambert. And Andrea is here too but I don't see Alice or Henri." Maddie must have made an involuntary face at Henri's name, because Joe stopped her.

"What about Henri?"

"He's just gross." Joe looked skeptically at her, so she added quickly. "No, listen, he really is gross, all male, macho pig." Joe winced at that. "But that's not all of it. His girlfriend Alice thinks he had something to do with Nina, maybe even her death." She waited to hear Joe exclaim that she must be on to something, but was disappointed.

"Joe, you have to admit there's something suspect when the girlfriend of a creepy guy believes he could be involved in a murder."

"Maddie, there's no law against being creepy. And Nina's death has not been categorized as murder."

"Creepy and now there are two bodies. You seem to be conveniently forgetting that bit."

"Maddie, we're taking care of that angle. The list." He tapped the list again.

"I'm not a child, Joe…"

"Then stop acting like one."

"Excuse me? I was the one who was almost killed; and found a dead body in my place of employment."

Joe took another agonizing breath. "You were not going to die, Maddie …"

"Oh, that's right, tell me that now, after I had to stay two nights in the hospital." Maddie swallowed both her outrage and tears.

"That was a precaution, but now that I see you're not going to stay out of my official investigation," he paused and almost made Maddie laugh at his dramatic presentation, "I'll say it again. Maddie, official investigation. I wish they'd kept you in all week."

Maddie stood dumbstruck. "Well, if that's all I can do for you, I have a class to teach."

"No actually, it's not all. What I'd really like to know is why there's a text from you on Toby Down's cell phone asking him to meet you at the studio at 8 am on Saturday morning."

"What?" Maddie nearly screeched. "That's not true. I never sent any such message." Maddie shook her hand in Joe's direction, but saw the look of disbelief on Joe's face and lowered her arm. "I really didn't."

While Joe opened a briefcase sitting on Peter's desk and reached in without taking his eyes off her, Maddie sighed elaborately. She began to feel nervous when he pulled a cell phone out of the case.

Joe's eyes finally left hers and went to the screen of the phone, where he scrolled through the received messages, then handed the phone to her. She looked down at the screen he'd opened and caught herself before she could scream.

"I'll need to see your phone, Maddie."

Maddie pulled her phone out of her handbag and didn't even bother looking into her sent messages before handing it to him. He scrolled down then handed the phone back to her. She reread the message that she had just seen on Toby's phone.

"But, I didn't send this."

"Who else has had access to your phone?"

"No one. Who would? I mean, I went home Friday night and went to bed. By myself."

Joe ignored her sardonic comment and tapped the pen he was holding against his bottom lip "The message was sent Friday night at 7:56. You were still at the Grass & Toad." Maddie nodded her head in agreement. Joe hadn't said anything, but by the length of his silence, Maddie guessed she should explain.

"Well, I went to the restroom a couple of times and left my handbag with Katy but why would she do that? She doesn't even know Toby. Then Renée sat with us for a few minutes. She's a nurse but I guess you know that." Joe ignored her tone again.

Maddie sat down in the chair immediately in front of Peter's desk and began tapping her foot against a leg. She noticed Joe glance down at her foot each time it connected with the chair, but she didn't stop.

"Do you want to know what I think happened?"

Joe seemed to wake up out of an unpleasant dream. "No, actually, I don't. If you left your bag unattended at the Grass & Toad, anyone in the restaurant could have rifled through it and taken your phone.

"I didn't say I left it unattended. I said I left it with Katy."

Joe brushed the crumbs of his muffin into his hand and tipped them into the wastebasket. "So, is that something you can do out in California?"

Maddie looked at him quizzically.

"Leave your handbag at a bar with someone you haven't seen in fifteen years?"

"I'm not even going to answer that."

Joe motioned to the door. "Now, if you'll excuse me. And you can take your phone."

"Won't you need to have it fingerprinted?"

"No."

Chapter Twenty

Maddie closed the door to Peter's office a lot more quietly than she thought she was capable and found the outer office empty. She took a deep breath and found that it did nothing to dissipate her anger. Just as she was about to hurl several choice expletives at the wall, Frank came in followed by a large man who was carrying what looked like electronic equipment. Frank caught the look of frustration on Maddie's face and paused at the door.

"Everything all right there, Maddie?"

"Yes, fine, Frank. Thanks. Just yet another reminder in a long list of reminders, that I'm not as important as I seem to think I am."

Frank drew his lips together and while he looked like he was on the verge of responding, he didn't say a word. Instead he added a shake of his head to his already disapproving expression. Whether he objected to Maddie's opinion of herself or something else, Maddie didn't know. The, until then, patient man standing behind Frank politely coughed, causing Frank to surface from his inner monologue.

"Right. This gentleman has to install these cameras." Frank scratched the top of his head, then his right elbow. "To make it safer for all of us." Before she could say that the camera would be a welcome addition to the studio, she saw Frank's expression change from concerned to bemused. Maddie swiveled her head 90 degrees, almost afraid at what she might find and could now see the sight Frank must have caught in the mirror hanging above the filing cabinet. Peter stood looking as if the sun was shining out of his eyes, clearly exhausted but ecstatic. Lifting his hands over his head as if he were holding a trophy he let out a woo hoo!

"Mother and baby are fantastic. We have our little Lauren Sophia."

Maddie ran up to him and gave him a hug. "Congratulations, Peter. And how's the father?"

"Great, great, great! I don't think I've ever felt this great. Kristy's sleeping right now and I'm just going home to collect a few things. They tell you what you're supposed to bring, but of course, we forgot half of them. But, first, I need a song. Come." He pulled Maddie and Frank by the arms out of the office and towards the classroom Frank had just swept.

"Frank, put something on, will you?"

Frank was grinning himself, Peter's joy infectious. "Now what kind of music would you like?"

"Anything, anything. Just turn on the radio and the first song on, that will be my baby girl's song."

"Peter, you may want to think about that again. The radio station could be that heavy metal stuff that Laura listens to." Frank grinned at Laura as she and Cathwrynn followed them into the classroom.

"I most certainly do not listen to such garbage, Frank. Give me Barry Manilow any day."

Maddie and Peter looked at one another before bursting into laughter. Between heavy metal and Barry Manilow, it was hard to know which was worse. When Frank turned the radio on, all four held their breaths and let out a collective sigh when they heard the words to *'I Can See Clearly Now.'*

Maddie laughed, as Peter slid to the stereo and raised the volume, simultaneously singing an off-key accompaniment to Johnny Nash and flapping his arms about in an effort to get the rest of them to join him.

Without much effort, he got Laura, Cathwrynn and Frank going but Maddie was laughing too hard and thinking that maybe the rain *was* clearing. Maybe everything would be all right and she didn't need to worry about why or how Nina and Toby had died.

"Maddie! Sing with us!"

Maddie had no intention of singing, but Peter's enthusiasm got the better of her and she belted it out, flapping her own arms around as they all jimmied and jiggled, or swayed and shuffled in Frank's case, and spun and clapped in Cathwrynn's, about the dance floor until the song's end.

Breaking up their carefree moment, a voice from the direction of the lobby pierced the joyful mood in the room.

"Hello, hello. Is anyone here?" The voice began sedately but within those five words had risen to irate consternation.

Maddie followed the sound of the voice belonging to Renée Lambert out into the hall. The nurse stood just inside the door, supporting herself with one hand against the wall, as she used her other hand to rub her shin.

"Those stairs are dangerous. I just lost my balance and fell against that pot. It should be moved before someone sues." Renée avoided eye contact with Maddie as she vented her irritation and Maddie wished that, as the realization of Renée's identity had hit her, she'd scurried into the restroom and hidden until the coast was clear.

"Hi, Renée, I'm sorry about that. I'll have Frank look into it." She covertly looked past Renée towards the pot and could see clearly that for Renée to have walked into it, she'd have had to have been walking flat against the wall of the building, an absurd path, as it was obstructed by several visible and substantial plants.

"We've got a first aid kit with some arnica cream, if that would help." Maddie smiled, hoping that Renée would leave and that she wasn't there looking for private tango classes.

Renée looked disgusted. "I don't need that crap. I only came here to say that I'm not taking classes here anymore. What the hell kind of place do you run?"

Maddie wasn't sure what Renée meant and must have looked clueless, as Renée immediately rolled her eyes and sighed. "Oh, for God's sake. It's not like everyone hasn't heard. Drugs are being sold here and now people have died because of it. I expect you'll be closed down." Renée turned as if to go, but Maddie stopped her.

"Wait a minute, Renée. What are you talking about? Drugs are not being sold here and the two people who died were not related to one another." Renée just pushed past her and rolled her eyes again, letting Maddie know her feelings.

"Renée, you were here when Nina died. It was unfortunate, but it was an accident."

"Yeah, maybe if you call taking drugs an accident."

"Do you know that Nina was taking drugs?"

"No, of course I don't. Why would I? I didn't even know her."

Maddie flinched. Either Renée had heard about the drug connection through inside knowledge as a nurse, or else, the sordid suburban grapevine worked a lot faster than Maddie had anticipated.

"If this is because Toby was into drugs, it has nothing to do with us. Toby only started coming to the studio three weeks ago."

Renée looked incredulous. "What do you mean? I had no idea Toby was into drugs. But this place is where it all happened." Maddie struggled against the certainty that Renée was losing her mind.

"But you just said that drugs were being done here and that people died because of it. You must have meant that Toby died because he did drugs, right?"

Renée had grabbed the railing on the wall and held onto it as if the world was about to turn upside down.

"I did not know that Toby did drugs. How dare you? I am a professional. How dare you imply that I knew?"

Maddie had been racking her brain to figure out what was bothering her and finally it dawned on her.

"Renée, why didn't you help Nina?"

Renée's already alabaster skin first paled further then produced a red spot on each cheek that grew until her whole head had a look of an overripe tomato.

"What exactly do you mean by that?"

"Just what I asked. Why didn't you help her? You're a nurse."

"And what business is it of yours? What? Am I a nurse all the time? Should I just be expected to work 24-7? Do you think I just carry medical supplies with me wherever I go?" Renée was spitting with every word and had begun to gesticulate furiously in Maddie's direction. As she stepped away from the increasingly unhinged woman, Maddie wished she'd just kept quiet.

"No, I didn't..."

"No, of course, you didn't." To Maddie's continued astonishment, Renée mimicked Maddie in a whiny voice.

From behind her, Maddie heard voices and in relief turned to find Peter and Joe at the door of the office, both with their eyes on Renée. Peter's eyes momentarily swiveled behind him as he instinctively hopped backed into the office.

Joe, on the other hand, strode over to the two women, his nostrils flaring, convulsively cracking his knuckles. He had his briefcase clenched under his right arm, but he managed to crack each knuckle in quick succession as he moved down the hallway. Maddie watched Joe's arrival and felt a fleeting twinge of compassion for Renée. It disappeared instantly when the nurse grabbed Maddie and brought her face to within centimeters of her lips.

"I will bring you down if you dare imply that I have taken drugs."

Joe had reached them by then and had taken Renée firmly by the shoulder, repositioning her on his left side and superficially using himself as a barricade between the two women.

"I was just heading back to my office and would like you to join me, Ms. Lambert."

Maddie watched as the unhealthy color drained from Renée's face. Her pinched features momentarily relaxed before she bared her teeth. Maddie held her breath, completely fascinated at the idea that Renée might bite Joe. But Joe must have used his special police superpowers to sense her intention, because with only the slightest squint of an eye and pressure to her right elbow, Renée's shoulders collapsed and she allowed herself to be taken through the door.

Maddie and Peter cautiously followed their departure and with a collective exhalation, watched as Renée pulled something from her bag and dropped it into a bush. They looked at one another and then back to the retreating pair.

"I think that woman is truly insane."

"Yeah. Insane and a litterbug." Peter shook his head sadly.

The odd couple had reached Renée's car and Joe stood over her, as she fiddled in her bag. Extracting her keys, she opened the door, apparently listening to Joe's instructions. Joe watched her drive away, then climbed into his own car and after a minute drove away as well.

Showing obvious relief that Renée had been escorted out of the building, Peter stood with his hands on his hips. "What was that about?"

Maddie wanted to spare him the drug dealing accusation, but knew that if gossip was spreading that the studio was a drug haven, Peter had to know.

"I know this isn't what you're going to want to hear, but Renée said that she wasn't going to take classes any longer and the reason was that we sell drugs."

Maddie had expected Peter to rant and rave at that news, possibly break down and cry, but instead he looked solemnly at Maddie and then exploded into peals of laughter. He laughed so hard tears spilled down his cheeks to nestle in the stubble of his chin. Then he bent over and started snorting as well. The uncharacteristic sounds brought Laura, Cathwrynn and Frank running into the hallway. They had wisely chosen to remain hidden while Renée was in the building but when they reached Maddie and Peter, both of whom were now in an unfamiliar hysterical state, they paused to assess the situation. Then, slowly, Laura began to laugh, followed hesitantly by Frank and softly by Cathwrynn.

The studio would have to think and act upon the supposed unwelcome reputation that it was garnering, but in the meantime, new bursts of laughter erupted as the five employees of the St. Claire Dance Studio reconsidered their studio alternately as a drug den, a whorehouse and a den of debauchery, unaware that the camera installer was watching them from the office in perplexed amusement.

Spent, the employees of the St. Claire Dance Studio got back to business. Peter collected several files from his office and prepared to leave to get back to his newly expanded family.

"Maddie, walk out with me, would you?"

"Sure." Maddie followed behind Peter out the front door. When the door was closed behind them, he turned around and held Maddie's eyes.

"Are you all right?"

Maddie was unprepared for the realization that she *was* all right. She'd been distracted by the display Renée had put on and Joe's undermining behavior prior to that, but overall she had to admit that she felt healthy and was simply looking forward to getting back to teaching. She smiled at Peter.

"You know, I am fine. I feel a wave of positive energy all of a sudden and I know that everything's going to be okay."

Peter looked at Maddie with raised eyebrows.

"I mean it. I think it's all going to be figured out soon."

"All what, Maddie?"

Maddie looked at Peter to see if he was joking, but the furrowed brow and wide eyes told her he wasn't.

"Um, the murders. What did you think?"

Peter looked to both sides as if trying to find an answer hidden behind the planters that Renée had tripped over.

"Maddie, I hate to sound like an over-protective parent or," he paused, unsure whether he should finish his sentence, "like a certain police detective, who shall remain nameless, but do you think you should be getting involved now?"

"Yes, I do. The whole studio is at risk if I don't." Maddie's heart sank. She had assumed that if anyone was going to understand why she had to know, it would be Peter.

"Maddie, it's not that I don't know what could happen to the studio. What I'm pointing out is that you shouldn't be the one trying to figure it out. Look what's happened."

"Peter, I wasn't trying to figure anything out on Saturday morning. I was just trying to make sure that no one had broken into the studio."

"But they had, and now we're where we are." Peter tapped the files he was holding against his thigh. "I think the police can do their job. Last week it was all fun and games talking to Andrea like Nancy Drew but now it's changed."

Maddie bit her lip, seven socially unacceptable retorts raging through her head. He was still her boss, though, and he had a point.

"Maddie. I care more about this studio and every single person working in it than you can imagine. Only my wife and daughter come before this place. That's why I want everyone to be safe. I need everyone to be safe."

Maddie blushed. "I'm being a bit of a princess, aren't I?"

Peter smiled in return. "Permission to be a princess granted, but just do it at home, preferably with bubbles and chocolate." Peter quickly hugged Maddie. "And now, I have a date. I'll be back in on Friday." He threw a kiss over his shoulder as Maddie watched him leave, a slight smile on her lips that didn't reach her eyes. She knew she'd given Peter the impression that she would be a good girl and leave police work to the police, but she also knew she had lied.

Chapter Twenty-One

If there was a rumor going around that the studio was a drug den, then she had to make sure that it didn't spread.

If there was such a rumor, the Shadylawn Retirement Village either hadn't heard or didn't care. Peter's waltz class showed up enthusiastically and on time. Maddie explained that Peter was a new father and she would be taking the class. She was pleased to have a group of people who hadn't heard about the events of the weekend and looked forward to focusing on them for the next hour.

After class, Maddie joined Laura and Frank in the office. She looked around the room in what she thought was a casual manner, but Laura saw it for what it was.

"Don't worry, dear, every last inch of this room has been cleaned and scrubbed. There's nothing stronger than Mr. Clean in here and nothing can hurt you." Laura reached over and squeezed Maddie's hand then briskly set about boiling the kettle, saying that what they clearly needed was a soothing cup of chamomile tea. Frank sat quietly, shaking his head as if trying to clear some water from his ear and only stopped when Laura put a mug of tea in his hand.

"I just don't get it. Why would people think that we sell drugs? That can't be right, can it?" Frank took a sip of tea and grimaced, placing the tea on Laura's desk, as far from him as he could reach, Maddie noticed with a grin. The tea wasn't very good, but Maddie drank it anyway.

Laura put her mug down and nodded emphatically.

"I'll tell you, I don't like saying it, but if someone were up to that kind of stuff, I'd put my money on Philip or Claire. They're young."

Frank appeared not to be listening any longer, but Laura tilted her head in thought and emitted a discreet huff. She leaned in conspiratorially toward Maddie and whispered.

"Or it could be Cathwrynn. She's so...well you know, airy."

True, Cathwrynn was whimsical, Maddie thought. But she also knew enough about crystal meth to know that Cathwrynn's fanciful behavior was the exact opposite of what a crystal meth user would be like.

Without warning, Frank stood up. "It really wasn't me, was it?" Frank ran his hand nervously over his belly.

"What are you talking about, Frank?" Laura tried to hand him the cup of untouched tea.

"You're absolutely sure it wasn't me who left poison on the floor and nearly killed Maddie?" He'd tightened his mouth in an effort to control shaking.

"No, Frank, it wasn't you." Maddie put her tea down and came to him. "And, Frank, I didn't almost die. I'm fine."

Frank was shaking his head. "But what if it was. I'm getting old. I'm not thinking straight so much anymore."

Laura looked at Maddie and then reached in a bottom drawer of her desk. "Listen here, Frank. This is the poison you used. It's for mice, not rats. Not nearly as strong." She glanced over her glasses again at Maddie, then turned back to Frank. "And the police already asked about it. They've checked everything here. It wasn't you, Frank."

Frank took a deep breath and smiled at Maddie. He then nodded slightly toward his still-full cup of chamomile tea. "Sorry about that," before turning and leaving the room.

Maddie sighed and Laura let out all the huffs she'd been holding in since Frank stood up, taking a cigarette out of the packet and sticking it between her ear and the tangled mess of her hair.

Maddie drained the last of her mug. "What if it's someone who dances here, not works here? Like Alice's boyfriend, Henri. He was a piece of work."

"You're right, but then it could be anyone. There must be two hundred different people dancing here, Renée Lambert for instance. She sure has a mouth on her."

"You're right. She keeps popping up. Here and at the hospital."

"Well, she is a nurse."

"Yes, but doesn't it seem a bit strange to you that she's a nurse, but didn't even step forward to help Nina. And then I saw her at the hospital. She was there when I was in bed and then again when I was discharged."

Laura sucked her lips. "I'm not sure what you're getting at."

Maddie looked down at her hands. She knew she had to verbalize the thought that had just popped, unbidden into her head, but she didn't want to. As if she read her mind, Laura melodramatically whispered.

"Do you think someone is trying to close the studio down? Like they're doing it on purpose."

Maddie's heart quickened at the thought of losing her job. She must have had a look on her face that reflected her growing panic because, Laura stopped the typing she was doing and lifted a hand to pat Maddie on the arm.

"Maddie, what is it? I was serious, you know."

Maddie rotated her head and tried to relax her shoulders before answering.

"I need this job."

Laura nodded knowingly and let out a long sigh. "Oh, I know, times are tough. I feel lucky that I've had steady work all these years." Laura gave a sanctimonious huff and tapped her computer keyboard. "Pays to keep up with technology."

"That's not exactly what I meant." Laura stopped Maddie by extending her hand and seizing Maddie's arm.

"I know what you mean. I saw the television show and the naked girl. But that doesn't mean I'd be opposed to hearing the story straight from the horse's mouth." Laura's hunger for scandal was wearing Maddie down so she told her a truncated version of her ordeal with Morgan LeRoux.

"The worst part of it was that the college didn't support me. I was halfway through my PhD when they told me that they thought it would be better if I took a break."

Laura huffed disapprovingly and reached for the cigarette at her ear and stood up, shaking her head.

"I'm sure that little hussy will get what she deserves in the end. What goes around, comes around, I always say.

Maddie gazed at Laura pensively, knowing she'd heard someone say that very expression recently but not remembering who it was. She was still thinking about it when Laura returned from her cigarette and began stuffing brochures into envelopes to be mailed.

"For sure, we're not going to be able to use the brochures that were out when the police came in and did their dusting. Good thing most of them were still in the boxes." Laura heaved a pile of brochures covered in grey powder directly into her wastebasket and swiveled her chair around to reach into a cupboard behind her desk. "Do you think they're worth all the money they cost?" She had picked up one of the glossy brochures and had opened the outer wings to show the entire middle spread.

Maddie took it from Laura and looked at it again. "Absolutely. In this competitive market, you have to look the part, even if you can't quite afford it. People see a brochure like that and they see professionalism and success. It may take some time, but it will pay for itself."

"Well, that may be so, but so much goes to waste."

"But, Laura, the office getting covered in fingerprint dust isn't something you could consider normal." Maddie felt a wave of laughter coming on again, but managed to subdue it to a giggle or two.

Laura waved her hand at Maddie dismissively. "I didn't mean this." Motioning to the room, she continued. "I mean people taking them and knowing that they're just going to put them in the trash. People like that Katy friend of yours."

Maddie straightened up from her position, collecting the stamp roll that had ricocheted off the table as she tried to use it. "What do you mean, Katy?"

"Oh, for goodness sake. Her mother has multiple sclerosis. She's been in a wheelchair for a decade. She sure as heck wasn't getting that brochure for her." Laura thought for a moment, as did Maddie. "Do you think she was here for herself, but was too embarrassed to say she didn't know how to dance?"

No, Maddie thought. *No. Katy wasn't here because she wanted to learn how to dance.* While she could simply accept the view that Katy was there to see her, an uneasy thought began swimming in her head. She didn't know what other reason Katy had for being at the studio, but she predicted that there was one.

"I knew her parents, Dee and John. But that was years ago. He seemed like such a good man. He moved over to Parsippany with that other woman, what was her name?" Laura stopped and tilted her head to the side as if waiting for an internal signal. "Ah, Georgia, that's it. And then they had a son and then the fire. So tragic."

Maddie remembered. She and Katy had been friends up to that point at the Junior High School. After her father left, Katy changed, becoming a much more cynical person. Maddie was glad that it appeared Katy had moved forward and succeeded in life.

Maddie begged off the last of the brochures saying she felt suddenly exhausted. Laura waved her away saying that, of course, she probably shouldn't have even come in today. Maddie was ruminating over the text message sent from her phone to Toby, smarting from the injustice of Joe's treatment all over again, when Alice Walters walked into the lobby.

"Maddie, I'm so glad I caught you."

Maddie did a double take. Alice looked like a completely different person. Her appearance hadn't changed, so much as her expression. This was the first time Maddie had seen her, *What was it? Happy! That's what it was.* She looked happy and confident.

"Alice. Hi, you look great. Our class is tomorrow, right?" Maddie felt a wave of anxiety as she thought maybe she'd gotten her schedule mixed up. With the events of the previous days, it would be forgiven, by anyone but Maddie.

A momentary look of unease passed over Alice's face, but was quickly replaced by a sheepish smile.

"Oh, no, you're right. It's tomorrow. It's just that...I came by to ask if I can reschedule it. I'm going on vacation tonight."

"Of course, that's no problem. Where are you going?"

"Oh, Henri and I are going to the Bahamas. He just asked." A wistful look now joined her smile.

"It's been so great. Ever since that woman died." Alice must have realized how that sounded, because she immediately clasped her hand to her mouth.

"Oh, I didn't mean that her dying was great. I'm so sorry."

"It's all right, Alice. It sounds like life is being good to you."

"Yes, that's just it." Alice looked behind her as if expecting someone to come through the front door. "I know that Henri can be, well, rough sometimes, but you just wouldn't believe the change in him in the last week."

Alice looked so happy she was almost pretty, the prominent veins in her neck and arms camouflaged by a healthy glow. She also looked as if she thought that the change in Henri could be due to her loving.

Running her hands down the sides of her hair, she continued. "He wants to get out of here and take me on a cruise. He just has to finish a last job today and we're leaving tonight. We're going to dance every night." Again, she looked around before whispering, "He actually broke down and cried after last Tuesday night. He told me all about his childhood and how he hates his job. You know he worked for MallCorps and they work them like dogs. But he's quit. Now he wants a change and he told me he never would have thought about doing it if he hadn't met me. I just can't resist a guy who cries, you know?"

Maddie didn't know what to think. Hopefully, Henri really experienced some sort of epiphany, and was being honest with Alice, but Maddie doubted it. Before she could reply, a horn hooted from outside. Not an impatient blast, but a couple of toots, followed by a pause and a couple more toots, as if the person behind the horn was playing along to music.

"Oh, that'll be Henri. So, can we reschedule for two weeks' time? Although, with all the dancing I'm going to be doing, I may not need so many private lessons." Alice spun around and floated out of the door, as Maddie thought that it would be a bit of a stretch to think that Alice was going to learn enough about Argentine Tango from Henri not to need lessons.

Maddie watched her climb into the car. So Henri worked for MallCorps. And Ricky and Nina worked at SynTech? MallCorps looked set to buy the riverside property. Was SynTech involved in the sale? And how did Jesse fit in all this?

Maddie could hear the swing music from Philip and Claire's class coming to an end and scooted out of the door before the class emptied. She didn't want to get caught up in friendly chit-chat while she thought about how Nina and Toby's deaths could be connected; and whether Ricky or Henri could have been involved. But why? There must be a connection she was missing. Maddie felt a headache coming on and left the building to get a coffee.

Chapter Twenty-Two

Maddie walked down Main Street and found herself gripping her skirt in an effort to keep herself decent. Halfway to the deli, she stopped in awe at an unfamiliar sound, then laughed at her stupidity when she recognized the sound as the wind. It was howling. She gleefully inhaled the turbulent air. Wind in LA blew gently, or wafted, but wind didn't make noise.

She continued towards Vito's with a thought fixed in her head that she couldn't dislodge. She'd been thinking about how Ricky and Henri could be involved but two women kept popping up and nagging at her: Renée and Katy. Crossing Elm, she cut through the library parking lot and ran straight into Maureen.

"Oh, hey there. You coming to see us?" Maureen as ever, was a veritable basket of sunshine. Maddie noticed that she looked particularly pretty that morning and told her so.

Maureen beamed. "Thanks, Maddie. I'm happy. Just went to the gynecologist and had my IUD taken out. We're going to get pregnant." She shot her hand up into the air, as if her team had just scored the winning goal.

"That's great, Maureen. Funny, pregnancy seems to be in the air."

Maureen looked dumbstruck. "You're not. Are you?"

"No, never fear. I'm not pregnant."

Maureen looked relieved. "Well, it's all one way or the other, isn't it? I just ran into Katy Clemments and she was getting her IUD taken out too. She said that it was time she started thinking about a baby, even if she didn't have a man. Sad, I think. But then, we're all different and that's what makes it all work."

Maddie thought that all the differences between people were what started wars, but kept the thought to herself.

Maureen was practically skipping towards the building. "I have to admit, though, I'll miss not getting my period, thanks to the IUD. Well, only until I get pregnant, right?" Maddie looked at her with amusement.

"I've never been pregnant, but I do remember my sister telling me that you don't have a period until you stop breastfeeding."

"I know, right? I'm going to breastfeed for a year."

Maureen stopped in front of the municipal building and looked expectantly at Maddie.

"So, you coming up?"

"Oh, no. I was just..."

For a couple of seconds, she thought about mentioning her unclear thoughts surrounding Renée Lambert and Katy Clemments. But no matter how Maddie thought about it, her explanations sounded lame and she couldn't link them to Nina's and Toby's deaths, so she said nothing.

"No, I'm on my way to Vito's and then back to the studio. Want to join me for a coffee?"

"Sure, I've got a couple more minutes."

The two women walked through the streets in companionable silence. They were passing a newspaper vending machine outside the YMCA, when Maureen snorted and pointed at the cover.

"Oh, heavens. This is so depressing."

Maddie read the large print splashed across the front page of the *Pembroke Telegraph*: "History Society

Loses Appeal: Riverfront Property to Go to Highest Offer. *"*

"I'm all for progress and I get that for progress we need change, but it sure is a sad day when we have to watch our heritage fall under the hammer of corporate greed."

"I have to admit, I haven't been keeping up with what's going on with the saga and local politics generally. With everything else that's been happening to me, the business with the waterfront seems far removed."

"Understandable. The fact is that's it's all coming to a head now, but it's actually been in the pipeline for about three years." Maureen danced through a pile of multi-colored leaves.

"About four years ago, the last of the Dodge family died, leaving most of the family wealth to charities and the town itself. The memorials and the municipal buildings were bequeathed to various philanthropic organizations and the mansion just out of town was donated to the Audubon Society. There wasn't any talk for a while about the riverside properties, because everyone had expected that they were to be donated to the Pembroke Historical Society. Then all hell broke loose. That was three years ago now. Well, somehow, through some big-wig real estate tycoon, a local real estate agent got hold of the rights to the property and has been working ever since to sell it. And now it looks like MallCorps is going to get it."

Maddie had been searching the depths of her handbag for change to buy the paper, when her hand stopped with the coins clutched in her hand and her stomach dropped straight down to her feet.

"Let me guess. The real estate agent is Katy Clemments."

Maureen raised her eyebrows and nodded.

"But how does she benefit? It wasn't as if she bought the property, did she?"

"No, that's just it. She didn't buy it, more like, she bought the rights to sell it. It's been agreed that the money MallCorps is willing to pay will go to the Historical Society but Katy will get a whopping 30% brokerage fee."

"How much are they offering?"

"$15,000,000." Maureen looked keenly at Maddie.

"Wow, that's almost a $5,000,000 commission for Katy." Maddie thought about that. Maybe that was why Katy had been acting unpredictably. She had a lot on her mind, and a lot of what was on her mind, was money.

"So the Historical Society would rather fight for donation of the property, even at the prospect of losing out on $10,000,000, rather than it turn into a fast food mini-mall.

"Yeah, I can understand that."

Once they'd turned the corner on Elm, they could see the riverside property beyond Vito's. The sight was so unexpected, both women stopped and stared at the spectacle. There were at least seven limousines parked in front of the building, all with their doors open. People, half in and half out of their vehicles, yelled into their phones. Protesters, made up of an assorted group of college students, young families and senior citizen, tried to break through a picket-line, carrying a banner across their width that read, in similar fashion to the front page newspaper article Maddie now held in her hand, 'Say NO to Greed! Keep our History Safe.' Maddie thought she recognized a few of the protesters from her Shadylawn Retirement Village classes and guessed that they'd been driven by the near-by mini-van to the protest.

"Wow, this has grown. I think I should call the station." Without another word, Maureen stepped away from Maddie and pushed a button on her mobile. Within seconds, she was talking to someone at the police station, but had turned away from the commotion of the protest.

As Maddie waited, she saw the crowd part and from within one of the buildings, Katy Clemments walked out with three men in suits. Alarmed, Maddie saw that one of the men was Jesse, speaking intently to Katy as it looked like she was trying to ignore him. She whipped around to see Maureen putting her phone away, but the younger woman must have seen the look of consternation on Maddie's face, because she immediately came to her.

"Maddie, are you all right? You're looking a bit lost."

"I was just wondering what Katy and Jesse Booth were talking about."

"Who's Jesse?"

"A man from the samba class. He works for the college in the environmental science department and writes about waste management. I just saw him up at the college and he said Ricky Russo has been helping him put together a pharmaceutical waste management proposal.

Maureen nodded slowly, but didn't say anything. She then asked Maddie to wait for just a second as she turned to make another call. This time the call was a lot longer and Maddie considered going in to Vito's, but curiosity made her want to see what was going to happen next. She took several steps closer to the action, in an effort to make herself more visible to Katy. If she could grab her attention, maybe she could get the scoop on what was going on.

At one point, she thought she'd caught Katy's eye, but in the next, Katy did a double take looking beyond Maddie. Her composure, up to that point impeccable in a breezy and charismatic way, slipped. If Maddie was correct in her assessment, a look of terror crossed her face. She recovered well though, for in the space of a blink, the panicked expression was gone and the cheerful and successful smile was back on Katy's face. Maddie gazed in the direction Katy had been looking and could see nothing out of the ordinary, just the protesters. Then she spotted Ricky Russo at the back of the crowd. She turned and looked at Katy but the real estate agent had disappeared. She whipped her head around again and found that Ricky had also vanished.

"She's strange, that one. Even in school, there was always a sense of uncontrolled energy around her."

Maureen had returned from her phone call. Maddie knew she was speaking about Katy.

"Hmmm...yes. You were always observant, weren't you, Maureen?"

Maureen chuckled. "Well, with you, certainly. I wanted to grow up so badly I just fixated on my brother and all his friends. You all seemed so impossibly adult to me. Especially you." Maureen grew pink but her smile was broad.

"Me? Adult? Now that's a laugh. I remember feeling anything but adult when I was 18."

"Well, you were to me. And sorry to have to cut this short, but I have to get back to the office." Maddie watched as Maureen responded to a text message.

"Don't forget my party." Maddie waved to Maureen and promised she wouldn't.

As she opened the door to Vito's, she noticed Jesse sprinting down the other side of the street and away from the riverfront commotion, and instantly thought of Robyn, hoping nothing had happened to her. Inside,

Vito and his half dozen customers were all pressed against the windows, watching the situation outside and debating the proceedings. The youngest in the room, a teenager with a homeschooled look about him, was adamantly defending the protesters.

"If we don't stop it now, the next thing you know, you're not going to be able to sit in here and have your coffee. Vito will have to close and we'll all be sitting over in the Long John Silver eating muffins baked last month and seven states away."

An octogenarian with hairs sticking out in several directions from his eyebrows and ears, but not a strand on his head, pounded his cane on the floor several times.

"Now, nothing like that's going to happen. Vito, you'll be here forever, won't you?"

"You got that right, George. I'll certainly be here as long as you're around, old man."

George smacked his lips together and nodded. When Vito saw Maddie, he immediately put the empty plate he'd been holding, onto the counter and swept her up in a hug.

"Ah, Maddie, I have been negligent. I should have come to the hospital to see that you were all right. I only found out yesterday." Vito released his grip and peered up at her. "Are you all right?"

"I really am fine. And if I say it enough, I know it will be true." She smiled, hoping that she didn't sound as depressed as she thought she did. Vito pursed his lips and shook his head in three economical bursts.

"You, sit. I'll bring a coffee. When do you parents come home?"

Maddie sighed. She'd wanted to walk a little and clear some of the funk accumulating in her brain, but she didn't have it in her to be rude. "Tomorrow night."

"Good. Until then, you come stay with me and Rosalinda." Vito presented her with a coffee and a mammoth piece of chocolate cake that she knew she wasn't going to be able to eat, and then rejoined the group back at the window. A middle-aged woman had been using her mobile phone to take pictures through the glass.

"I'm going to send these to the paper. They shouldn't be able to do this."

A man sitting with her, and the only person in the deli who didn't seem enthralled by the events outside, briefly took his eyes off the paperback novel he was reading and glanced in the direction his wife was focused.

"Look, the reporters are already there. They're not going to need your pictures."

"Well, then I'll post them online so everyone can see."

Now the homeschooled teenager joined in. "That's right. That's how revolutions start these days."

Maddie's phone rang. *Thank goodness*, she thought as she motioned to Vito that she had to answer it. She left the building without having touched the the cake.

"Hello...Hello? Damn." She thought she heard a female voice say her name, but the reception in that area was shocking and she couldn't make out anything further. Looking at the screen, she saw the call was from a local number. Assuming the television crew's equipment was responsible for the poor reception, she walked quickly away from Vito's and the riverfront with the phone still to her ear. As she rounded the corner and came out on Main Street, she ran directly into Jesse, who was also on his mobile and in their collision, both phones went sailing through the air and crashing to the ground.

"Oh, Jesse, I'm sorry..."

"No, Maddie, I'm sorry, I wasn't even watching." Jesse bent over and retrieved both phones, handing Maddie hers. "Sorry, I've been such a spaz. I've been expecting a phone call and when it came in, the reception was bad. I had to go halfway down Main Street."

"Oh, so that's why you were running."

"What?"

"Oh, I just mean that I saw you run this way and I wanted to talk to you."

"Oh." Jesse moved from foot to foot. "What was it you wanted to talk to me about?"

Maddie felt like a complete idiot and wouldn't have blamed him if he thought she was stalking him. "Oh, nothing now. I mean it's not that important. I guess you have to get back to the protest."

"Protest? Oh, yes, that. I do need to get back. See you soon."

Maddie turned away as quickly as Jesse, and vowed to head straight back to the studio. Her phone beeped, indicating a text message and she looked down at the screen to see who it was. Behind her, Jesse's voice called.

"Maddie. Maddie."

She turned to find him holding his phone in the air and waving it frantically towards her. Unsure if it was Jesse who had texted her, she looked down again and read the screen. Then, like a puppet being manipulated from above, her head jerked up and her eyes rested on the figure of Jesse running towards her.

"Sorry, again, Maddie. Funny that we have the same phone." His hand extended toward Maddie with her phone held between his thumb and first finger. "Here, this one's yours." She must have looked unsure, because he looked at the phone in his hand and then the one in hers.

"See, they're the same except mine has that sticker on the back." Maddie didn't need to look at the sticker, she knew she was holding Jesse's phone, but she looked anyway. The sticker was a red speech bubble with white letters that said *Pick Me*. They exchanged phones, both looking at their own screens. Maddie's was blank, but Jesse read his screen. Immediately his head popped up and his mouth opened and closed several times before he said anything. He had turned an unnatural shade of pink, as he stuck his phone into his back pocket.

"That was just some information I was waiting for. This deal..." He motioned to the commotion at the riverfront building. "There's a chance that it can be stopped."

"What do you mean? Is there something illegal going on?"

"I really shouldn't say." Jesse looked around conspiratorially and then stepped closer to Maddie.

"Look, it's all just coincidence. I'm doing my research for the environmental science department and I've met some people who could help put this building in the hands of the town."

"Do those people work at SynTech?"

Jesse looked scandalized. "How did you know?"

Maddie didn't say that after reading the text on Jesse's phone, things were beginning to fall into place. "It was just a guess."

Jesse's phone rang again. He looked at her, as if begging her to understand something, although Maddie didn't know what or why, and after an awkward good-bye, they turned in opposite directions again.

Maddie walked aimlessly, unsure of where to go. Should she go to the police station and tell Joe she'd seen Jesse's phone? But then, what would she say? That she read a text on Jesse's mobile and it bothered her?

The thought sounded absurd, even to her. No, she'd go back to the studio as planned. But the text she read was as clear in her head as if she were reading it from the screen:

She knows. Do not underestimate how dangerous she is. Find the toxic paperwork and you will kill the deal. Do not contact me again.

The text was from Henry Levitt. Maddie knew without having to be told who Henry Levitt was. She had always felt uncomfortable saying Henri with that ludicrous French accent. She walked back to the studio and sat on the front steps with the newspaper she'd picked up earlier, trying in vain to keep from thinking about how Jesse had become involved in the mess in her head.

The first page dealt with the riverside development and though she scanned the whole article, there was nothing in it she had not already been told. She considered passing over an obituary article on Nina, but was struck by the first sentence, a quote she recognized as being by Rainer Maria Rilke. *She who reconciles the ill-matched threads of her life, and weaves them gracefully into a single cloth—it's she who drives the loudmouths from the hall and clears it for a different celebration where the one guest is you. In the softness of evening it's you she receives.*

Maddie shuddered, not sure whether it was the exquisiteness of the poem or the incongruity of the recipient.

The obituary went on to list Nina's involvement with a halfway house in Chester and her love of animals. Growing a little emotional, Maddie read that Nina's first job out of school was at the Silver Star Diner and that she had saved enough money to send herself to County for an associate degree in bookkeeping. Then she worked at a real estate agency while she was at

Seton Hall where she graduated at the top of her class. The obituary was heartbreaking, because it was so mundane. Nina was a typical girl from New Jersey who lived a typical life and now she was dead. At the bottom of the page, Maddie noted that the author of the obituary was Richard Russo. After thinking about that for several minutes, her eyes popped up to the middle of the paragraph again. Her first bookkeeping job was with a real estate agency and she graduated from Seton Hall. Maddie stood up and went back onto the studio. Things were definitely falling into place.

Chapter Twenty-three

Maddie woke in the dark and fumbled for the light beside her bed as she fought off a wave of fear. Something had jolted her out of her sleep but as she lay with the light on, all was silent around her. She heard a dog barking and got out of bed. The window in her room was open, letting in the cold night air. She shivered as she closed it. From the look of the dark sky splattered with stars, she'd been asleep for several hours. She breathed deeply, counting to ten as she exhaled and then inhaled again. She tried to concentrate on happy thoughts and happy people like Peter and Kristy and their baby and the hope of a baby for Maureen and Tim, too. Back in bed, she tried to read but she must have drifted off to sleep, because she felt herself jolt back to reality and in that second had a realization that made her sit straight up in the bed.

No matter how hard she tried to leave Katy Clemments out of her thoughts about the murders—probably out of misplaced childhood loyalty, Katy remained firmly in view. She'd been trying to figure out the connection between the two victims, but maybe what she needed to do was put Katy into the middle and figure out how they both knew her. She turned on lights as she ran down to the kitchen and rummaged around in her handbag until she found her address book with Joe's business card, creased where she'd folded it in her anger, but clipped onto last week's page. She paused when she caught sight of the time, 11:30 pm, but dialed the numbers anyway. He'd said to call if anything out of the ordinary happened. And what she was thinking was out of the ordinary. The phone rang only once before it was answered.

"Joe, it's Maddie. Before you ask, yes, I'm fine. I'm at home."

She could hear Joe exhale. "What is it, Maddie?" The way he said her name made both her head and her heart hurt.

"What do we know about Toby Downs?" She could now hear Joe's intake of breath.

"Maddie, please. You need to stay away from this case. It's a lot more serious than we thought at the beginning. I don't want to have to keep saying these things to you."

"Joe, I can help. Tell me, what do you know about him, and I mean besides the drugs?"

"The drugs are a significant piece of this investigation, Maddie. Though why the hell I'm even having this conversation with you, I don't know."

"Doesn't matter. The drugs have something to do with his death, but not everything. I think they've been clouding the real issue."

"So, first off, Maddie, yes it does matter. Each piece of an investigation matters and a mistake, even a small one, along the way, can kill a case. But, of course, since this is all an amusing game to you, that wouldn't matter."

"I know it's not a game and I'm deadly serious, too."

"Fine. Second, please trust that the Pembroke Police Department is perfectly capable of looking at Toby Downs and his drug involvement and looking past it to get to how he ended up dead in a closet."

"Please just tell me what you know about his childhood."

Joe was silent for a moment, then sighed. I'm going to say goodnight. I suggest you do the same.

Maddie sat on her end of the phone silently, her head pounding and her stomach feeling as if she was going to slip out of her body.

"Do you know anything about his parents?"

"Maddie. Go to bed."

Neither of them spoke for a full minute. Maddie had been thinking, trying to dislodge the thoughts from her head and relegate them to the realms of the preposterous. but couldn't. "I know why they died."

"WHAT!"

Oh damn. Maddie realized she must have said that out loud. She hadn't meant to.

"Nothing. I'm going to bed. Good night."

"Oh, no, you don't, Maddie. I'm coming over there, now." Joe had already stood up and was grabbing the clothes he'd thrown onto the floor, trying to get them back on with the phone held to his ear.

"Joe, no, really. I'm going to bed. I didn't mean anything. I just haven't been getting enough sleep."

"Maddie you stay on the phone with me. I'm coming over and I want to hear your voice every step of the way."

"At any other time, Joe, that would sound completely provocative. But as it is, I'm really tired. Good night."

She hung up, but not before she heard Joe's outraged voice screaming her name.

She ran back to her bedroom and pulled on the same clothes she'd been wearing earlier that day. She had to get to the studio to pull off what she wanted to do. She would save the studio from any further controversy and deliver a solved case to Joe, all in one fell swoop.

Stepping out into the cold night air, she decided to leave her bicycle and drive down to the studio. She pulled out of the drive hoping that Joe had not reacted faster than she had and was childishly pleased when the streets remained empty all the way to the studio.

Within two minutes, she had parked by the back door of the studio. She used her key to enter the dark building and without thinking, or letting herself get freaked out at being alone there again, she let herself into the office. This time, the door was locked, and she turned on the light. Luckily, there were no surprises and she let out a shaky breath, realizing that her tension levels had been steadily rising since she'd left the house. Shaking herself free of the anxiety she'd been carrying by taking action, she immediately opened the file cabinet that held personnel records. Ricky Russo's file was exactly where it ought to have been. She grabbed it, sought his mobile number and sent a text. Pushing the send button, she let out another breath. It was done. Now she had to wait to see if she was right. If he showed up, she'd call Joe and tell him she'd figured it out and had the one person who could tie it all up at the studio and ready to confess.

Maddie waited for Ricky in the office, feeling safer in the enclosed space than she thought she would in one of the open classrooms. Nevertheless, she hugged herself, both to keep warm and as a comfort. *Just keep breathing,* she thought. The message she'd sent to Ricky was a spur of the moment decision and the longer she waited on her own, the more she regretted having sent it. Fighting down a wave of panic, Maddie got up and poured herself a glass of water from the cooler. She couldn't stop now, no matter what. And she was doing it for a good reason. She was sure that another incident at the studio would cause students to panic and quit, leading inevitably, to her unemployment. If she got Ricky on her side, then she could tell Joe everything she knew. If she could just get through this, she promised herself, as she sank back into Laura's chair, she'd divulge all the information she had and not get involved again.

She heard a sound from the front door that made her jump. It wasn't a key in the door kind of sound, but a pulling-on-the-door-to-see-if-it-was-unlocked kind of sound. Because she expected Ricky to have a key, the noise made her nervous. She stood up and moved to the wall, then shimmied along with her back flat against it until she came to the door. Cautiously, she stuck her head out and promptly bumped into Ricky, causing both of them to stifle yelps. Without any hesitation, he took her by the shoulders and stared into her eyes. His face was close to hers and she could see the hairs poking out of his left nostril. Maddie absurdly wondered if she'd caught him in the middle of plucking his hairs and worried that he was going to go out looking like that.

Ricky was breathing heavily, not the in and out yoga breaths that Maddie thought would calm him but short, ragged breaths that sounded like he was preparing for an eruption. He still had his hands on Maddie's shoulders and, unsure of his intentions, she braced herself. He looked maniacal for a moment, but that passed and he dropped his arms away from her, stepping back as he smoothed the fronts of his trousers down in an unnecessary display of vanity that betrayed his nervousness. His apparent anxiety led Maddie to hope that Ricky wouldn't cause her any harm.

However, while he may have been nervous, his words demonstrated that he was also angry.

"What the hell are you playing at?" His voice had taken on a snarly tone that reminded Maddie of a caged animal. "Do you think this is funny? You know what she's capable of doing?" Ricky moved further away from Maddie and began pacing the room, reminding

Maddie again of a wild cat, caged and hungry, ready to pounce on the first available meal.

"Listen, I am so out of here. This has gone way too far and I'm not going to go down with her. I had nothing to do with Nina and that kid dying." Ricky now sounded as if he was trying to convince Maddie that what he was saying was the truth.

Maddie found it hard to start speaking. Her throat had dried and she found her hands shaking as she pulled them in close around her again.

"I know." She sucked her breath in again and let it out slowly. "I know, but the police are going to need to know why, and you're the only one who can tell them." Ricky was already shaking his head, but Maddie carried on. "I'm going to tell them what I know but it's not proof. You could give them proof." This was the delicate bit, and for a minute, the world around her was spinning. "You owe it to Peter to clear the studio of any wrong-doing, if nothing else."

"Oh, Miss Goody-Two-Shoes, you are completely out of your freakin' mind."

Then they both heard a sound at the back door. Running into Ricky the way she had, she'd forgotten about the unexplained sound at the front door. She could feel her heart pounding in her chest and had an almost uncontrollable urge to pee. Then she whimpered. Ricky looked alarmed too, but then pulled his limited height upwards and hardened his face. They both knew who it was going to be.

"How…" Maddie began, but wasn't able to finish when Katy Clemments walked into the office with a gun in her hand. Maddie's brain seemed to stop working. *This has to be a joke, or a nightmare.* She felt tears spring to her eyes as she edged over to the desk with the idea of using it to prop herself up. Katy's screeching voice paralyzed her.

"Don't move at all, Maddie. Just stay the hell still."
Katy floated the gun she held somewhere between
Ricky and Maddie and it appeared to dawn on them
simultaneously that if they stayed apart, she wouldn't
be able to shoot both of them. Not at the same time
anyway.

Katy didn't seem to recognize this though. Almost
reiterating the words that Ricky used, she directed her
first thoughts to Maddie.

"Just what the hell are you doing? Why did you have
to get involved in this?"

Maddie was briefly able to stifle her fear with a
feeling of anger that she couldn't hold down, even if it
meant getting shot.

"How could I not get involved, Katy? Two people
are dead. Were their lives worth five million dollars?"
Maddie could see the change in Katy as she heard the
words.

"What's wrong with the riverfront property? It's a
waste problem, isn't it? Nina knew about it and she was
blackmailing you. That's how she came into money."
Maddie didn't take her eyes off Katy and her gun, but
turned slightly to Ricky. "That's where she got the
money to support you, didn't she, Ricky?"

Ricky didn't say anything but a coldness passed over
Katy's expression that made Maddie's knees weak.
With only her life to lose and a sense of righteousness
to bolster her, she continued.

"You and Nina met at Seton Hall University and
then you got her the job at Raitt Realty. That's how you
knew one another. So, when she saw paperwork at
SynTech between the two of you," Maddie's glance
passed between Ricky and Katy, "she put two and two
together. Then Nina started blackmailing Katy and with
her new-found wealth, lured you away from Andrea."

From the grimace on Ricky's face, she knew she'd hit on the truth.

Katy gestured wildly with the gun, causing both Ricky and Maddie to duck.

"The first one was an accident. I didn't mean that. Like the note said, it was a test. If she went further with it, then I'd do something serious."

"I know. You thought Nina would have the drugs to save herself, because you knew for a fact that she always had them with her. Ricky, you told Katy that, didn't you?"

Ricky looked outraged. "Yeah, maybe I told her that, but don't go thinking that I had anything to do with her dying. I didn't tell her so that she could use it against her." He directed his next words at Katy. "You bitch. You killed her and you didn't have to do that." Maddie's resolve strengthened. She knew Ricky hadn't meant for Nina to die, but he was partially responsible.

"Earlier that day you met Nina, even though everyone else thought you were out of town. She was stung by a bee, so she'd had to use her adrenaline and she'd been on such an emotional roller coaster with you, she didn't think to replace it before coming out that night to samba class." The enormity and sadness of Nina's death visibly hit Ricky again. His body caved in on itself and he buried his head in his hands.

Katy sighed dramatically. "Right, this is all sweet but I have things to do," She took a step closer to Maddie, whose mouth opened but no words came out. It looked to her as if Katy had chosen to focus her murderous intentions on her.

Maddie wasn't sure what Katy would do next but she had to stall for time. Why hadn't she told Joe to come to the studio?.

"And then, Toby. How could you kill your brother?"

Katy's eyebrows shot up for a nanosecond. "Half-brother."

"Yes, half-brother. He's the child who survived the fire that killed your father and..." She was cut off sharply by Katy.

"Don't say it. Don't ever say that bitch's name. Don't even mention her existence. She deserved to die and I'm glad she did." Katy grew more irate, as she paced the room, continually using the gun to make a point as she jabbed it into the air. "It was her fault my father left and she got exactly what was coming to her."

"But Toby was three when they died. He was a boy. He couldn't have even remembered his parents."

"My father was taken away from me and that wasn't fair." Katy stamped her foot. "Toby never should have been born."

"What did he do to deserve to die? Did he tell you that he wasn't going to help you anymore? Was he going to turn you in?"

Katy was shaking her head and looking at Maddie in a way that clearly said that Maddie had it all wrong but Maddie didn't stop. Her voice was growing hysterical, but she thought that if that's what it took to keep Katy from shooting her, she would keep talking.

"What? Was he going to turn you into the EPA so that you couldn't make your millions on the riverfront development?"

Katy strangled a laugh as it escaped from her mouth.

"No, little Madeleine Fitzpatrick, he didn't. He would have helped me do whatever I wanted, whenever I wanted. He was a drug addict with no backbone. But then, something happened to him." Katy's voice parodied a Disney voice-over. "Something miraculous. He told me that he'd fallen in love." Watching Maddie's quizzical look, Katy became outraged.

"With you, you stupid bitch." Her voice changed to an evil sing-song.

"He'd just met you and his whole life was going to change. He had found something that brought meaning to his life." She said the last four words with such rage, Maddie thought that the next second could be her last.

"Oh, and now you're going to say that you didn't know. Or what? That you didn't mean to do it? Well, too late. There was no way I was going to let him be happy." That was when Katy stopped her haphazard pacing and aimed the gun directly at Maddie.

"I was never going to let him be happy."

The next three seconds were erased from Maddie's memory. She tried to form a clear picture of what happened, but her brain chose to protect her from the most frightening experience of her life.

Later, she was told that Katy fired her gun three times. The first bullet didn't hit Maddie, because Ricky had lunged forward, successfully knocking Maddie out of the bullet's path, sending it instead into his shoulder. Her second bullet went wild and hit the Monet print hanging next to Laura's desk. Before she could shoot again, another gun was cocked from the doorway where Joe was standing, his gun aimed at Katy.

Katy had time to turn around, see Joe and aim for him. Maddie was told that Joe yelled to Katy to put her weapon down, but she didn't—instead she fired. Luckily, her aim was not good and hit him in the arm, but not before he took aim and shot, hitting Katy in the left side of her chest.

Maddie did remember the sirens, seemingly hundreds of them. She saw Peter at some point, before she was taken in an ambulance to County Hospital again. Maddie was also told that Katy was pronounced dead on the scene and Ricky and Joe were both taken to the hospital to have their wounds tended to. Maddie spent the night at the hospital, but was released early on Tuesday morning into Vito and Rosalinda's care.

Peter called, asking how she was and telling her that he'd spent several hours at the studio with the police that night, much to the chagrin of Kristy who was already making schedules for baby care. Maddie started crying when she heard that, congratulating both of them through hiccups, as if she had only just heard that they'd had their baby. Rosalinda heard her from the other room and came rushing in to make sure everything was all right.

"I just can't believe that miracles still happen in such an ugly world."

"I know, darling, I know." Maddie accepted the hugs and tea from Rosalinda.

She spent much of the next three days crying and sleeping. Her parents arrived home from their trip to South Africa, as planned. Her mother, an inventive cook who took pleasure in making meals out of arcane ingredients and self-imposed rules, limited that week's menus to all of Maddie's childhood favorites. Every time Maddie tried to say she wasn't hungry and was just going to take a cup of tea to bed, the smell of whatever her mother was making would change her mind and she'd end up at the table with her mother and father. Slowly her life began to take on a familiar patina.

She suspected that she would remember the days shortly after Katy's death as the closest she'd felt to her parents since she'd become an adult. Instinctively, they seemed to treat her like a child when she needed to be a child and encouraged her to act like an adult when they saw she needed that, too. She knew that she would have to take on the role of adult again soon, *but not quite yet,* she thought, drinking the hot chocolate her mother had made and licking the custard off the side of her mother's second batch of cream puffs.

Chapter Twenty-Four

On Maddie's first day back at work, Peter called a staff meeting. It was Thursday, and having missed two weeks of classes, she'd grown increasingly anxious over the prospect of having to talk about the night Katy died. However, her greatest concern was whether she still had a place at the studio. The moment she walked into the office, she knew that she needn't have worried. Peter, Frank, Laura, Cathwrynn, Claire and Philip were all there, looking as if they were about to open their Christmas presents, a box of pastries from Vito's waiting on the desk and the intoxicating aroma of coffee ready to be consumed. Stretched above their heads was a banner that read "Welcome Back, Maddie. Tango Teacher Extraordinaire."

Frank walked over to Maddie as she hovered in the doorway, overcome by relief at finding out that she was truly home, and wrapped his arms around her enthusiastically. Then Peter hugged her and the rest of the group nodded encouragingly, or in Cathwrynn's case, lifted her hands up to Maddie's face, palms upwards, then tilted her head and let out a long breath. Finally, she smiled at Maddie and dropped her hands.

"Your soul has prevailed over physical reality." Maddie spontaneously hugged Cathwrynn and grinned, not minding the fact that she had no idea what Cathwrynn ever meant.

Peter gave her an extra squeeze and spoke close to her ear. "You don't have to talk if you don't want to." He then pulled away. "We have a lot to discuss today

and if you just want to be a spectator, that's fine."
Laura gave Peter a disapproving glance that made
Maddie smile. She knew that Laura wanted every
gossipy detail and, that she wasn't too pleased to be
told that she might not get it.

Philip, with his mouth half full, added. "Yeah, you
can just stuff your face if you want to."

Claire reached behind Philip and grabbed a custard-
filled pastry. "You pig. Maddie's not like you."

"I think I'll just start with a coffee."

"Okay then, we might as well start. As you know,
I've been looking out for a new Latin teacher and I
think I've found the perfect replacement for Ricky." A
shadow crossed Peter's face as he took his glasses off,
polished them on his shirt and replaced them. "Ricky
has been released from the hospital and with some
physio will recover, but he has to remain in town to
wait to find out how he will have to answer for his
involvement with Katy."

"Oh, Jiminy Cricket! We all want to hear the story
from Maddie. Let's just sit down and get it all out, so
that we can get back to work." Laura took a stance that
assumed everyone agreed and she was right. Even
Cathwrynn lowered herself into a seat next to Laura's
desk, ready to listen.

"Madeleine, on behalf of all the staff, I would like to
say that it is often most fruitful to expel dangerous
energy within the embrace of the group." The rest of
the room had gone quiet, save for Philip's rhythmic
chomping. Cathwrynn seemed to take the silence as a
sign that the entire staff was in agreement. "The
redeeming energy will banish anything harmful that
remains. Although, I have to admit, I've already danced
the worst of it out and the healing has already begun."
At this point, a flush crept up Cathwrynn's face, almost
matching her hair color. She then looked first at Peter

and then at Maddie and smiled the most poetic smile that Maddie had seen outside a Renaissance painting.

"Thank you, Cathwrynn. I can't tell you how much I appreciate that." Cathwrynn rewarded Maddie with a sigh.

"Maddie, I want to hear how you figured it all out. And all by yourself." Laura looked around the room, as if daring any of the other staff members to disagree with her.

Maddie took a large sip from the coffee Frank had poured for her. "Well, that's not true, not really." There was a discreet cough from the door and Maddie swiveled to find Joe standing, his eyes fastened to hers, his good hand unconsciously rubbing his injured shoulder. Maddie's mouth opened, but nothing came out.

"Well, thank you, Maddie, for giving the Pembroke Police Department some credit." Joe stepped into the room and nodded to the rest of the inhabitants. Alarmed, Philip jumped off the corner of Laura's desk where he was perched and swallowed the last of his pastry noisily then coughed until Claire slapped him on the back. By this time, Maddie had closed her mouth. "But please, Maddie, I'd like to hear the story from the beginning too."

Maddie scrutinized Joe's face for any sign of anger or sarcasm and found neither.

"Okay. Well, to start, Katy Clemments married for convenience. While she was paid half a million to do so," Maddie nodded through the incredulous stare from Cathwrynn and a look from Laura that said she knew Katy was no good, "she also made a connection with her husband's grandfather, a real-estate tycoon and not-so-nice-guy named Franco Leonardo Raitt. When I read Nina's tribute, written by none other than Richard Russo, and saw that she had attended Seton Hall, the same school Katy attended, and that her first bookkeeping job was with a real estate agency, I guessed the agency was Raitt Realty."

Joe took over the story. "We've since uncovered that Franco had used Ricky's nefarious skills at various times and he introduced Russo to Katy when the opportunity arose. The original illegal dump occurred seven years ago in Denville and Katy's been moving toxic waste around ever since. The riverfront property was simply the latest location for the dump."

Claire had paled all the way up to her shaved head. "So the way she dealt with the toxic waste was to transfer it to another project she controlled, and when the time was right, move it?"

Joe nodded.

"Unfortunately for her, the timing went wrong. The Historical Society laid claims on the property and demanded the property be handed over to them as it had been written in the Dodge Estate will."

Maddie picked the story back up. "When I ran into Andrea at lunch, she said that Nina had come into money and that was the only reason Ricky was back with her." Frank shook his head at this point. "She may have been saying that because she was jealous, but I wondered where that money had come from. It all came together when I realized that Ricky and Nina worked together and that Nina and Katy knew one another. Katy had Russo move the waste again, and that's where Nina came into the picture. I guessed that Nina saw the shipping documents that Russo used to hide the movement of the waste. Nina was smarting from her break-up from Russo and so did what a woman scorned does—she blackmailed Katy because she thought the only way she could hold on to Ricky was by supporting him financially."

Joe had been standing in the doorway but finally took a seat next to Maddie. "We're certain, at this point, that Katy orchestrated Nina's death, but we think that it was unintentional. She wanted to scare Nina, not kill her."

Philip reached for more food, but Claire moved the box away from him and patted his stomach. Admonished, Philip took a sip of coffee, "But how did you know that Nina had seen documents that you didn't even know existed? That's a pretty big jump."

But I did." Maddie looked pointedly at Joe. "I found a note in my dance bag the day of the samba class. During the confusion of Nina's behavior and then her death, it must have fallen out of her bag and ended up being pushed into mine. It was typed on a bad copy of a shipping manifest. I ran into Ricky after Nina died when he was carrying several files. I knew instantly that I recognized them but it took me several days to remember that I'd see them on the back of the note intended for Nina."

Joe nodded appreciatively, a sly smile creeping up at the corners of his mouth. "And why did you assume that it was an accident that she died."

"It seems that Nina had been with Ricky the day she died. She kept going on about how she was back together with him and that they'd practiced that day. In class that night, I heard her talk about swelling and how she was feeling better. I guessed that she'd been stung by something and had used her adrenaline, then forgot to replace it."

Claire moaned. "That poor woman."

Frank got up and offered the box of pastries around. Maddie took one and between mouthfuls continued.

"Katy must have paid Nina for several months, but I bet Katy wasn't happy about it. Meanwhile, she reconnected with her half-brother, Toby, the son of her father and his lover. Katy must have convinced Toby she wanted to get to know him, but, in reality, she was seething with hatred and revenge. She killed Toby in cold blood." Maddie's voice caught and she turned her head away from Joe before continuing.

"Katy must have grown tired of Nina and decided she wanted to scare her out of the whole blackmailing business. She found out that Nina danced in Russo's class and got Toby to become involved, so that she could figure out a way to get at Nina. Laura, you told me that."

Laura jumped at the sound of her name. "Me?"

"You told me that Toby really wanted to get into the samba class and was irritated that he couldn't because he had no experience. Then, when I told him that I was teaching that night and that he was free to come by, he was really happy. I mean really happy. I should have known then that something wasn't right."

Joe could hear the recrimination in her voice. "No, Maddie, you couldn't have. And you have to stop beating yourself up about it."

"So Katy was able to get to Nina with a carefully placed box of chocolates, which were meant to appear to have come from Russo as a lover's gift. The chocolates were filled with marzipan, and, as we know, within minutes of eating them that evening, she was dead."

"But I thought Nina could smell nuts a mile away?"

"According to Andrea, she could. She must have believed Ricky had given them to her and so discounted the smell, because she thought they were from Ricky."

"But what made you suspect Katy in the first place?" Laura sat at the edge of her seat, eagerly awaiting the next installment.

"Katy came into the studio, ostensibly looking for a dance class for her mother. But later," Maddie looked to Laura, "told me that Katy's mother has been in a wheelchair so she couldn't have been looking for a class for her. While I thought that was odd, I realized that it didn't mean there was criminal intent on her part. It became suspect later when I ran into Maureen, Joe's sister. She told me that she'd run into Katy at the gynecologist's when she was..." Maddie turned pink and looked sideways at Joe, "um...having her birth control device removed, and Katy had said she was doing the same."

Even Joe's face flushed. "But why did you suspect that?"

"It was because of what Maureen said next. She said that the one thing she was not looking forward to was getting periods again. Which meant, if Katy used the same method of birth control, she wouldn't be getting periods. Then she would not need a tampon, which is what she borrowed from me when we were together at the Grass and Toad and she went to the restroom. That was when she must have taken my studio keys and my phone to text Toby."

Philip had gravitated back over to the food and this time Claire ignored him. Claire leaned over to Cathwrynn. "Good thing I'm the one who gets lifted in our dance."

Cathwrynn's eyes sparkled. "I get lifted in my dance, too."

Peter, who'd been inordinately quiet thus far, spoke up. "So fill me in. Where does Renée Lambert fit in all of this?"

Joe let out a wry laugh. "Nowhere, except that she happened to be in the same dance class as Nina and, oh yeah, she was buying drugs from Toby."

"Damn, and she's a nurse. She should be ashamed." Frank shook his head for the hundredth time.

Joe finished the coffee that Laura must have poured for him. "And Henry Levitt, AKA Henri, while not a guy you want to bring home to Mother, was not involved in either Nina or Toby's deaths."

"But what was he doing there with Katy when I saw them at the riverfront development?" Maddie passed her mug to Laura, who then put it in a plastic tub for washing.

"He was part of the MallCorps acquisitions team. Not a company with great environmental credentials but not illegal. The company knew nothing of the contamination problem, which was why Katy was becoming desperate. She knew they would pull out of the deal if they found out and then she'd have a history of chemical fraud to have to explain. She had to silence everyone involved, so that she could deal with the problem before they handed over the property."

Maddie stood up as Joe sat down. "That's right. And Jesse worked at the college and with SynTech. That's how he knew Nina. She was the secretary who delivered the information Jesse was collecting for his environmental impact report. He didn't know Katy, but he knew Ricky because Ricky had tried to put pressure on him to steer the Historical Society away from the riverfront development."

Joe nodded. "And Jesse knew Henry, because he was working with him to try to stop the development falling into MallCorps' hands. Henry had leaked the information that could have brought the deal to a standstill."

"Henry Levitt? You mean he turned out to be one of the good guys?"

"Seems so. He quit MallCorp last Friday."

Everyone in the room watched as Maddie paced between Peter's door and Laura's desk.

"So, what it comes down to is that Nina was in love with Ricky and wanted to keep him. She saw that her only chance to get some decent money to do that would be to blackmail Katy, but she didn't realize that she was dealing with such a volatile psychopath and she died because of it. And Toby was the wrong person for Katy, no matter what the circumstances. She would have made another excuse to kill him if he hadn't fit so perfectly into her plans to scare Nina. She was that unstable."

The room was quiet until Laura's squeal and announcement. "So I did it!"

Joe's entire face screwed up as he looked at her and Peter nearly fell off his chair. Philip and Claire looked at one another, as if the other had an answer to Laura's outburst. Frank appeared not to have heard and Cathwrynn started humming.

"Laura, you weren't responsible in any way." Maddie knew Frank and Peter had taken the past few weeks hard, but Laura was the last person she thought would break down now that it was all over.

Laura had been gazing around her with a satisfied nod, before she guffawed. "I did it. I was the one who gave you the vital clues. You never would have figured it out if I hadn't told you about Katy's mother being in a wheelchair. And then there was Toby and his desire to learn samba. Again, me." She then pulled the packet of cigarettes out from her pocket and took one out. Peter coughed.

"You know, I just may have a new career path in law enforcement, don't you agree, Detective Clancy?"

Joe couldn't keep the grin off his face, although luckily he didn't have to answer, as Laura had waltzed out of the office, presumably to smoke her victory cigarette.

Joe stood up. "Well, folks, I have to get back to the office. Maddie, I was hoping to speak with you." Maddie noticed Joe wasn't looking at her, but instead had his eyes already out the door.

"Um, yes. I'll be right back, Peter." As she followed Joe out of the office and then down the hall and out the front door, she wondered if he had bad news for her.

She hadn't heard from Joe since the shooting and was upset about that fact. Every time her mother said that the police were on the phone to speak to her, she anticipated it would be Joe and was disappointed each time when the voice of a junior officer came on the line. At the same time, she had wanted to put off talking to him as long as she could. She thought she knew Joe like she knew her own name but had been proven wrong in her short time back home. Not because he'd given her a chance to know him again, because if anything, he was actively avoiding any semblance of a relationship.

Her current misgiving was due to an epiphany of her own. Some time in between teaching people to Argentine Tango and people being murdered, she'd made up her mind to stay in Pembroke. While her future remained uncertain, she was able to dismiss Joe's indifferent behavior. It was an irritation, but one that she would no doubt escape when she'd made her permanent plans. Now, she wanted to stay and she would have to figure out what Joe's role would be in her new life. Maybe their relationship would dissolve into nothing more than friendly nods on the sidewalk, but the unexpected feelings that Maddie had experienced the past few weeks made it necessary for her to confront the situation. Joe stopped and turned swiftly to Maddie.

"So."

"I'm sorry, Joe, for the mess I made of things. I don't know what came over me. I guess I just want to explain..." Maddie paused for a breath and then barreled into her account of events.

"I just...I don't know if you saw it, but I was a choreographer out in California." Maddie paused, hoping Joe would indicate that he'd seen the infamous production, but Joe stood expressionless in front of Maddie. "Well, it didn't go quite as I expected." At that statement, Joe looked at her quizzically. "What I mean is..." Maddie could feel her face grow red. She didn't want to be discussing a situation about another woman's genitals with Joe. "What I'm trying to say is that things in California went a little..." Joe coughed into his good hand, evidently getting impatient with Maddie's preamble. "I'm just...that is, fifteen years in California was a long time and I feel like I've come home."

Maddie waited for Joe to say something and felt herself grow increasingly irritated that he remained silent. Finally he said softly, "So, was her Brazilian wax a choreographic choice or was that wardrobe?"

Maddie stood completely still, her mouth slowly forming a tentative smile.

"You big, fat jerk. You watched it."

Joe broke off into a booming guffaw, actually slapping his hand to his knee. "Of course, I saw it. I think everyone in Pembroke saw it. My favorite bit..."

Maddie cut him off. "Okay, I don't think I want to know. Why didn't you say something?"

"What, and miss you turning fetchingly pink as you tried to tell me that TV standards for nudity have been increased, due to your choreographic exploits? Not a chance."

Maddie placed her hands on her hips. "Well, it seems you've been doing your homework."

"Always." Joe looked unnecessarily out the window. Without looking at Maddie, he continued. "I just didn't expect you to come back here."

Maddie followed his gaze. "Neither did I. I really want to explain…"

"No, Maddie, you don't have to."

"Yes, I do have to. I feel like I've been passing through my own life, kind of like a visitor, and I don't want that anymore. I want to be here. I thought if I took a stand to help Nina, that I would wake up, that I would actually be taking part in my life rather than letting things happen to me."

"Maddie. I would like to see you again."

"What?"

"I would like to get to know you again."

"But what about Tracy?" Maddie swallowed hard. "Oh, God, I'm so egotistical. You just meant as friends, didn't you?"

"Maddie, stop. I did not just mean as friends." Joe let his good arm hit the side of his leg in frustration. "Or maybe that's what we will end up being. I don't know. But what do you mean, what about Tracy?"

"Well, I mean, what are you going to tell her?"

Joe looked at Maddie with a glimmer of mischief. "I'm going to tell her that my ex-girlfriend from high school, my first love, has come back to town and I would like to get to know her again."

Maddie looked at Joe in awe. "You've got to be kidding me."

"No, I'm not." Unable to stop himself, he laughed. "Maddie, Tracy and I are not going out anymore. We broke up a year ago and it was a mutual decision. There's no problem there."

"But…what about dinner and all those kids?"

Joe stopped laughing. "All those kids are what that dinner was about. I try to eat with Tracy at least once a month. Tracy and I broke up and can deal with it, but her kids have been through a lot with their dad dying and I'm not about to disappear from their lives, just because I've stopped dating their mother."

"Wow. I feel like an idiot."

"Don't." Both were silent, but came back to life when they heard Claire and Philip, coming down the hall. When the young couple saw them they did an about-face, and shot into one of the classrooms.

"So, how about you go out on a date with me? Do you think your parents will object?"

"Actually, yes, I think they will. But I'm going to do it, anyway."

They stood eyeing each other quietly.

"So, will you be at my sister's birthday party tomorrow night?

"Um..." Maddie had been thinking of the party quite a lot and wasn't sure that she was comfortable with the idea of being around a lot of people she didn't know, but who would undoubtedly know about the deaths at the studio. She was about to say that she probably wouldn't make it, when she looked at Joe. He took her hand in his good one.

"Come to the party, Maddie. We can consider it a prelude to a date."

Maddie smiled. Joe had grown up and so had she, but the Joe she knew fifteen years ago, was also there in front of her.

"That sounds great, Joe. Just what the doctor ordered. I think there may be a Southern Comfort with my name written on it."

"Ugh, Maddie. Do you still drink that stuff?"

"Yes, Joe, I do. And don't knock my drink. I believe if pushed, I could come up with some of your teenage habits that the kind people of Pembroke will find very interesting."

Joe's lopsided grin showed his dimple off perfectly and Maddie felt her stomach flip.

"I'm sure you could, Maddie. Just stay out of my investigations, will you?"

Maddie smiled innocently. "I'll try, Joe. I really will."

THE END

ABOUT THE AUTHOR

 Kate O'Connell spent her youth in Europe, her teen years in northern New Jersey and her twenties in New Mexico, before moving back to Europe and then on to South Africa. To this day, her accent comes from an amalgamation of those places and no one can tell where she comes from. She likes it that way. She also likes to consider herself a librarian, though she has no formal qualifications, compelling the local librarians to keep a sharp eye on her. She does, however, have a lot of education. She received her BA in Theatre and History, her MA in Dance History and Criticism, and her MPhil in Dance Studies.

Kate's research focused on the Argentine Tango community in London and while learning about the dance, she started teaching and performing. She still teaches classes and workshops and occasionally pushes the living room furniture aside so that she and her husband can dance.

Kate writes novels now. She also swims daily in the Atlantic Ocean and is tortured weekly by her Pilates instructor, and she has made it her mission to teach her daughter everything she knows about making room on the dance floor.

You can visit Kate at her website: www.dyingtodance.com.

Printed in Great Britain
by Amazon.co.uk, Ltd.,
Marston Gate.